Between

Christine Morris

Opening Spaces Books are available for order
through Ingram Press Catalogues

Christine Morris
Visit my website at www.christinemorrisauthor.com

Printed in the United States of America
First Printing: April 2015
Published by Sojourn Publishing, LLC

ISBN: 978-1-62747-085-8
Ebook ISBN: 978-1-62747-086-5

For Steven, Evan and Ellis who gave love, support
and space for me to find my way to write these words

& particular thanks to Jill, Geri, Mitzi, Denise, Erin, Judi and Steve R.
for adding your advice, support, expertise, love and inspiration

& finally a world of gratitude to Tom and Rama
for knowing that there was a book in there
and knowing how to get it out.

PART I

ILA

I la Dean sprung up in bed, her amber brown hands bracing her from behind, loaded and taut. Her toned arms appeared almost black in the early morning darkness. Wildly, her brown eyes darted around the room, whipping her long, kinky curls side to side. She struggled to get her bearings.

Into the small room, Ila coughed, the stark sound sharp and abrupt against the quiet. She blew out hard through her flared nostrils, as if trying to remove an invisible invader. She squeezed her burning eyes shut, letting the sting dissolve, then opened them and searched through watery eyes for the source of the smoky scent. She found no trace of smoke, no fire. Ila relaxed a bit, pushed her covers into a pile in the center of her bed, and crossed her long, bare legs in front of her.

"Holy crap," she muttered, sitting up taller and wiping a stray curl out of her eyes. "What the hell was that?"

Ila was used to having strange dreams. From a very young age, her mother had taught her how to interact with them. She knew it was an unusual ability—"Unique," as her mom's friend Mave had called it. She didn't announce this part of herself to her world at large. She only trusted it to a select few friends. And even with them—those who knew her from childhood—she still felt somewhat guarded.

For the most part, Ila's dreams were good, but this one was horrible. Her nostrils still stung. Images burned in her mind's eye. Fires. Charred earth. Water. Molten, disappearing ground. The scent of smoke heightened in her nose. She shook her head to remove the images and the smell.

This one is going to be hard to let go, she thought as she swung her feet to the ground and untangled herself from the last of her crumpled covers. Ila staggered upright, stretched overhead and stumbled forward, her feet slapping awkwardly on the worn wood floor. Through her open window, the light call and response of the morning songbirds contrasted the dark images in her head. She gazed down, still not fully awake, and studied the first rays of sunlight filtering through a crack in her heavy curtains. She watched, groggy and entranced, as light and shadow danced across her dark floor, the branches outside creating movable works of art through the slit in the curtain.

Ila turned and brushed back the dark, heavy curtain hiding her window. Sunlight gathered behind the far off hill, building and preparing to burst sunrise into the morning sky. From her upstairs window, she peered into the shadowed driveway below. Her father's truck was already gone, leaving a familiar empty space. *Typical,* she mused. Her mother's old car, one of the only remaining traces of her, sat alone in the grey, colorless driveway. Its white paint gleamed lustrous and bright, even bathed in shadows. Ila sighed heavily, then lifted her eyes back to the orange-red light on the horizon and inhaled deeply.

As Ila watched, the golden sun swelled brilliantly into the red-orange horizon, contrasting the calm, blue-white sky above it. A warming breeze rolled through the window and fluttered Ila's dark curly hair. The smell of warm earth and cut grass filled her, clearing out the last remnants of smoke.

Reluctantly, Ila peeled her eyes away from the radiant sunrise and paused while her eyes adjusted to the dark room. Then she padded across the hall into her bathroom, leaned into the tub, and spun the shower to life. The drum of falling water soothed her further while steam gathered, rising and filling the room. Ila moved to the sink as warm mist emerged from the heated water, floating and dusting her hair and face as she pulled her toothbrush from its home. She stared into the mirror, barely noticing her own brown reflection as it slipped into the fog. The images from her dream materialized like a faded picture coming back to life. Charred earth. Lava oozing, surrounding and swallowing mounds at a time. She heard a faraway scream.

"Eve?" Quickly, Ila turned the shower off. Her ears strained against the silence as she lowered herself and sat on the smooth hard edge of the tub, squinting out the partially open bathroom door. She turned back. It only took a second, but the shower was gone. In front of her stood a large, thick piece of aged wood, wide and solid. She raised her eyes and followed the grey grains until the back of her head touched her neck. A shiver ran down her spine. The door was enormous. Suddenly, she heard a loud *crack* from outside the bathroom door. She twisted toward the exit, her heart pounding, and watched her bathroom door disappear. Ila stared, horrified and unable to turn away, as distant ground swelled up, cracked, then split apart. One huge slice rose slowly, dramatically, and then hastily plummeted, disappearing swiftly beneath rising, turbulent water—like a giant, earthen Titanic.

"Holy crap," she whispered hoarsely. Blood rushed through her ears, racing to keep pace with her barreling heartbeat. Beads of mist gathered into drops and slid down her brown skin. Still as a panther, she squeezed her eyes shut, untangling and pulling herself from the images. She gripped the knob tighter.

"I am awake. *I am here*," she claimed, just as she was taught. She squeezed her eyes tighter, demanding fiercely through gritted teeth, "*I. Am. Here.*"

Slowly, tentatively, she opened one eye, seeing first her white knuckles gripping the white shower knob. Her chest fell as she exhaled her long-held breath. Her grip softened, and her smooth brown skin slowly regained its warm color. Ila dropped her hand heavily, letting go of the knob completely. She inhaled deeply, lifting and expanding her whole body, then blew it out in one long steady stream.

"Holy shit," she whispered, scanning the empty bathroom with nervous eyes. There was her pedestal sink, her shower, and the cool white tile beneath her feet.

After a long moment, she stood and turned the water back on, finally noticing her toothbrush still gripped tightly in her other hand. Sharply, Ila threw it into the sink, the light clank barely audible over the drumming water. She kicked the door closed, roughly stripped off her clothes, climbed under the steaming hot water and stood motionless as it seared into her skin.

EVE

A light midnight breeze rustled the faded pink curtain and brought the cool scent of jasmine into the room. Eve Pierce sat on her sagging bed, her long pale legs crossed underneath her. She brushed a thick, brown lock of hair behind her ear. Immediately, it sprung free. She stared absently past the once gallant canopy ruffle and out into the darkness beyond her smudged window. Unconsciously, she picked at a small piece of fuzz on her summer pajamas. Restlessness grew around her. Her mind moved, as it usually did, to Jay and his beautifully warm dimpled cheeks that smiled at her from somewhere inside. She shook her head, as if she were shaking him out of her mind, tired of the empty hole that seemed to follow thoughts of him.

"Oh, man," she grumbled to the empty room. "Is this all there is? When will my life *really* start?"

"It's already started." A voice, soft and feminine, rang into the dark quiet room.

"Bullshit!" Eve boldly shot back, instantly regretting it and clamping her hand tightly over her mouth. She held her breath as her eyes darted through the empty room. A deep chill ran down her spine as the hairs on her arm prickled up. The room was dark and silent beyond the haggard light trickling from the ancient lamp on her side table. The only sound she heard was the rapid thumping of her own heart.

"Really? Then why are you talking to me?" The voice rang melodious. It seemed to come from everywhere.

Eve jolted upright. The roar of her own blood rushed loudly in her ears.

"If it hasn't started, then you'd still be all alone in your head." The voice was soft and gentle.

Eve spun around on the bed, searching the room for another presence. Finding none, she scurried backward until she bumped her back against the headboard. She yanked her quilt up around her shoulders, tucking it tight in an attempt to quell her growing sense of exposure. Short, tight breaths escaped her lips as she hugged her unsteady hands around her knees, making herself small and compact. Except for the familiar furniture guarding her walls, the small room was completely empty. Shadows stretched from the dim yellow stream of her burdened lamp. Eve sat completely still, frozen, as a part of her reviewed the events of the unusual conversation.

She exhaled deeply, fighting to keep it smooth. "That's true," she answered finally, her voice cracking only slightly. "This is different."

"You going to go with it?" The rich melodic voice seemed to be smiling.

"Yes," she answered without hesitation, "Yes. I'm in." She shuddered but relaxed slightly, unsure why she answered yes.

"Well then, let's go."

Eve remained still on her bed, the wooden headboard awkwardly torquing her neck. She pushed the discomfort from her mind and felt her chest rise and fall easily as her breathing slowed and lightened. Her lamp glinted off the glass, stinging her soft green eyes. Whisper silent, she slid her arm out and clicked off the tired lamp; the sharp sound was hard against the calm quiet of the black room.

Outside, the moonless sky sparkled with the faint light of flickering stars. All sound vanished as she strained her ears to hear something—a car, a cricket, her breath—but all she heard was the vast emptiness that roared through her mind as the black enveloped her. Everything around her faded as her eyes locked onto one bright star pulsing rhythmically in the thick, dark sky.

What now? Eve's mouth felt too heavy to speak aloud.

"Nothing now. The Star. That's all there is right now," the melodic voice answered her silent question. The star continued to pulse gently, settling her mind.

Eve sat still, her eyes fixed on the star, the rhythm soothing her entire system. Then slowly, in front of her, a door materialized. Its thick grey wood was worn smooth. Her nostrils flared as she inhaled the sweet, warm fragrance that wafted across her nose. Cautiously, she reached out a trembling hand. Her wide palm touched then molded to the grains of the immense door. Her eyes slid closed involuntarily. Under her hand, the smooth, deep grains rose and fell as she brushed lightly across the wood.

Wait! she thought. *Wait. This doesn't make sense.* She felt her rumpled bed underneath her and tried to feel the headboard behind her back. The star pulsed vibrantly just above the door then shrunk smaller and smaller, until it finally disappeared completely.

Wait!

"Don't wait. Go."

Wait, she thought once more. She lifted her hand from the door and opened her eyes.

"Wait," she whispered. The scene froze. The word 'Wait' appeared, large and opaque, and floated like a cloud around the door. She lifted her hand off the door and stretched out one finger, running it through the word. The letters moved from solid to gaseous. From here to gone.

Eve placed her palm on the door again, unsure how this was happening. *Am I dreaming,* she wondered, *like Ila does?*

"Yes and no." The answer was harmonious, as if it were now a chorus of sound, echoing softer and softer until the sound finally evaporated.

Eve noticed a round metal knocker at the edge of the door. She ran her hand around the thick circle of metal and tried to lift it up. It didn't budge. She traced the small bumps on the metal, and her heart filled with a collision of sadness and loss. Without warning, her eyes filled with tears. Slowly, she peeled her hand off the metal. As she did, she felt the metal pull on her, as if the metal was touching her as much as she was touching it, like they were somehow magnetized together. She sat up and peered into the metal circle.

Suddenly, she was standing. The floor under her feet was black and void, as if there were nothing there. She gazed around, curiously aware of her own relaxed ease. Around her was only darkness. And the tall grey door. Eve reached out and ran her hand around the circle of metal again. The coolness drew her hand into the middle, and her finger touched the firm wood. A low gasp escaped her lips as the door softened under her fingertips. Gently and slowly, it widened around her hand. Eve pushed. She felt the door expand and stretch around her fist. The more she pushed, the more the door gave way, straining lazily under her pressure. A shiver ran down Eve's spine as the smooth elastic of the once hard door encircled her whole wrist, swallowing her entire hand. She stayed completely still. Then, from beyond the door, she felt a slight pull.

With a shudder, Eve looked down at her arm, still in the door. Instantly, the surreal scene shocked her mind back to the present. All at once, Eve ripped her arm out of the hole and cradled her hand to her chest. Her heart pumped chaotically, her hand light and tingly as she peered into the metal hole. Then, tentatively, she reached one finger inside the ring one more time.

It was completely solid.

"What's happening to me?" she whispered hoarsely.

The door began to fade and darkness fell like a blanket across her eyes. Heavy and suddenly exhausted, Eve's body tilted, then fell gracefully backwards. She landed with a soft bounce on what felt like her own bed. Her eyes were wide open, but she saw nothing. She couldn't move. The star appeared again, bright then dim, pulsing over and over across her small room; her half open window emerged from nowhere and framed it perfectly. In the distance, she heard an echo of soft melodic chimes. A light breeze ruffled her curtain ever so gently as the familiar night jasmine filled her nose.

Eve struggled for consciousness as her eyes fluttered shut against her will, the entire scene fading from her mind as she fell into a deep, dreamless sleep.

MAVE

M avel Harkins leaned her middle-aged body forward in her kitchen chair and held her head in her hands. The room was soft and warm in the predawn quiet, lit only by the yellow glow of the stovetop light. Her folded form cast a long shadow across the linoleum, blending smoothly into the dark corners of the room. The haunting images from the night—the red-hot fiery glow swallowing the ground like a ravenous villain—lingered, refusing to leave her mind.

"This is not good," Mave whispered to the empty room, shaking her head slowly.

She pushed the heels of her dark brown hands into her closed eyes, as if this could erase the remaining discomfort. She felt the roughness of her calloused palms against the soft creases of her almost black face. She cradled her hands gently over her eyelids and pushed the images, literally and figuratively, from her mind. The edges of the vision began to blur, residual reds and browns lingering momentarily, then slowly retreated, leaving in their wake an empty void.

"Isaac," she whispered to the vacant room. "If you can hear me, Isaac, I'm worried. This... this is different... you hear?" She lowered her voice even more. "Ila... and Eve... I just don't know. I keep seeing it this time... this same horrid image. And I wish so much that I could talk to you."

The silence that followed her words cut into her heart with a force that caught her off guard. Deep within her chest, the old familiar ache returned. She had not felt this pain for quite some time. She had thought it was finished.

Mave hugged her knees up into her chest, curling her body into a ball on the kitchen chair, and stared out blankly across the dimly lit floor, her body still as the room around her. She fixed her eyes on one speck of light on the dark wall and let herself feel his absence. When she could bear it no longer, she inhaled deeply, unclasped her hands, and pulled herself up tall in her chair, pausing briefly with closed eyes.

"Okay … enough now, enough," she chastised herself, throwing her eyes open and abruptly heaving herself out of the chair. She crossed the room quickly and stood before her devoted coffee machine. Out the kitchen window, the first light of day stretched blue across the horizon. She smiled sadly as she flipped on the machine, its red light glaring grimly into the shadowed room.

Just then, headlights flashed onto the wall beside her, the gravel road outside churning and grinding heavily under the weight of a vehicle. She turned, peering out into the early morning dawn as a truck groaned to a stop in front of her large wooden barn. Following behind it was a single horse trailer. Mave squinted out the screen door, the warmth of the day only a hint in the cool morning air, and searched the unrecognizable trailer and cab.

"Now who in the world could that be?" she muttered to herself, glancing at the clock. "At this hour?"

JAY

Jersey Lang pulled up to the stoplight. As usual, his aged BMW almost stalled.

"Piece of shit," he muttered, forcing the clutch in with his left foot. Using his right toes to brake, he revved the engine with his right heel.

"Only two more legs and I could really drive this thing."

He jerked the gear into neutral, moved his foot heavily onto the brake, and looked in his rearview mirror. The morning light lit his face, warming his rich, brown skin. He ran one hand over his coarse, tightly clipped black hair and turned his head from side to side, scrutinizing his appearance. *Good*, he thought, *didn't miss anything*. He caught sight of his eyes and began his usual ritual of looking from one eye to the other. His high cheekbones bordered his eyes, causing them to appear even more different. He peered into his left eye, blue and light as the sky. He turned to his right eye; it was so dark brown there was almost no difference between it and his pupil.

"I look like two totally different people," he whispered to no one.

Just then his phone rang. As he peered down, Eve's wide smile greeted him. He slid his finger across the screen and brought the phone to life.

"Good morrrning," he drawled out as he plugged in his headset.

"Morning," Eve grumbled back. "You close?" she asked.

"Yeah, just a few blocks away."

"Okay, good. I'm almost ready." She hung up before he could say anything else.

"Nice talking to you, too," Jay muttered to himself as he popped out his earphone. "Yes, I'm doing well. Thank you so much for asking." He shook his head then smiled wide, the light dimples in his cheeks softening his face, making him appear younger than his seventeen years.

"Eve Pierce...." He punched the clutch a little too hard and jammed the car in gear. As the light turned green, he caught first gear and screeched away from the line, and arrived at Eve's house in record time.

Hearing his honking, Eve flashed her blinds to let Jay know she was coming. She grabbed her bag and breezed through the empty hallway, slamming the screen door in her wake.

"See ya!" she hollered over her shoulder to no one in particular, her long thick hair bouncing out behind her. Her mother was already at work; her brother was nowhere to be seen. She leapt over the two concrete steps that led her out into the world, and reached for Jay's metal car door. As soon as her hand touched it, sparks flew.

"Yow!" Eve shrieked, shaking her hand viciously. Smoke floated up, sneaking off into the light sky.

"What the hell?" Jay's door squeaked loudly as he threw it open and jumped out. "You okay?" He banged the back quarter panel as he ran around. "Piece of shit!"

"Yeah, I'm fine. It's really strange, though. My hand ... it's funny. I don't know. It feels weird. It's okay, I guess. It just feels ... weird."

"Should we get it checked out?" Jay took her hand in his and turned it over. He shivered slightly as the warmth of her pale skin touched his.

"Nah, let's just go. What's the schedule for today?" Eve said, changing the subject. Gently, she pulled her hand back without meeting his eyes.

"Mavel's." Jay looked at her and smiled. Eve looked up and watched as one side of his mouth curved slightly higher than the other. The soft pink of his full lips was a shade lighter than his warm, brown skin. She glanced into his eyes. Her cheeks warmed. She pressed her lips together and raised an eyebrow.

"Right, of course. Ila will be there already, I'm sure. To Mavel's then." Eve tilted her head, warmly returning his smile. "Sorry I grumped at you."

"S'ok."

Jay opened her door, and Eve slid into the well-worn seat. Jay landed behind the wheel and revved the car to life once again. He thrust it into gear and slowly eased away from the curb.

"I love that woman." Eve broke the silence.

"Huh?"

"Mavel." Eve rested her elbow on the door and stretched her hand out the window, fingers pointing into the wind. "She seems so much older than she is, don't you think?" Eve smiled wide and settled back against her sun-warmed seat. The air around her hand guided it up and down, waving it rhythmically as they drove. The morning sun bathed her face. She closed her eyes and let the sunlight burn red through her closed lids.

"Yeah, sometimes she does seem like she's at least 103," Jay replied, smiling, stealthily watching her bask in the morning light. "And I'm not too sure she ever tells us the truth about her age, anyway." He thought about it for a moment then shook his head.

"Ah, well, she may just be timeless," he said finally.

MAVE

J ay and Eve traveled the rest of the ten-minute drive out of town in
silence. The gravel crunched under their tires as Jay pulled his car
onto Mave's long drive. Dust rose in a thick cloud behind them, and
then was swept in a swirling haze into the green field. Eve leaned her
head out the window—the sun momentarily blinding her—as the fresh
smell of damp earth filled her nose. She turned her face up to the early
summer sky, rested her shoulders on the door, and stretched her legs
out across Jay's lap. Jay slowed as they entered the tunnel of foliage.
Eve gazed up at the small white blooms that dangled off the towering
limbs like tiny chandeliers. Shiny mahogany bark contrasted the white
blooms and played in shadows across her face. Jay watched her light
skin move into and out of the shadows as her lips pulled into an ever-
widening smile; he waited patiently for the question he knew was
coming.

"What are...?" Eve started to ask, her voice strangely strangled
from the strain on her neck.

"Tibetan Birch or Birch Bark Cherry."

Jay looked back out the dusty windshield, smiling ear to ear, his
cheeks lifted high, his dimples in full sight.

"Why can't I ever remember that?" Eve wondered. "They're the
most beautiful trees I've ever seen." She peeled herself off the door,
slid her legs back to her side of the car, and leaned forward. The noble
trees stood slender and tall as they lined the lane. Gently, they swayed
back and forth, as if waving them in.

"Dunno." Jay smiled at her, keeping his eyes on the lane. "But you
forget it every time. There's somewhat about them ... something
magical, though, don't you think?"

"Mmhmm, absolutely."

They pulled up to Mave's barn and parked next to Ila's shiny white car.

"I knew she would be here." Eve smiled wide. "My sister from another mister."

Eve and Jay burst like a whirlwind through the screen door. They entered the bright kitchen and threw greetings around as they helped themselves to some of Mave's get-your-bones-seriously-moving coffee. Ila sat back in her kitchen chair, eyebrows raised, as she watched them playfully push each other out of the way in mock competition for the brew. Then, Eve plopped down on the vinyl chair next to her. She paused for just a second to inhale the eye-opening scent, and sipped noisily from the steaming cup. She looked over the mug at Ila, a satisfied smile slowly creeping across her face, and surveyed her friend's unusually serious expression.

"You look terrible."

Ila looked down into her porcelain cup and suppressed a smile. "Ah, good to see you, too, sunshine."

Eve leaned over, careful not to spill her scalding drink, and gave her a loud, sloppy kiss on the cheek. "I'm sorry, that was awful—I just meant you look exhausted. What gives?"

"I don't know." Ila wiped the wetness off her cheek with her shoulder. She stared into the remnants of her cup. "I'm just off today. I had a pretty crazy-ass dream last night."

"Language!" Mave bellowed from the back.

"Sorry, Mave!" they hollered back.

"Yeah?" Eve said, lowering her voice, urging Ila on.

"I had this crazy-ass...." Ila lowered her voice, too, and grinned. She glanced toward the doorway, then started a third time.

"I had this crazy dream last night I just can't seem to shake."

Jay and Eve held their wide mugs to their lips and blew soft ripples across their coffee almost in unison. Eve nodded, leaning forward. Both sat waiting for the story. They loved hearing about Ila's dreams. After a long silence, Ila peeled her eyes from the depths of her cup and looked back and forth between them, the wrinkles in her forehead deepening as she surveyed her own memory.

"It's not a good one. I keep seeing it. Images of charred earth. Burning fires. Earthquakes. I think that's what it is anyway. It's hard

to tell. Then the land just tips up and slides right into the water. Gone."
Silently, she set her cup on the speckled Formica table, rubbed her
hand, and stared passively out the screen door. A fly hovered, buzzing
just outside the door, then found the small hole near the handle. It
crept through and entered the warm kitchen. For some reason, Ila
didn't want to mention the door.

Mave's footsteps creaked up the wooden hallway. She leaned
casually on the doorframe while she carefully scrutinized each of them.
The light chatter of birds from the bush outside grew louder in the
silence.

Ila looked at her. "Did you ever have that one, Mave?" she asked.

"Yes," Mave replied. "I know that one."

"I've been having that one for a few weeks now. It's even starting
to come in while I'm awake." Mave's brown eyes steadied on Ila as
she studied her unreadable face. She noticed the dark circles under her
eyes and watched Ila rubbing her hands nervously back and forth as if
wringing them out. Ila swished palm across palm absently back and
forth. Then she looked up and saw Mave watching her. She stilled her
hands, interlacing her fingers, and then brought them quietly to the
table. Almost immediately, she picked up the sugar spoon and started
turning it over in her hands.

"Have you had it more than once?"

Ila shook her head.

Mave looked across the wide kitchen and out the screen door
toward the barn. Her own forehead creased as she let herself fall into
the images.

"It's always the same reel over and over for me. Like it's stuck or
something," Mave said finally. She padded across the faded yellow
linoleum, her dark bare feet soundless on the floor, and paused at the
cabinet, her hand resting on the silver handle.

"It's a little different than usual."

The cabinet creaked loudly as she opened it, silencing the birds
outside the window. Mave reached in and pulled out an oversized
brown cup—the "trough" she called it—and filled her mug from the
last of the coffee. The pot sizzled as she slid it back onto the hot burner.

"It's something, all right," Ila said. "It sucks. I feel horrible, and I can't seem to shake it." She pulled her hands under the table and started squeezing one hand in the other. Her hand was starting to feel prickly.

"Don't worry, it'll fade. That's how it goes for me anyway."

Jay and Eve looked at each other then gazed down at Eve's hand. Mave and Ila followed their eyes.

"What?" Mave asked.

"Well, um…," Eve hesitated.

"Tell them," Jay urged.

Eve nodded and looked up. Mave's brown eyes surveyed her kindly but intently and waited. Eve adjusted herself in her chair, tucking one long, slim leg underneath her.

"My hand. It's felt weird since I woke up today. It seems okay, but it feels really strange: tingly and light. But"—she took her hand and held up her cup—"using it like this feels totally fine. Totally normal. This morning, when I touched Jay's car, it sparked. Or something. It didn't hurt. It's just really weird…," Eve trailed off.

Mave set her cup down and picked up Eve's hand; holding it gently, she turned her palm up. Faint pink lines divided Eve's palm into asymmetrical shapes. Mave put her dark hand palm to palm on Eve's, her dark lines matching and syncing up with Eve's faint pink ones. She brought her other hand underneath, sandwiching Eve's pale hand between her own. Warmth filled both of Mave's hands. Her thin arched eyebrows rose higher as she looked down at Eve, surprised.

Finally, she spoke. "It feels *good.*"

Eve looked up. The sunlight behind her caused Mave's short kinky hair to frame her head like a wooly, misshapen halo. "I *know*, right?"

"Really good." Mave chuckled. "Well, it can't be all bad then if it feels this good." She put Eve's hand down and gave it a gentle little slap. "Let's put that thing to use then! Come on, lazy bones! Let's get this party moving!"

"Lazy bones," Jay mumbled. "Who are you calling lazy bones, woman?"

Mave leaned over and smacked him playfully on the back of his head.

"What's wrong with you, mister? You don't talk like that around an old lady. Youth these days."

Jay choked, almost spitting out his coffee.

"Dang, Mave! You must have been dreaming craziness last night, too! You're what, thirty?!"

"Forty-three!" she shot back. "Forty-three. But I'll be darned if I don't feel like I'm 103," she said, only half joking. She rubbed her hands briskly across her face, then across her thick, black hair. "Lord." She shook her head clear.

They all looked at her. At that moment, standing in the light of the kitchen, silhouetted by the morning sun, the yellowing floor and walls reflecting on her, Mave glowed radiantly.

Eve looked at Jay, trying to hide a smile. "You were only off by sixty years." She giggled. Jay joined her, the sound of his deep laughter ringing through the open kitchen. Ila shook her head slowly from side to side as they continued to infect each other, cracking up at their own inside joke. Her grin stayed as she scolded them. "Okay, you guys ... now, it's not all *that* funny."

"Come on, let's go, funny man." Mave snatched her large coffee cup in her hand, tilted it up, and emptied it in one long gulp. She brought it down on the table with a commanding *Thump!*

"Let's get moving! Youth these days...." Mave mocked exasperation as she walked over to the door tsking and shaking her head while she drew on her multicolored socks, leaning easily against the pale yellow walls for support. "Where's the respect?" Over her socks, she slipped on her worn leather boots, stamping each fully for punctuation. She launched open the wooden screen door dramatically, the door spring groaning poignantly as if to accent her question.

Jay emptied his cup, sauntered over to the door, and slung an arm over her shoulder. They wobbled together across the wooden porch, the screen door slamming behind them. Jay matched his long legs to Mave's short stride and moved them awkwardly across to the steps.

"Respect is out the door! Who gives a rip about respect? Bah!" he taunted, teasing. "But there's love! There's always love, Mavel!"

Mave reached up and hugged his head. They waddled down the steps together, arms entangled. "You're a nutter, son. You know that, right?"

"Loooove!" Jay replied, his deep smooth voice carrying across the yard. Mave matched him with her light, rich voice, harmonizing with him. "Lift me up, love!" they sang the words repeatedly as they wobbled around in their weird awkward embrace, heading down the well-worn path to the barn.

Ila and Eve both watched them go, eyebrows arched, smiling.

"Damn, they're fun to watch," Eve said.

"I know. They're both nuts. Hey, you okay? For real?"

"Yeah, I am. I feel a little like I dreamed about this or something," Eve said, looking at her hand. "But of course, I can't remember."

Ila nodded. She rubbed her own hand briskly under the table then stood and stretched her arms wide, her muscles hugging her bones intimately. Her delicately laced t-shirt drooped casually, contrasting her sound arms. She swayed over to Eve.

"Love, love, love," she sang out low and sweet. She wrapped her arms around Eve and heaved her up to her feet. Eve stood and hugged her back.

"Lift me up, love. Pick me up, love!" they sang loud and purposely off-key as Ila hoisted Eve up and spun her around the empty kitchen. She set her down gently and they each slung an arm over the other's shoulder. They continued singing loud, giggling, and waddling out the door as one.

They zigzagged their way across the porch, the wooden door slamming once more, as they followed clumsily down the steps, wobbling and giggling down the same dirt path to the barn.

BEAST

S till stumbling and giggling, Ila and Eve shuffled up to the barn as one. They lowered their voices but kept their embrace as they approached the large sliding doors. The sweet smell of hay and the musty scent of grain filled their noses. A scraggly calico cat bumped and brushed across Ila's leg.

"Mave's got a new animal," Ila whispered. Eve raised her eyebrows and shook her head.

"I don't think so. I've seen that cat before." The cat deserted Ila and began to bump against Eve, weaving back and forth through her legs, purring heartily. "Okay, kitty," she leaned down and stroked her once. "That's enough."

"No, no, not this one. It's a cow or something." Ila turned, smiling, and walked around the corner of the barn to the hidden side door. Eve caught up with her and stepped through the door Ila held open. Carefully, she took the door from her friend, well aware of the spikes of rough wood ready to lodge themselves in her thumb or finger, or both.

They stepped into the cool feed room and cautiously felt for the metal feed bin to guide them until their eyes adjusted to the darkness. Crunching over the stray pieces of grain mixed into the dirt, they crossed the small room and stepped over the wooden partition into the main aisle of the barn.

Tied in the middle of the room was an enormous black beast. At the sound of their footsteps, the animal turned and locked eyes with Eve. Then it looked directly at Ila.

"Holy shit," Ila whispered.

"Holy cow," Jay corrected from across the room. "Technically, though, it's a Cape buffalo. Or African buffalo as some call it."

Jay had his hand on the shaggy beast and was grinning wide at them.

"Now don't they look suspicious?" Ila recovered first, squinting at Mave and Jay. "What's the story, guys? How the heck did you come into the possession of a—what did you call it?"

"Cape buffalo."

"Of a Cape buffalo? Here? In Moira?"

Jay grabbed a large grooming brush and started to rub the animal's side. Its thick skin waved and morphed under Jay's rhythmic movements.

"He just showed up," Mave said. Eve and Ila would not be surprised if this beast really did just "poof" right onto Mave's farm. They just might have believed it with the right backstory. They braced themselves for it. Jay looked over at them, staring back wide-eyed at the animal, waiting.

"Nah," Jay said, laughing. "We're just messing with you. He was trailered over here early this morning from an older couple over in Seren."

"What was he doing there?" Eve asked.

Mave answered slowly. "*Well*, the couple *said* they found him grazing on the side of their house a month or two ago. They kept him at their place, just like a cow. I'm not sure they were being completely truthful, though. They say he's a gentle little thing."

"I don't think they were lying about that." Jay rubbed the huge animal's haunches. The beast leaned into the caress like an oversized cat.

"Yeah, okay, but he's definitely not so little." Ila walked to the animal's other side. She grabbed a brush from the dusty box on the floor, gripped it with both hands, and began to mirror Jay's rubdown. Ila began to feel small vibrations in her hands. Gradually, they grew into a soft, light ringing. She stopped and cocked her head to one side.

"You hear that?" Ila asked. The sounds faded as soon as she stopped moving. Eve watched her friend. Ila was staring off, looking beyond the animal.

"Earth to Ila…," Eve called gently to her.

The animal turned to look back where Ila was standing.

Ila shivered involuntarily.

"Why's he looking at me like that?" Ila asked, wary, watching him from the corner of her eye. Slowly, she started brushing again.

"Oh, he likes you," Mave cooed as she came over and started scratching and rubbing the animal with both her hands.

"Yeah, but where's that sound coming from? Don't you guys hear it? Like wind chimes or something."

"No, I don't hear any wind chimes," Mave answered, but she stopped rubbing him. She stepped back slowly.

Eve looked from Mave to Ila. "What's going on, you guys?"

Jay looked at them over the animal. They both had a faraway look in their eyes.

"Hellooo...." Eve snapped her fingers rapidly at Ila and Mave, walking cautiously toward the animal. Small sprinkles of dust flurried up, glinting in the sunlight. She stopped a few feet from the buffalo, tentatively raising her hand, willing it to stop shaking, and brought it toward the beast—just above his wide, dark nose. His warm breath moistened her arm. "Damn, he's huge."

"Language!" the other three said in unison. Eve jumped at the noise, and the beast turned his head to look at her with one eye. Eve froze. The animal sniffed her hand. He opened his mouth and stepped one foot forward.

"Stay still," Jay told her. "You're fine."

Eve didn't move. The beast stretched his thick neck and leaned his head toward her hand again; his rough horns swooped out like a comical hairpiece above his large black eyes. He blinked casually and Eve squinted, staring deeply into his eye. Far inside, a speck of light shined brightly. The animal opened his large mouth, showing his square, off-white teeth. Without warning, his thick, bumpy tongue reached out for her hand.

"Stay there, Eve," Jay said. "He just wants to greet you."

Eve felt his tongue, warm and wet, slide across her hand. She looked down; her mouth pulled into a grimace, and she surveyed her dripping hand covered with stringy beast saliva. Her hand tingled. Ila looked at her own hand as it, too, began to tingle and vibrate. The animal shot a sideways glance to Ila. Again, Ila heard the soft and harmonious chimes. She shook her head to clear the sound.

"Um, thanks?" Eve pretended to rub the fringe of fur around the animal's ears while she wiped the goo and slime off on him.

"He's one gorgeous beast," Jay said, still rubbing his leathery coat. "Why'd they let him go, Mave?"

"They said they just got a feeling he was at the wrong place." The animal turned his gaze to Mave. "Said they didn't think they should keep him. And they said they found me on the Internet, which is really peculiar, because my site is down right now. And it clearly says I only take horses, not cows."

"Well, I guess they knew you were firm on that rule." Jay chuckled.

"I know, I know. It's odd. I never have trouble turning anyone down. And people ask *a lot*. But for some reason, I just could not turn this guy away."

"Must be his charming ways," Ila said.

As if on cue, the beast lifted his tail and dropped a load on the floor.

"Oh! That is *nasty!*" Eve said, backing away. Ila hooted with laughter. Once more, the chimes rang, as if only in her head.

Jay pulled out the metal shovel, poised just for these occasions, and scraped up the waste. He dropped it with a ceremonious *thrump* into the plastic bin next to the stalls. Then he moved to the beast's shoulder, bent down, and leaned into the animal. The buffalo picked up his foot in response. "Good man!" Jay praised, reaching into his back pocket and pulling out his metal hoof pick. The animal let him clean his hoof, as if he had done it all his life. Then Jay gently dropped the buffalo's leg back to the ground.

"He's in good shape," Jay said, shaking his head. "His legs are sturdy. His eyes shiny." He moved smoothly from one foot to the next until he had circled the animal. Then he slid up next to Eve and rubbed the beast's head. The wet, black nose nudged his hand, giving Jay his own version of being slimed.

"See anything, Mave?" Jay wiped the slimy film onto his faded jeans.

"Nope. I think he's good. Hooves look strong, healthy, sturdy. He's been well fed."

"Where you going to keep him?" Ila asked.

"I'm thinking on putting him in the field with the boys. I think it will be a good fit. You agree?"

Jay nodded. "Absolutely."

"Let's put him up in the corral first. Just to make sure. Food and water, boy?" Mave asked the animal as she slapped his side heartily. The buffalo jerked his head upwards, his bumpy white horns barely missing Eve. She jumped back out of the way and slinked over next to Ila.

"Okay then, let's go." Jay stood next to the buffalo and clicked a metal buckle onto its halter. The animal's wide head turned in Jay's direction. Jay leaned back to keep out of the horn's path, and the thick curved edge barely missed him. Jay lengthened the lead rope between them then clucked his tongue to coax the animal forward. The beast swayed easily side to side, swishing his long tasseled tail back and forth behind him. Dust rose around them, puffing lightly, then settled back down in a light, satin mist.

"There go two fine looking young men," Eve called. Impulsively, she stuck her fingers in her lips and blew out a low, sweet whistle. Jay and the beast looked back in unison, pausing in the shadows, both faces hidden in silhouette. Jay turned away quickly, hoping no one saw the color rise, warming and flushing his brown cheeks with pink.

"Indeed," Mave agreed as Jay and the animal stepped out into the bright yellow sunlight. A small grey songbird swooped past, bravely inspecting the new resident. Then another joined in. And another.

"Let's get this place in order, shall we? Or should we just stare at those two for a while?"

Eve's cheeks burned bright red. She brought her hands up to either side of her face, trying to hide her glowing skin. The left side of her face cooled down immediately beneath her tingly hand.

"Oh, I'm good to stare," Ila said, coming to Eve's rescue. Her own hand felt thick and warm again. She slid it behind her, slipping it into her back pocket. Eve looked over, and Ila put her free arm around Eve's shoulder.

"I hate cleaning horse poo. This is much better." She leaned into Eve and rested her head on her shoulder. Her coarse curls tickled Eve's cheeks as the light lavender scent of Ila's hair washed around

Eve's nose. She relaxed. A lone bead of sweat rolled down her temple, and she swept it aside with the slightest movement of her finger. Mave stepped in front of them. "Here you go, ladies." She reached her arms out to the girls. In one hand, she held a rake, the handle worn smooth from years of constant use. In the other, she held a pitchfork, its handle equally as smooth. She clanged them down ceremoniously on the dry, dusty floor. A small puff of dust rose on each side.

"All right then," she said with a mischievous smile. *"Now,* can we get to work?"

BEAST

The sun gleamed steadily from its midday position, casting no shadows in the warm afternoon. Occasionally, one of the horses in the field would blow out through his nostrils, creating a short break in the quiet lunchtime lull.

In Mave's kitchen, dishes and glasses chinked and clattered. Cabinet doors thumped both as they opened and closed. Jay licked the remnants of Mave's infamous aioli spread off his knife and set it down, adding its clank to the symphony of kitchen sounds. He squeezed the thick French bread into a manageable bite.

"How's your hand?" Jay nodded at Eve before he took a bite.

"I forgot about it completely." Eve opened and closed her fist. "I think it's feeling more normal. Maybe a little sparkly." She shook her head and chuckled at the absurdity of her words, turning her hand over and back, inspecting it. "It still feels good," she said, "just not as tingly."

Ila felt her own hand matching Eve's description. She wasn't sure why, but she didn't want to tell anyone about it. She was used to handling things herself. But something like this she normally would have shared.

"That's moving in the right direction." Jay took a bite and wiped at the edge of his mouth. Eve watched him out of the corner of her eye.

"What are we doing this afternoon?" Ila watched Eve watching Jay.

"Depends on Mavel. What else you need today, Mave?" Jay put his sandwich down and wiped his mouth fully.

"We're in good shape here, for now. Actually, I'd love a ride over to your place to ask your dad about our new friend," Mave said. "But let's check on him before we leave. I want to make sure he's good out there."

Mave slid her chair back from the table, signaling the end of her lunch.

"How you doing, love?" Mave stole a glance at her as Ila sidled up alongside to help with dishes. Ila focused her attention on the twist tie she was fastening around the bag in her hands.

"I'm fine, I guess." The morning's ominous beginning had faded from her mind, just as Mave had predicted. She kept her eyes down. Ila knew that once she looked into Mave's eyes, there'd be no holding back. Mave's penetrating gaze always elicited the deepest of secrets. Ila didn't want that. Not now. Not yet. Something was brewing inside of her, and she wanted to keep it to herself, at least for now. She changed the subject.

"So, you're really going to keep him, Mave?"

"What?" Mave looked at Ila blankly. She had been watching and listening to Ila so intently, looking for clues to explain her unusually quiet distance, that she had no idea what she was talking about.

"The *beast*? You know, that humongous buffalo that no one in this whole state, probably in this whole half of the country, would have on their farm." Ila looked directly at Mave and rolled her eyes prodigiously. "Come on, Mave. You're slipping there, eagle eye."

Mave widened her eyes, repressing a smile. The kid was good. She knew how to redirect like a pro. Mave recovered quickly and let it drop, not wanting to push Ila. The kid had been progressively more guarded, Mave had noticed. Maybe the distraction of the animal would prove helpful somehow.

"Oh, *that* him," she replied just as sarcastically. "Yes, of course. He just might be a weary traveler far from home in need of good company and shelter." Mave looked out of her small kitchen window and spotted the animal looking back up at the house. He seemed to be looking in the window directly at her. Mave shivered, her tone turning serious. "He most certainly is mysterious. Look at him down there; he seems to be fixed right on me."

Ila leaned over and spotted the animal down in the corral standing completely still; not even his tail was moving. The buffalo was staring unwaveringly back at the window. Ila shuddered, too.

"Dang, he is intense. You sure he's safe?" Ila heard a soft low chime ring deep in her ears. This time she knew for sure no one else could hear it.

Eve and Jay gathered the remaining dishes off the table and joined them at the sink.

"Yeah, for some reason, I do." Mave answered, eyes fixed just as intently on the animal

"Shall we?" she asked, pulling her gaze away and glancing around the warm, clean kitchen.

They slid unhurried into their shoes and stepped into the afternoon sun that stretched like a yawn across Mave's wide front porch. Small birds swooped gracefully across their path, diving and darting after insects in the warm air. Down at the corral, a soft breeze waved across the thin coat of the still-as-statue buffalo, while flies circled his enormous head like electrons to an atom. The group situated themselves on varying levels of the slatted fence. As soon as they were still, the animal rotated his huge head toward them. With the speed of a slow moving train, he turned his body and began a slow shuffle across the corral to the fence it shared with the horses' field. The loose cloud of flies hovered along with him.

The animal reached his wide neck over the smooth, timeworn dip in the fence rail, and Boss—Mave's tall Palomino horse—ambled over, shaking his large head, his long blonde mane flowing like a rippling flag in his wake. The horse stopped a few feet away from the new resident and blew out hard through both nostrils. The buffalo inhaled deeply, raising his head and stretching his nose as far as he could. Even at their distance, they could see his large round nostrils flaring and drawing in the scent.

The buffalo replied with a long, slow breath. Boss stepped closer, until he was nose to nose with the beast. They stayed here, sides rising and falling, and shared breath back and forth. Ila looked at Mave, eyebrows raised.

Mave stepped onto the bottom rung of the fence and whispered, "It's how they greet each other—at least how horses do."

Ila nodded and turned to see Boss stepping away, replaced by Bean, the littlest of the bunch. The black beast was double his size, dwarfing the miniature black and white pony, yet the buffalo lowered his head as far as he could toward the pony. Bean stretched, lifting his small head and bringing his flaring nostril as close as he could. They greeted each other in the same respectful manner. Satisfied, Bean backed away and walked out into the afternoon sunlight. From the fence, Ila and the others watched the silent ritual unfold as this greeting continued through all four of the remaining horses in the field.

When the last of the horses turned and casually sauntered away to graze, the buffalo bobbed his head up and down, which they all now knew meant *something*, then shuffled over to his hay pile and tugged a mouthful from the mound. His jaw rolled in a rhythmic circle as he scanned his sunny surroundings from the comfortable shade of the sprawling willow tree.

Mave cleared her throat and broke the serene silence.

"Well, I guess he's fine." Beast looked over at her and nodded imperceptibly. Mave narrowed her eyes at her strange guest, shaking her head unconsciously, her kinky twists of hair moving like a malfunctioning compass, pointing recklessly in varying directions.

"Ah then," she squeezed her lips together briefly then stepped down into the soft, silky dirt. Across the quiet corral, they heard the beast contentedly chomping, making his way through the coarse mound of hay beside him.

"Shall we go?"

One by one they piled into Jay's car, careful to keep their bare skin from touching the blistering faux leather seats. Jay cranked the car alive and lured the engine into a steady purr. Eve studied his forearm, musing over the slight variations of his muscles tensing and releasing as he eased through the gears. Ila caught her eye. Eve pulled her mouth into a sideways smile and turned, unruffled, to look out the side window. Jay eased the car forward, driving with the same relaxed vibe the animals on the farm had radiated.

ZOE

J ay guided his car easily, weaving them through the shadowed, tree-lined back roads between farms. They were each so immersed in their own inner world that the transition from spacious fields to the town buildings went largely unnoticed. Only when they turned onto Jay's lane, lined by well-groomed hedges and thick green lawns, did they notice they had arrived at their destination.

Jay cleared his throat as he pulled on the brake and looked across the passenger seat to the side entrance of the house his family had occupied for generations. The house sat almost regally in the old part of town, surrounded by acres of fields filled with horses of their own. At one point, there had been a large interest in developing the land around their house. Jay's family refused vehemently. His father had no need or desire for finances over open space. Their fields rolled out around their house in a large circle, spacious enough that the small stream trickling through the back pasture wasn't even noticeable from the house or the barn. His father wouldn't have it any other way.

"I don't think my dad's home," Jay spoke low, not wanting to pull them too abruptly from their inner worlds. "I don't see his truck anywhere."

Often, one of the first things to be noticed when pulling up to Jay's house was a massive black, four-door pickup truck with a simple drawing of a horse on it. The image sported the widest, toothiest grin one had ever seen—on a horse. Under the picture was the name of Edge's business, "Happy Horses." Jay hated it. Eve loved it. Ila laughed every time she saw it.

"Yeah, no cheese truck," Ila said. She giggled to herself. They had started calling it the "cheese truck" years ago because of its big, cheesy smile.

"Is he traveling?" Ila asked between chuckles, trying to keep herself in check. She couldn't help laughing every time she saw the truck—the image was joyfully ridiculous to her. Eve kept her head turned away from Ila, trying to keep from influencing her unraveling. Whenever they saw it, they both fell into echoing spasms of laughter.

Jay smiled, shaking his head. He was used to their laughing ritual. "No, he has a clinic tomorrow, though. He's probably out getting ready."

The scent of fresh cut lawn mingling with the smell of the summer hay met Ila as she cracked her door open and stepped into the sunlight. All of a sudden, a strange feeling washed over her. She looked over at Eve, who was wringing and squeezing her hands absently. Ila started to rub her own.

"Come on, you guys." Mave wrapped her arms around them both, urging them forward and nodding to Jay. "Let's find your mom."

On the sprawling, wraparound porch, they stopped to tug off their boots. Mave, closest to the front door, felt a warm current of air float out across her arm. She raised her head slightly, searching the moist air for a whiff of Zoe's creations.

"Your mom cooking today? It feels warm in there."

"Dunno," Jay answered, cracking open the screen door. A burst of thick, humid air hit him full force. He gasped.

"Oh my God, it's crazy hot in here!" He threw the door open wide, and they were all hit with the oppressive heat.

"Mom!" Jay called, diving straight into the house. "Hey, Mom! Where are you?"

Ila, Mave, and Eve looked at each other, instantly covered in tiny beads of sweat. Ila wiped her hand across her damp brow. Sweat gathered on the back of their necks and face, making slow, weaving descents down the various parts of their body, as if skiing down their skin.

"Jay, what's up with the heat?" Mave hollered into the house. They were hesitant to enter.

"I don't know." Jay's voice was distant and hurried. The thick air sat motionless, hovering at the entrance. "It wasn't like this when I left this morning." He checked the thermostat on the living room wall. It was off.

Jay hollered all through the downstairs, searching frantically for his mom. Breathing was difficult, as if oxygen were scarce.

Ila, Mave, and Eve inched their way in the door. Ila hollered breathlessly to Jay from the doorway. "Jay! Call them!"

Jay appeared in front of them, drenched in sweat, and pulled out his phone. He wobbled hard, and Mave cinched his arm, holding him steady.

From the kitchen came a slow rolling ring.

"There! That's my mom's phone." Jay gulped some fresh air before he ducked back into the house and found the ringing phone on the sparkling granite counter. Then he spotted his mom's boots barely peeking out from behind the island counter.

"Shit! Mom!" His voice cracked. He fell to his knees beside her unmoving body. Zoe lay on her side, her knees bent in toward her chest, her arm under her head. Her light brown face was relaxed and easy; the soft lines around her eyes barely noticeable. She looked ten years younger than usual. If it weren't for the location, it would appear she had simply decided to take a little nap.

"Mom!" Jay gently shook her leg. "Mom. Hey. Mom. Wake up." His voice was softly urgent.

"Is she breathing?" Mave nimbly knelt down by her head. "Zoe?" Mave leaned in and whispered close to her ear, so low they barely heard her. Mave held her own breath while she willed Zoe's chest to move. She placed her weathered hand on Zoe's side, and felt her ribs slowly rise and fall. "Yes, okay, she's got air." Mave closed her eyes, said a silent 'Thank you," and blew out a long shaky breath. "And a heartbeat. Don't move her. Ila, Eve—you guys, throw open some windows!"

Ila and Eve scurried through the rooms, tugging each white-framed window wide open. The fresh, clear air hit the thick haze of heat with a contrasting force, and the room filled with mist. It feathered down, settling over them in a whisper light wash.

"Hey, Z, you okay? Zoe?" Mave was talking softly, stroking her friend's hand, her face.

Zoe began to stir. She made small noises until they formed into a sound. "Ee."

"E," she repeated. "E, where've you been?" She reached out her thin long fingers and touched Mave's cheek. "Oh, honey, I've missed you. Oh, my! Look at you. You're so old." She started to chuckle. "Wait, who's that man with you? Wait, I know him … E!"

Ila stopped short in the doorway. The warm brown glow of her skin began to drain away, turning her face ashen. She backed up and bumped into Eve. Eve wrapped her arm around Ila's shoulder. Ila was shaking.

Ila whispered anxiously into Eve's ear. "There's a man over there—look—standing next to Mave." Ila nodded into the kitchen as a translucent man slowly straightened up from beside Mave and Zoe. He looked directly at her. He smiled, wide and warm, and placed his hand gently on Mave's shoulder. Then he began to fade until finally disappearing completely.

"What man?" Eve whispered back. Her eyes darted from Ila to Mave. Mave was pale, too. She was looking down at her own shoulder.

"Mom, it's me, Jay. Mom. Hey, how do you feel?"

Zoe blinked her eyes. She squeezed them shut, then opened them wide and worked hard to focus.

"Jersey?" she asked, tentative, unsure.

"Yeah, Mom, it's me. You okay?"

The mist was clearing, and the house was cooling off fast. Drops of water fell from the ceiling. One landed on Zoe's cheek. She touched it.

"Why is it raining inside?" she asked.

"We don't know. It was crazy hot when we got here. You were passed out on the floor. When we opened the windows, it misted up."

"I don't feel well." Zoe pulled her knees closer. She moved her head to rest on the hard stone floor. It felt cool and refreshing.

"Easy, girl," Mave reminded her. "Don't move too fast. Get her some water, hon." Mave nodded to the girls.

Eve started to pull away from Ila, and she felt her begin to tilt and sway without support. Eve grabbed onto her again. "Can't," was all Eve said as she guided Ila over to the couch. Jay stole a glance at them. Mave silently filled a cup and brought it over, waiting patiently as Zoe pushed herself upright and leaned heavily onto the wooden cabinets. Zoe took the cup and sipped deeply. Then she dipped her fingers in and wiped the cool water around her flushed face.

"I don't know what happened." Zoe rubbed her forehead, brushing her damp hair out of her face, and adjusted her salmon-orange scarf on her head. "Um, did your dad just leave? Shoot, I don't really remember. Is he here?"

Jay shook his head. "His truck's gone. We thought you'd know."

"Um, maybe I do. Let me get my thoughts straight. It is really hot in here."

"Zoe," Mave said slowly, "who were you just talking to?"

"I was just talking to you, Mave." Zoe wrinkled her forehead. She looked across the bright room at Eve propping Ila up on the couch. "Wasn't I?"

"Damn, that's weird," Mave said. They all looked at her. Zoe raised her eyebrows at Mave.

"Language, hon," she chided quietly.

"You were just talking to someone." Mave looked at Ila through the wide doorway.

"You called them E," Ila added softly. She didn't look up. She was acutely aware that was the name Zoe often called her mother. She squeezed her thin brown hands together in her lap.

Eve looked at Jay, brows raised, questioning him with her eyes. Jay shook his head and shrugged his shoulders back. He nodded at Ila. Eve shrugged in response.

Mave bit her lip as a shiver billowed down her spine. She let herself gaze beyond Ila, out the wide picture window into the pasture.

Isaac. The name echoed hauntingly in her mind.

EDGE

E dge Lang's short grey hair resisted the bursts of warm afternoon
air that flew through the cab of his truck. He rolled past the aging
Wellstop, the large value goods store, and slowly passed the empty
Moira High School as he headed out of town. Once he emerged from
the winding, tree-lined country road, he spotted Mave's faded barn
roof, standing like a weary sentinel across the undulating green fields.
He smiled to himself in the quiet, the deep grooves in his lightly
tanned face curved into their well-worn path. He didn't know exactly
why he was driving over here at this time of day, but he had a feeling.
And just like he told his clients, "It's all about the feel."

Edge pulled down Mave's lane. Both birds and insects buzzed
back and forth across the gravel road, playing their own version of
chicken with his vehicle. Edge spotted Mave's truck as he approached
the house. He pulled up next to it.

"Hey, Mavel!" he called as he slammed his door shut. "Mave! You
around?" He crunched his way across the gravel to the house, the hard
soles of his dusty cowboy boots thumping dully up the stairs. At the
door, he rapped his calloused knuckles next to the greying screen.

While he waited, he ran his gnarled hand around the knocker next
to the door. He had never thought twice about it before, but today it
caught his eye. He reached for it, its smooth metal cool in the warm
afternoon. He pulled on it, but it didn't budge. Edge retraced the circle,
feeling something pull at him from deep in his mind. The tranquility of
the afternoon settled down around him like a cloak. He shook his head,
remembering why he was here.

"Mave?" he called into the house again. Silence. Even the birds
seemed to now be resting in the still afternoon. Edge headed back
down to his truck then paused, cocking his head to the side, as if

listening for something, then turned and followed the fence line down to the corral.

Without thinking, he waved his hand over the tall grass beside the fence. From under the shade trees, Boss stepped out and ambled across the field, falling into stride with Edge. His blonde head bobbed up and down with each step.

"Hey, fella! What's new around the spread?" Edge snuck a handful of long grasses expertly out of their stalks and handed them across the top of the greying fence. Boss leaned over and nuzzled them out of his hand.

As they walked along—man on one side of the fence, horse on the other—they fell into a smooth, easy rhythm and continued this way to the corral. Boss swished his long tail carelessly as he stopped a short distance away from the large fur-covered mound peacefully lying under the swaying willow tree. Edge squinted into the corral, and then hauled himself onto the fence. The board bowed and groaned lightly under his sturdy frame. He squinted again into the shadows of the tree and was greeted with the light scent of musk and hay.

The dozing form slowly raised its head, and Boss crept closer and breathed into the beast's nostril once more. Then he turned and walked back to Edge's spot between the dividing fences. Boss leaned close in and blew. Edge could feel his warm breath and the tickle of his whiskers.

"Thank you, Boss," Edge said as he rubbed the soft white fuzz on his pink nose. "You're a good host, buddy."

Edge approached the corral gate, and, in one smooth motion, neatly swept the lock up, creaking the metal gate wide open. Across the dusty circle, the large animal watched with subdued interest, staying relaxed in his spot but following him intently with his eyes.

"Hey there, mister, when'd you get here?" Edge clanked the gate closed and walked off to his side, careful not to stand directly in front of the animal. A shallow breeze swept across the animal's fur, ferrying its earthy scent over to Edge once more.

Standing sideways, Edge waited about two feet away from the animal, while the old willow tree moved in a lazy dance around the two of them. Light moved and shifted across the dry, hay-specked dirt.

With a slight groan, Edge squatted down and leaned one forearm across his faded jeans. He reached his other hand down and scooped up a handful of loose dirt, and then let it sift through his fingers, sliding like fine silk, back to the ground.

"This bum knee has been giving me trouble."

The animal gave a slight nod. Edge lifted an eyebrow and turned his head, looking more directly at the animal. The leaves cast strange shadows on both their faces. Edge gazed eye to eye with the buffalo across the short distance between them, catching a fleeting light dancing across the animal's eye. Edge grinned, the corners of his mouth pulling his smooth, whiskerless jaw into a wide smile.

"You, my friend, are going to be interesting. You're a bit mysterious, you know?"

Just then, Edge's phone buzzed. The buffalo jerked his head to the side. Edge felt the closeness of his heavy horns as he reached into his back pocket and pulled out his phone. He squinted at the screen.

"Gotta grab this one, fella. Be right back." A small black bird inched its way closer and closer to the large animal, cocking its head in a quick, jerky motion and staring intently. The buffalo nodded and the bird leapt to his back.

Edge heaved himself upright, turning his back to the animal. "El-lo?"

"Dad!"

"Hey there, Jay, to what do I owe the honor?"

"Dad! Holy man! I'm glad I got you. You all right?"

EDGE, MAVE and ZOE

"Yeah, son, I'm fine. Why? What's going on?"

"We don't know, really. The house—it was so steaming hot. And mom. She was passed out on the floor and—"

"Is she okay?" Edge cut him off, already leaning toward his truck.

"Yeah, she's fine. She's okay now. We think it was the heat. She's better now. Hey, where are you?"

"I'm at Mave's. I can't find her either. Have you been here yet?" Edge relaxed his shoulders and turned to the buffalo. The bird on its back was busy searching through his light scruffy hair for tiny insects.

"Yeah, I was there all morning. Mave's here. She was looking for you."

Edge sighed out relieved breath and walked back beside the animal. He eyed the small mounting block just on the other side of the fence. "Hold on a second, son." He slid the wooden stool under the lowest fence rung, wiped his hand across to clear the dust, and sat down with soft grunt. He brought the phone back to his ear.

"Let me guess," he said smiling, "she had questions about a large black fella." Edge chuckled. The creases around his eyes deepened. Jay laughed.

"I'll ask her."

"Let me talk to your mom a minute, son."

Jay handed the phone to Zoe. She took it in one hand and brought the other to the back of her neck. It was wet, even though her thick twists of shoulder-length hair were pulled up and off her neck. She adjusted her scarf, gently shaking out her puff of hair, and walked into the other room.

Jay smiled at Mave. "Dad wants to know if you had a question about a large black fella."

Mave choked on her water. "Damn, that man sure is direct," she said. She raised her brows. "Oh, my. That was twice, wasn't it?"

They nodded.

"I'm going straight to hell," she muttered, shaking her head.

"Well, if you're going to hell for two 'damns,' then you'll sure as shit have good company," Ila sputtered out.

Mave's smile was all the acknowledgement she gave. She followed Zoe into the other room. They stood side by side in front of the picture window. Mave ran her hand over her springy hair then sat down on the window seat, hugging a pillow into her lap, and looked out over the wavy green pasture. The horses grazed lazily in the distance. Mave stuffed another pillow behind her and leaned into the wall, watching the horses inch their way around the pasture. It was like meditation to her. Zoe sat down beside her.

"Okay. Bye, baby." Zoe handed the phone to Mave and leaned into her friend's shoulder.

"Edge, you kook, I've been waiting for a large black fella half my life. You know, one that's as dark as me." She laughed as she scolded him. "Wouldn't you know it? When he shows up, he's completely hairy and has four legs."

Edge laughed. "Mavey, Mavey, Mavey. Oh, darling, one of these days. You just be patient. Although he is one good-looking dude."

"I don't know, Edge." Mave looked out past the horses roving on the horizon. She took Zoe's hand. "I think my opportunity just might have passed." She caught her reflection in the window. Her dark, round face smiled sadly back at her. Zoe leaned her head on Mave's shoulder, her long twisted locks tickling Mave's neck. Mave watched Zoe as she lifted her amber brown face, smoothed her hair, and then leaned into her once more.

"Black I certainly am," Mave said quietly. She thought of Isaac for the third time. "I don't know, Edge. It's been a long while. And you've seen how this town is changing. I—" Mave broke off, inhaling deeply. "I'm not sure if this is my place anymore, you know?"

"Hey there, girl." Edge softened. "Hey, listen—that wife of mine still next to you?"

"Yep," Mave said as she leaned her head over to rest against Zoe.

"Look at that beautiful woman." Mave saw Zoe's face next to hers in the window. "See that beautiful brown skin? I love that woman more than anything on this planet." Edge instantly thought of Jay. "Well, you know what I mean. That woman has my heart and soul. Her beautiful brown skin is just one of the things I love about her. Love is love, Mave. You, of all people, know that. And you never know when it will come for you."

Mave smiled, pulling her lips to the side. "Mmmhmm," she drawled out slowly. She brought her hand up and touched Zoe's cheek with the back of her fingers. Her own features were lost in the darkness her face reflected; her eyes, the only part she could see, stared back into her.

Edge paused. "Mave," he said, softening his voice, "you know you're not alone, right? And you know that being the beautiful, mysterious dark woman you are, living here in Moira was the right thing for you to do, remember? It's never simple, Mave. And it's certainly never easy ... but we're here with you, girl. We're waiting, too, in our own way."

"Mmmmm," Mave answered again, not committing to an answer. Zoe squeezed her long, thin fingers around Mave's short, thick ones.

"Look, Mave," Edge started again, "look, just because he's not here right at this moment ... it doesn't mean...," Edge paused, strangely at a loss for words. He looked over at the buffalo lounging casually next to him. The animal was looking directly at Edge, the light in his eyes flickering. Edge squinted, staring hard into those eyes, searching. It was as if shadows were moving deep within, as if he were seeing only a portion of a scene. Edge leaned forward, straining to decipher the images before him, but they remained cryptic. Then, instantly, words popped back into his head.

"Mave, it's not completely over, and you know that. We didn't know how this was going to come around, but we always knew that it would, didn't we? And I don't even know what that means. You hear me?"

"I know. I've been seeing it. And now Ila has, too. Edge, it truly scares me." Mave's voice fell.

Feeling the tears welling up, she gritted her teeth to hold them back. She turned her head away from the room and quietly handed the phone to Zoe. Zoe gently received the phone from Mave's hand and leaned away. She touched the top of Mave's head as she stood up, then lifted the phone back to her own ear.

Ila sat on the overstuffed couch watching Zoe and Mave across the room. They had this way about them. One touch and the other nodded or shook her head. Something, an imperceptible language, almost like Edge with his horses, transpired between them. *That's why happy horses sound so corny,* Ila thought, *because it's so much more than that. It is happiness, yes. Contentment. Safety. But it's love, too. Absolutely.* Ila nodded to herself. *Love in action.* Ila turned to Eve.

"I've never seen Mave like that before."

"Like what?" Eve leaned around Ila and stole a look at Mave.

"Sad, I guess. Alone. She looks"—Ila's heart squeezed in her chest as her own familiar aloneness crept up on her—"lonely."

"Yeah, she gets like that sometimes," Eve said. "Feeling different … alone. Maybe lonely. I never thought of it like that."

"She talks to you about that stuff?" Ila felt a pang of jealously shoot through her.

Eve nodded and looked down at her hands. She looked at Ila's brown one then back at her own lily white one. She squeezed her hand shut then opened it, stretching her fingers wide.

"How is your hand anyway?" Ila asked, erasing the distance threatening to come between them. She took Eve's hand, flipped it over and back, and then held it softly between her own.

"Fine." Eve brushed thoughts of her hand away. "Why don't you ask her about it, Ila? It might do you both good to talk about that kind of thing."

"I don't even know what 'that kind of thing' is," Ila said more sharply than she meant. Gently, she placed Eve's hand down, contrasting her harsh tone.

"You guys have more in common than just dreaming, Ila," Eve said. "You hear me?"

"Yeah, I hear you," Ila answered. "But I'm not so sure about that."

Eve's chest fell as she blew a loud breath out across her lips. "You'll never know if you don't ask her."

"I *said* I hear you. But I don't really know what I'm asking about." Ila sighed pointedly. "We're so alike in many ways, Mave and I, but it's more on the outside, you know? More the wrapping, the package, you know? You and she are the ones more alike. At least on the inside. You guys and your feelings." Ila picked up a picture and gazed at a younger Edge and Zoe with baby Jay, suddenly feeling very alone in the world. Her eyes began to cloud. She blinked back hard against the threatening wetness. She turned her head away and set the picture gently back on the shiny, dark table.

"Look, Ila, I just take more chances with people, you know? I can't help it. You don't like to do that, I get it. You don't want to let people know how soft you are on the inside. How things get to you, how sensitive you really are...."

Ila spun and looked through her smoldering eyes at Eve. She pushed herself off the sofa and clenched both hands into loose fists. Her jaw squeezed just enough that Eve saw the taut muscle working under her skin. Ila fixed her gaze on a shiny spot on the wall behind Eve. Eve didn't relent.

"I don't push it with you, Ila, but you're making it hard on yourself. Mave is good to talk to. About anything. Outside or inside. And, if you have forgotten, she's your friend. Yeah, she's older, but she's a really good friend. And a really good person. That's what friends do, right? They talk about shit they don't understand."

Eve stood up and put her hands on her hips at the other end of the sofa. Her feet were wide, as if she were blocking the way. She inhaled deeply and watched Ila closely. Seconds passed. The distant scream of a red tail hawk broke the heavy silence. Ila peeled her eyes away from the light on the wall and looked at Eve. Her brown eyes were flecked with gold, vibrant and fierce. But Eve felt something in there, something behind her fierce gaze. Ila stared deep into Eve's green eyes, unseeing. For a brief moment, Eve glimpsed something in the depth of Ila's eyes and it wrenched Eve's heart, as if she had been physically hit. Then it was gone.

Ila blinked her eyes and relaxed her arms and hands. She glanced down quickly then back to her friend. Eve hugged her arms around herself. Underneath, she was shaking.

"Damn, Eve, you didn't have to go all Shakespeare on me with that soliloquy." Ila turned up the corner of her mouth and smiled slyly. She squeezed then shook out her hands, shifting from one foot to the other, and wiped her moist palms on her thin, faded jeans.

Eve walked over and slid her arm around her friend.

"You're okay, tough girl," Eve said, bumping Ila's hip. "You're going to be just fine with all this. Trust me."

Ila smirked at Eve then flashed her a covering smile. "Of course, I'll be just fine," she said. *That's what I'm afraid of,* she added in her head. *I want to be more than just fine.*

EVE and JAY

"**D**o you want me to head back?" Edge asked Zoe.

"No, Ji," she answered, "I'm okay."

Eve hugged Ila tight, the tension in her own arms and shoulders fading. She lingered an extra moment and let Ila melt into her shoulder. Ila nodded and her full lips pulled into her signature sideways smile once again.

"I'll be right back," she mumbled, pulled away, and traipsed to the bathroom.

Eve watched Ila and her two different-colored socks slide across the hard stone floor. She thought of Mave and her multicolored socks and smiled silently regarding her two friends' similarities.

Jay leaned leisurely next to the doorway, resting his socked foot casually on the wooden baseboard.

"Really, Ji, I'm okay," Eve heard Zoe finishing up across the room.

Eve leaned into the wall next to Jay and caught his clean scent slightly mixed with leather and hay. Her eyes slid shut as a small shiver ran through her. She peeked out of the corner of her eye to see if he had noticed. He was staring out across the room, seemingly caught deep in thought. Eve drew her hand up in front of her and pretended to examine her nails. Then she began picking absently at her finger. She brought it up to her mouth and started nibbling her nail—an old nervous habit.

"Why does your mom call him 'Ji'?" she asked softly around her finger.

"Huh?" Jay jumped at the sound of her words. Eve stifled her smile behind her hand. Jay blinked and turned to face her, leaning his shoulder casually on the wall. She could see him trying to decipher what she had said. Eve nodded to his mom and smiled as she brought her hands to the wall and turned to face him.

"Why does your mom call your dad 'Ji'?"

"Oh," Jay's mouth broke into a wide smile. "Sorry." The soft creases at the edges of his mouth hinted at dimples. Eve felt her heart quicken in her chest. She steadied her breath, working hard to overcome her body's organic response.

"She says it's because when they met, he was more agitated, more 'edgy.' She's the one who started calling him that in the first place. Edge. It stuck. He had nothing to do with it." Jay imitated his father's deep, slow drawl, "'No say,' as he tells it. He said it was like this huge river that he found himself being pulled into then dragged along in."

"I don't understand."

"That's exactly what I said. He said the whole world had been conspiring to call him 'Edgy,' starting with one gigantic tsunami of a force—that would be my mother. She was the only one who could get away with it, too. That's how he tells it anyway—the only one brave enough. *She* says someone needed to give that man a dose of reality." Jay smiled. Eve loved his smile. She mirrored it back to him.

She pulled her gaze away from his mouth and fell into his eyes, never knowing which one to look at. The brown and blue were both so clear in their own way. They pulled her back and forth. She felt silly, like she was trying not to notice the difference every time she looked at him. Jay gazed down at her, watching her darting eyes. He smiled. Eve felt her cheeks warm but held his gaze. Jay felt warmth spread across his own cheeks. He looked over her shoulder at the stone mantle and drew in a long shaky breath, trying to slow his heartbeat down. He glanced at Eve and quickly tumbled his words out.

"Mom shortened it to 'Ji.' She likes to tell it as an eastern thing. Like in India. That it's a term of endearment and respect—J-i—like how they call Gandhi Gandhiji. She says it all straight faced. God, she adores him." Jay looked over at his mom still on the phone with his dad. "For all his toughness, for all his drive, for all that he is. She really and truly loves 'Edge-ji.'" Jay smiled warmly.

Eve was quiet. *Yeah. Love*, she thought. *I know that one.*

But she doubted her own parents ever did. They couldn't even be in the same room together. They couldn't stand one another. When she was young and she had to go to the other's house, she would ask to be dropped off at the corner. She could feel all the anger and hurt both of them had for the other. It jittered under her skin, jumbled and bumped chaotically all around her. It got worse as their worlds got closer. It was like they each had their own bubble, but when they got close, their bubbles were chemically explosive. Two ingredients both perfectly fine on their own, but together—kazow!—a huge nightmare.

"Yeah," she said, bringing herself back to the present. "That's pretty cool," she finished lamely.

Jay nodded. Neither looked at the other. A breeze floated in the open windows, coaxing the sweet scent of gardenias through the warm room. Eve closed her eyes and inhaled deeply, lightly lifting her chin, as if following the scent. Jay watched her through his long, thick eyelashes.

Mave cleared her throat from across the room as Zoe slid her phone in her back pocket.

"All right y'all, ready to head out?"

Jay pushed himself off the wall, brushing his damp palms on his jeans.

"To where?"

"Back to my place."

Zoe stretched her long, thin arms up and rolled her head from side to side.

"You all right there, girl?" Mave asked as she pushed herself up, her thick, sturdy frame a contrast to Zoe's long, thin body.

"Yep." Zoe's soft pink lips pulled into a wide, toothy grin. "Okay, then, people, let's beat this Twinkie stand!"

"Oh my, you did not just say that." Mave chuckled, shaking her head.

Zoe, the only one in shoes, spun on her stylish but weathered boots and clacked lightly across the stone floor. Mave padded after her in her multicolored socks. She approached Eve and Jay, both of them trying to avoid her gaze. Around them, the air was warm and light, much warmer than where she had been sitting. She eyed both of them. Jay ran his usually steady hands over his head. Mave's perceptive eye saw them shaking ever so slightly. Jay felt her gaze and began rubbing his head, trying to distract her. Mave reached for his vibrating hand and met his eyes squarely. His other hand became motionless on his head as she willed him into her deep, seemingly endless eyes. Mave glanced at Eve, the soft pink fading from her cheeks. *You'll be all right, mister.* Mave thought. She gave his hand a little squeeze and started to let go.

I know, I know, Jay responded in his own head, not even realizing he had heard Mave's thoughts. Mave paused momentarily then gently dropped his hand.

At that moment, Ila walked back into the room, shaking the last drops of water off her hands. The three turned and looked at her. She stopped short and furrowed her brow.

"What'd I miss?" She looked from one to the other, stopping on Mave. "*What?*" she demanded. "What'd you all do?" She glanced behind her and turned in a full circle. "Why's it so hot in here again?"

Mave held out her arm and waved Ila over. "Come on, child, let's get moving." Ila walked over and let Mave draw her in and guide the door. Ila looked back over Mave's shoulder, brows still furrowed, trying to figure out what had transpired. She caught Eve's eye then glanced at Jay, and realization washed over her. Ila smiled, nodding to herself, then relaxed under Mave's warm embrace as they moved outside.

Eve, followed by Jay, strode out after them, silently sliding on their dust-covered boots, and walked, nervously quiet, side-by-side to the car.

Mave squeezed behind the driver's seat, bounced and scooted all the way across, and rolled down the dusty window. Ila followed her, sitting in the middle.

"Grab the front, Zoe. We'll be fine back here."

Zoe slid the front seat into place and plopped down, keeping the heavy door open. She brought her hand to the soft curve of her neck and sighed happily as a breeze gently ruffled her hair.

"Phew, it's hot in here!"

Eve flopped in next to Ila, pulled the driver's seat into place, and cranked down her window. "Let's go, let's go!" she commanded lightly, bouncing up and down on the worn seat, mostly to ease the jitters she felt inside. Mave and Ila bounced on the seat next to her. Sweat beaded on Mave's brow.

"All right there, happiness and sunshine, calm down." Mave drew the back of her hand across her wet forehead.

Jay jumped in, revved the engine to life, and clunked the aged car into reverse in one swift motion. Zoe rested her elbow on the window and settled back into the warm seat. Mave leaned into the breeze that began to flow around them as they pulled out of the lane.

The low, steady beat on the radio drifted into the quiet. Jay leaned over and turned it up. On his classic station, Smokey Robinson's smooth, high voice sang out, and they all began to bob and sway to the rhythmic beat. The twangy guitar licks rolled out over the funky bass line. Zoe swayed side to side then reached over and turned the volume up louder. She added a light harmony to the chorus.

"Going to a go-go."

Mave and the others joined right in.

"Everybody's...."

"Going to a go-go."

"Baby, come on now...."

"Going to a go-go."

"Don't you wanna go?"

BEAST

J ay's car arrived at Mave's place in a light cloud of dust. Laughing and singing, they tumbled out of the noisy car and headed straight for the barn. Edge and the buffalo sat in the cool shade of the willow tree, silently watching them.

Mave squinted across the corral, looking for the animal in the shadows. The rest of the crowd noisily congregated behind her.

"Shush, you all." She swatted behind her as her eyes searched, as if the quiet would help her see. Finally, she spotted Edge resting casually next to the animal.

"He's gorgeous, isn't he?" Mave lifted the metal latch and swung the heavy gate open.

"Oh, wow," Zoe whispered, glimpsing the large form next to Edge. She took a step back. "What *is* that?"

"Come on in." Mave held the gate open for her.

Zoe hung back.

"I'm good here. For now."

Zoe stepped aside and let the others through. Nervously, she rubbed her lips together and adjusted her bright scarf on her head. She took the gate from Mave, the cool metal comforting to her sweaty hand, and steadied herself as she kept a wary eye on the animal. She stepped just inside the ring and slipped the gate closed, stopping there. The others moved closer to Edge, climbing onto various spots along the tall fence. So far, the buffalo had been nothing but gentle, but he *was* huge. Only Edge had the inclination to sit on the ground next to him.

"Dad, you're either crazy or brave, and I don't know which."

"I've been called both, son. I like both sides of that coin—I'll take either," he said, winking at Jay.

"What are you gonna do with this guy?" Edge asked Mave.

"Keep him," Mave answered. She raised her eyebrows, surprised at her own answer. "I guess I'm going to keep him," she nodded, satisfied.

The beast gave a quick nod. "Guess he's good with that, too." Mave walked over to the animal's shoulder and gave it a confident pat. Even lying down, his shoulder was higher than her hips.

"What do you know about Cape buffalo?" Edge asked her.

"Not much," Mave admitted. "Not much at all. The folks from Seren didn't tell me much when they dropped him off this morning. I'm not even sure they knew what he was. Nice people—but I thought it strange they had this kind of animal in their possession."

Edge nodded. "I would have thought—between you and I—we would have known about him, even if he was way over in Seren." Edge turned to his wife.

"Hey, Zoe, whatcha doing way over there?" The animal turned and looked toward Zoe.

"Hanging," she answered, her voice cracking. She was clearly uncomfortable with the attention from the buffalo. The animal looked back to Edge. Edge nodded and the animal turned back to Zoe.

"Did he just ask permission for something?" Ila asked. "I swear it looked like he was asking you permission."

"Yep." Edge nodded. "Yes, he did. He is one respectful young fellow. I wonder where he learned that. It doesn't sound like his previous owners would have taught him much."

Ila shrugged, pleased to have noticed something about the animal. "It sounded like they treated him just like a cow."

"He's one smart cow," Edge said as he kept his eyes on the animal. The beast heaved himself onto his front feet. Mave backed away. Edge stood and dragged his stool away, giving the animal space. The buffalo lurched forward, rising to his full height. Edge let out a low whistle. Casually, the animal moved straight toward Zoe. She looked as if she would jump right out of her skin, but true to her nature, she stood her ground. "They should get along well," Edge said, nodding at the two of them. "They're a lot alike. Very herd oriented. Family is the most important thing, probably for much of the same reason. But when they're threatened, even if it's a poorly matched fight, they'll stay and stand their ground. They fiercely protect what's important to them. Very group, collective orientated, but not afraid to be an individual, make an individual choice. In Africa, they are given a wide berth. They are said to be unpredictable—"

"Ha!" Jay interrupted. "That *is* like mom!"

"Better watch it, son," Edge said smiling. "In Africa, they are known to attack. Often they say it's unpredictable, but I bet dollars to doughnuts that they have a darn good reason. But somebody just hadn't read the warning signs. That's how it usually goes when someone says an animal does something for no reason. I have yet to find a case where an animal doesn't have a way of communicating their fear or agitation. Humans just seem to be ignorant of the signs," Edge finished.

Ila nodded, keeping her eyes locked on Zoe and the animal.

The buffalo took his time approaching Zoe. Another small black bird swooped down and hovered over the large animal, deciding this wasn't the time, and flew to the fence to watch. Zoe stood statue still. The animal stopped an arm's length away. His musty smell, mixed with the earthy scent of fresh hay and grass, swirled around Zoe, touching her on a primal level. Her dark brown eyes locked on his vacuous black ones. Every cell in her body seemed to be electrified. Slowly, courageously, she reached her hand out to touch him. As soon as her trembling fingers reached his short dark coat, Zoe felt herself relax, a deep sense of calm washing over her. She widened her gaze, taking in the full size of the massive animal standing in front of her. The animal shook lightly from head to toe. Zoe watched his short coarse hair wave with the movement, as if it were in slow motion. Then, simultaneously, they both turned toward the waiting group. Side by side, as if they were long lost companions, Zoe and the animal covered the short distance to the group across the corral.

"I think he'll be fine here," Edge quietly said to Mave.

"Whooo, that is one brave animal," Mave replied, chuckling softly.

"You've got that right." Edge nodded.

Edge teased Zoe as they walked up. "You really had him fooled, lovie. You let him think he was leading you."

"He's unlike any animal I've ever been around, Ji—any. And we've had some soulful beasts in our midst."

Zoe slid up next to Edge. He nodded and wrapped a strong arm around her. She held onto his arm with both her hands and leaned into him.

"That's it!" Mave said, "Soulful Beast." She took a piece of stray hay off the ground. The animal walked up and stood directly in front of her. "I hereby dub thee Soulful Beast." She tapped him on each shoulder. "Beast for short." Beast gave his quick nod of acceptance then carefully turned his massive head and walked toward the horses' field.

"I guess he's ready to go in with the boys," Mave said, raising her eyebrows.

"Looks like it," Edge agreed.

Eve moved closer to Jay. Ila leaned forward on her perch.

"Think it will be okay?" Ila asked.

Jay nodded but didn't speak. His dad knew horses well and had even owned some cows growing up, but this was new. Jay rarely got to see his father in a totally new situation. Often he saw him with new people, but he was basically repeating the same situations over and over—teaching different people how to read their animal's language. Rarely did he get to observe "new neural pathways being created" as Mave often put it when new situations were happening.

"Good for the brain!" she would tell them. "Keeps you young!"

They always protested, telling her the same thing. "We're trying to grow up, here, not get younger!" At least in the beginning that's what they had said. But that only encouraged Mave to go on about how the brain forms new paths—using terms like "neuroplasticity." To them, it became blah blah blah, so they learned not to complain. In the end, though, they had learned.

Here's to new neural pathways. Jay smiled to himself as he watched the scene unfold.

Edge shifted, taking a wider stance, his hands moving modestly at his sides. Jay watched his dad and noticed the tapping of his fingers and thumbs together. Initially, Jay thought it was a nervous tick, but then he saw the rhythm, the pattern, and he felt the energy of his movement. Then Jay knew exactly what he was doing. Edge was "calming his field"—that's what he had called it when Jay asked. Jay remembered the conversation. *"Not in the new agey, airy fairy out there kind of way,"* his dad had told him. *"But in the practical, palpable way that settles into your cells, into your bones."* Jay had felt it way back then. If you stood near him, you always felt it.

Mave had her own version of this practice. Today, she rhythmically waved her palms at her sides. It reminded Jay of playing the tambourine. Both Mave's hands were synchronized in subtle, rhythmic movement. You had to look hard to notice it. He realized that what they were doing fell under the radar of our everyday mind. *Maybe that's why people are drawn to these two,* Jay thought. These two individuals who loved time alone more than anyone else he knew, attracted people wherever they went. They always seemed to have a small crowd gather around them. It was like moths drawn to light. They were irresistible. Jay smiled. *Peeps,* he thought while watching them, *you gotta love your peeps.*

"Hey, Jersey," Edge called over to Jay, his fingers still moving, "get the gate, would ya?"

Jay slipped carefully off the fence and walked to the metal gate separating the corral from the horses' field. He slid the latch up, swung the gate out into the field, and positioned himself between the metal gate and the corral fence, just in case. Stepping up onto the bottom rung of the fence, Jay rested his upper body on the gate and drew in a long breath and held it.

At the sound of the latch opening, the other horses lazily picked their way over to Boss and stood waiting. They paused a short distance from the opening and gave plenty of room for Beast to enter. Beast walked to the opening and looked back to Edge. Edge nodded. Then Beast swung his head over to Mave. She nodded, too. Beast turned to Jay and gave a quick jerk of his head. Then he stepped out into the deep green field, making his way over to the horses. Bean shook his head up and down, his jet-black mane rising and falling in a continuous wave, and stepped out in front of Beast. Then he turned and walked back into the field, his mane flying like a banner in the wind. Beast followed. The others fell into line behind. Bean led Beast to a large pile of green alfalfa hay. They heard a soft *huff* from the buffalo. Then the animal leaned down and casually pulled a tuft of hay into his mouth, grinding it round and round. Every so often, he would look up and pause, a stray piece dangling from his lips.

Mave cleared her throat. "All right then. That's a wrap! Tea time, y'all?"

"Yes, ma'am!" Eve answered. "Tea time it is!"

The others chimed in agreement as they fell in laughing at themselves. Jay swung the gate back around and clanked it ceremoniously into place.

Ila glanced one final time at Beast, his dark eyes staring, penetrating her mind. She turned quickly and followed Mave and the others up to the house.

ILA and EVE

"Jay, I really do need some shoes on my boys this week. That work for you?"

"Yes, ma'am," Jay answered. "For you, Mavel ... the stars are the limit!" He finished with a dramatic sweep of his long arm as he bowed in her direction.

Zoe and Edge shook their heads from inside Edge's truck. "Thanks for the tea, Mavey," Edge drawled out in his deep voice. "See you soon."

Zoe blew a kiss from her side of the truck, and Mave waved them all off then turned and headed into back into the house.

"Want to meet at the Roadhouse later?" Jay asked the girls as the dust from Edge's truck settled around them.

"Absolutely!" Eve loved the Roadhouse.

"Sure," Ila said, a little less enthusiastically.

"What?" Eve asked Ila, sensing her hesitation.

"I'm just tired, I guess. I don't think I slept well last night. With that dream and all."

"Want me to ride with you?" Eve asked. She glanced at Jay.

"Sure," he said. "Ditch me. That's cool."

Eve's face fell.

"Hey, I'm only kidding. Go. I have to grab a couple of things for this week anyhow." He smiled widely. "I know you can't really ditch me," he said as half of his mouth rose higher into a crooked smile. "Work for you, Ila?"

"You know it." Ila walked to the passenger door of her car and climbed in.

Eve hugged Jay tightly. "You're the best," she teased. "Who could ever ditch you?" She gave him a swift peck on the lips and quickly let him go, her soft lips lingering for a split second. She slipped into the driver's seat, started the car in one swift movement, and stared out the back window as she reversed over the loose gravel. Ila raised her eyebrow. Eve caught it out of the corner of her eye.

"Not a word if you know what's good for you." Eve turned and looked straight ahead down the tree-lined lane. She smiled and waved out the window, still not looking at Jay.

Ila lowered her voice, deep and creepy. "Take me home then, woman."

Eve raised hers. "Of course, m'lady," she said with a flourishing gesture of her hand, "whatever you wish."

Eve punched the gas a little too hard and shot gravel out behind them. Jay jumped to the side and watched them drive away. He rubbed his fingertips over his lips, still feeling a slight tingle from Eve's kiss. *Damn,* he said to himself. *She just kissed me!*

Ila and Eve drove down the back road in silence. The sun slowly lowered itself across the western sky. Traffic was starting to pick up around them. Cars swooshed by from the opposite direction. Ila was the first to speak.

"Do you think I really should talk to Mave?"

"Huh?" Eve glanced over, not understanding.

"You know, about my stuff. About being an African-American, brown-skinned woman…," Ila paused, collecting her thoughts. "About being a half-white, dreaming, motherless woman. All of that, I guess." She nodded to herself. "Yeah, about all of it, really."

"I don't follow."

"Well," Ila began slowly, "here's the thing: I know you don't see me as any different than you. You're like my sister. I guess. I don't really know what that's like—having no siblings and all—but I imagine it would be like this." Ila paused, moving her hand back and forth between them. "It's just that no one really talks about these differences, these very obvious differences in backgrounds…." Ila squirmed in her seat. She had never broached the subject with Eve before. "I'm not sure, it's just that…."

Eve squinted at Ila, trying to follow.

Ila talked faster. "I know it shouldn't matter—I know that. But it does. To me. Right now, anyway. I don't have a mom. That's fucked up. I know there are lots of kids like that. But I don't have anyone in my family that looks like me, literally. You know? My dad ... even if he was a decent dad—which he's not—he still doesn't look like me, doesn't know my experience in the world. Barely anyone at school looks like me. And to top that, I do this weird dreaming thing—my mom, she taught me that. But no one mentions her. Sometimes I feel so damn alone. Like I just don't fit. Anywhere."

Eve stayed silent.

"How could you know? Of course, you don't know...." Ila smiled wearily. "Well, Mave, she's the closest thing I have to family that actually shares my complexion." Ila hung her head. This was coming out all wrong. She tried again. "I know it's more than skin color, I know that, but I don't know. Something in me really wants Mave to get me, to meet me, to notice me as a brown-skinned woman, a black woman, to talk about what it's like."

"What it's like? Here in Moira?"

Ila nodded.

"But Jay," Eve began, "he's mixed like you. What about Zoe? Haven't you and Jay ever talked about it?"

Ila shook her head. "I guess I want a woman to talk to me about it, to walk me through this deal of growing up. I love Zoe, but I'm just closer to Mave. Maybe it's the dreaming stuff. No one ever mentions race. Mave has never said a word that makes me think she sees you and me any differently. Except way back. Before you moved here. She showed me how to take care of my hair. My dad had no idea. I had some serious nap—" Ila stopped herself. "Some serious tangles."

"I've been told I have nappy hair before." Eve giggled. "One of the preschoolers was combing my hair once; she told me so. You know, it must be true if a four-year-old tells you something."

Ila smiled. She reached out and combed her fingers through Eve's long wavy hair. "This in no way can be considered nappy." Just then her fingers caught and tangled in Eve's hair.

"Mmmm hmmm," Eve answered smugly. "Told you."

Ila wrestled her fingers from Eve's hair then poked them into her own corkscrew curls. "I guess...," she said finally, dropping her hands heavily into her lap, "I guess I just want somewhere I truly belong."

"Now *that* I get," Eve said, nodding, staring ahead and watching the road disappear under the car as they drove. "Seriously, Ila, I think you should just talk to Mave. She's as much family to you as anyone, right? I'm sure she could help you, sort it out with you. She's definitely no stranger to this stuff"—Eve hesitated, glancing up, searching for the word—"this heart shit." She smiled.

Ila nodded. "I guess so." She hesitated, inhaling shakily. "I guess I will."

"Atta girl," Eve said, slapping her on her thigh.

Ila rolled her eyes. "Atta girl?"

Eve nodded, turned, and stopped short in her own driveway. She threw the car into park, and unbuckled, letting the belt clank loudly against the door.

"All right, then. See you, sister!" Eve leaned over and gave Ila a quick, tight hug. "Roadhouse at 8?" she asked as she swung the driver door open and slid out. She closed the door behind her and leaned back through the window, waiting for Ila's answer. Behind her, a group of young kids squealed. Ila looked past Eve as the children darted across the street in one large group. Ila couldn't help noticing none of them had brown skin. Eve followed Ila's gaze over her shoulder. The gaggle of children had already disappeared into someone's backyard.

Ila crawled her way awkwardly across the console and flopped into the driver's seat.

"Sure!" she said with mock enthusiasm. Eve shook her head then bounded up the front steps to her door, throwing it open enthusiastically.

The Roadhouse, Ila smirked, shaking her own head. She shifted the car into reverse with a proper thunk and turned to look over her shoulder. Her chest fell as she let out a long, slow breath. *Yippee.*

THE ROADHOUSE

E ve pulled her small pickup next to Jay's dinged up BMW at the far end of the crowded roadside parking lot. She was late. The warm summer sun was just disappearing behind the massive neighboring oak, bathing it in golden light. *Dang, that looks like a giant, multi-limbed deity or something,* she mused.

Eve looked back at the Roadhouse. Its exterior, draped with reclaimed 200-year-old barn siding, was something of an enigma. Its rustic outside led you to believe you were stepping into an old saloon, which was far from the case. It looked especially seasoned in the rich, golden light of the sunset. Eve gazed back and forth between the golden tree and the faded wooden décor of the building. *Looks like East meets West.* Eve stood silently in the parking lot. Birds chattered invisibly from deep inside the cover of the immense tree's rustling leaves. Eve shivered even though the breeze feathering across her skin was warm and moist.

The sun slipped ninjalike below the horizon. Light pinks and muted violets diffused around the fading golden glow. The tree's limbs turned darker, more ominous, silhouetted by the glorious sunset. Eve shivered again and turned away from the tree. The warm glow from the Roadhouse windows drew a smile across her face. Her ears tuned into a soft beat rising up, growing louder and louder, approaching fast.

As if shot out of a cannon, Ila's white Jetta flew around the corner, music rhythmically streaming out the windows. She screeched into the parking lot. Eve jumped back against her car as Ila skidded skillfully to a stop next to her.

"Jesu Cristo, woman!" Eve scolded Ila over the music. Ila cut the engine, and the chaos of noise settled to the ground like a blanket.

"What?!" Ila yelled into the quiet night, her ears still ringing from the music.

"You drive like a bat outta hell!" Eve's mouth threatened a smile.

"You can't even mess up this parking lot," Ila said, lowering her voice to a normal range. "Vince even has the parking lot groomed to perfection. Just like every other aspect of this place. See? No mess." Ila waved her hand behind her car and walked around to Eve. "Not one tiny pebble out of place. And, you know, I'm an excellent driver." Ila grinned mischievously.

The granite lot beneath their feet *was* packed down expertly. Eve looked around. The lot flowed naturally into paths on either side of the building. Ila linked her arm into Eve's.

"No, darlin', I wouldn't. No, I *couldn't* mess up the Zen of this place."

They walked up to the inviting red doors arm in arm, the granite pebbles grinding lightly underneath their feet as they approached.

The entrance greeted them warmly, ready to usher them in.

"That tree sure is trippy in this light, almost otherworldly…," Ila commented as she pulled the front door open for Eve.

"I know. I was just thinking the same thing."

Eve stepped into the glowing light of the restaurant. The soft murmur of the crowd rose up around them. Delicate rhythms fell like soft rain, seeming to come from nowhere and everywhere. Ila let go of Eve's arm and surveyed the room. Eve looked around, too, at friends and families gathering, visiting, and eating. Vince, the owner, had filled the room with booths. He designed the rooms around flowing, continuous lines, minimalist in its use of only the necessary elements. Vince had told them once that he had wanted a simply designed establishment, one uncomplicated that appealed to the sensitive side of people, especially those more affected by environments. He had said that the world was moving fast and flashing loud enough, and people needed places like this, places that spoke to the soul. He kept the lights low and warm. The booths were high, so sounds were kept to a minimum and comfort was maximized.

"This place sure is mellow," Ila said.

"Relaxing to the system, Vince calls it."

Ila nodded absently. The place was packed. Vince appeared from the side room, tray loaded, hurrying back to the kitchen. He smiled widely when he spotted Ila and Eve. He put his free hand in the air as he approached them, beginning their traditional greeting ritual.

"Your place rocks!" Eve vowed.

"And rolls!" Vince affirmed.

Eve met him promptly with her left hand. A loud *crack* echoed through the room as their hands collided. Instantly, Vince dropped his tray, dishes crashing loudly on the hard entrance tile, and cradled his tingling hand. The room fell silent. All eyes turned on them.

"Oh, God, Vince! Are you okay?" Vince doubled over his hand. Eve bent down to help him. "Vince! Oh, man, I'm so sorry! I didn't smack you hard. Let me see. Here." She took his hand in both of hers. In Eve's hands, his grew warm. Vince furrowed his brow and looked at her strangely.

"I ... I think it's okay," he said, pulling his hand from hers.

"Just a minute," Eve said, "hold on a sec." Eve felt the warmth, but she felt something else—a flow, a connection that pulled Vince and her hands together. Then, just as soon as it started, their hands cooled down. The force that seemed to pull them together slowed then separated. Eve looked up at Vince. He stared back at her.

Ila felt a bead of sweat form then slowly descend along the side of her face. She reached a shaky hand up and smoothed it into her skin, looking from table to table. All eyes focused on Eve and Vince. Ila's heart thumped loudly in her chest. She placed her still shaky hand on Eve's shoulder.

"Hey, no big deal," Eve said, looking from Vince to Ila. "Just rubbing your hand a little, getting the sting out. See?!" she said, holding up his hand. "All better! Sorry, Vince, don't know my own strength." She tried to lighten the situation. Vince chuckled for the crowd. "Yep, all better! Keep eating folks, I'm okay!"

Eve squatted down and started to clean up the mess. Vince and Ila joined her.

"What the hell was that, Eve?" Vince's voice was low and sharp.

"I don't know, Vince. I'm really sorry. My hand has felt weird most of the day."

"Well, now, so does mine," he said, turning it over, examining it. "It's the strangest feeling. Like nothing I've ever felt before. Light. Tingly."

"I know. It feels pretty good, right? I really don't know what it's all about." She looked him in the eye. Ila kept her gaze down, slowly loading the broken dishes onto the emptied tray.

"Vince, I'm really sorry. I didn't mean to do anything to your hand, really." Her eyes pleaded with him. He held her gaze for a few seconds. Eve felt her shoulder tingle slightly. Then she noticed the weight of Ila's hand and felt her friend there, behind her, supporting her completely. Vince looked from Eve to Ila and back again.

"No harm, no foul," he said finally, exhaling deeply. "It does feel pretty good," he admitted. The three of them finished stacking the last of the broken dishes on his tray in silence. "Just please, don't do anything like that again. Deal?"

"Deal. Thanks, Vince."

"He's over there," he said, nodding toward the other side of the room.

"Okay," Eve said, "you got this?"

"Yeah, get outta here before you cause more trouble." Eve didn't wait for him to say anything else. She stood up and brushed her hands on her loose, linen skirt, smoothing out the small creases that had started gathering. Ila followed her across the room, her mind spinning from the encounter.

"Wassuuuuup?" Eve drawled as she slid into the booth, bumping Jay and making him scoot over.

"Apparently, you are freak," Ila said, raising her eyebrows to her friend. "And no one talks like that."

"Except you!" Eve shot back cheerfully. "Zing!" She held out her hand for a high five. She stopped in midair. They all looked at her hand. "Well, it's my right hand, at least," she said, bringing her hand slowly back to the table. "Jeez, you cause a little crackle in a room and people get all freaky."

"Actually," Jay said quietly, "I think they got scared."

Eve looked at him. So did Ila.

"They were all staring at you, Eve." Jay's voice was low and serious.

"So?"

"So, I just don't want you to have any trouble, okay? Cool it on the high five action, all right?" Jay shot back.

Eve furrowed her brow. "Trouble with what? These people? Come on, Jay, they're a little reserved, a little quiet maybe, but these are good people."

"Look, people get different; they change when they're scared. People are generally scared of what they don't understand. Just don't give them any other reasons to be scared of you, okay?" Jay sounded irritated.

"Okay," Eve said. "Damn, Jay, lighten up, would you? It's not that big a deal. These are my peeps, our peeps, remember? They've known us for a long time."

"Yeah, okay," Jay said, shifting in his seat. "Let's just change the subject."

"I don't know if I'd really call these my peeps," Ila said slowly, looking from table to table.

"What do you mean?"

"Well, I'm just not sure…," Ila trailed off.

Eve looked at her, waiting. Jay did, too.

"I don't know. These guys…," Ila met Eve's eyes. "I'm just not sure I'd call them 'my peeps.'" Ila stopped and watched Eve closely. Eve looked down and started picking at a spot on the table.

Ila took a deep breath and continued. "Remember what we were talking about earlier? In the car?" She didn't wait for an answer. "Look around, Eve. Look at Jay. Look at me. Then look around at the other people in the room." Ila lightened a little and sang to her friend, "Which one of these is not like the other?" Ila saw the edge of Eve's mouth curve slightly.

Jay stared hard at Ila. She felt his eyes boring into her.

"Are we going there?" he asked when she wouldn't look at him.

"I guess we are," Ila said, sitting up, turning to face him squarely. "Why not? We never talk about it, Jay. Why is that? Doesn't it bother you that you're more brown-skinned than anyone in this room? Even me?" She held her arm next to his. Her yellow-brown skin looked pale next to his darker, reddish brown arm.

69

"Ila…," Eve began.

"No, Eve, we're not going to change the subject. *THIS* is the subject tonight." She looked back at Jay and waited. Her eyes were wide and fierce. Her hands were poised on the table, as if she were ready to pounce.

Jay stared off over Eve's shoulder. He wouldn't meet her eyes. Or Ila's. He stayed silent for a long time. The waitress brought over the menus, looking from one face to the other.

"You guys okay?" She set a small wire basket on the table. The smell of warm, fresh bread wafted up and mingled into the smokey-sweet air around them.

"Umhmm," Eve answered without looking at her. Jay stared, unblinking, across the room. The waitress placed the menus on the table and disappeared back into to the busy room.

Their menus stayed closed as Eve and Ila watched Jay. Eve could see his jaw clench and relax. Ila watched his eyes. Finally, after what seemed like forever, Jay blinked and tuned to Ila. "All right. Fine. Let's talk about it."

Ila sat back and crossed her arms across her chest.

"Let's." Ila answered, relieved.

Eve leaned in close to Jay. She looked up at his face, as if she were trying to solve a puzzle. "What were you *doing* just now, Jay? What was that? I've never seen you like that before."

"Basically, I was trying to keep my cool and not storm out of here." His chest fell as he let out a long, slow sigh and leaned back in the booth. "You know how my dad and Mave were doing that thing with their hands this afternoon?"

Ila nodded. Eve blushed. "What do you mean?"

"That stuff with their hands. How it got all calm out there in the pasture." Jay was impatient. "Didn't you notice?"

Eve's cheeks turned bright red. "Notice what? Your dad and Mave basically communicating, somehow, on some level, with a 'Soulful Beast?' Yeah, of course, I noticed. I *felt* it. But I have no idea what I was feeling. I don't know. We never talk about this shit, Jay. And I think it's weird that we don't." Eve sat back and crossed her arms tightly around her.

"Sorry, Eve, I wasn't trying to insult you or anything." Jay softened his tone, his eyes full, watching Eve. "It's just that I've seen him do it a million times. *'The calming of the field,'* my dad calls it. It's never the same, exactly, but he always does something like that when he's calming himself down, tuning into the energy of a situation. He told me once a long time ago, way long ago ... he told me that he was getting in tune, like how you tune a guitar. He said it's like tuning into the song of the universe however it's played at the moment."

Ila smiled and relaxed her arms on her chest. She nudged Eve's foot with her own.

"You know, I guess we probably did talk about this stuff a bit when we were younger, now that I think about it. Before you moved here." Jay nodded in agreement. "Sorry, hon, I guess you just slipped in so naturally, you know? You just seemed to understand and accept everything that came with this weird little town you moved to. I guess I assumed...." She looked at Jay. "We assumed? You just seemed to have a natural understanding of things ... people. Oh, hell, I don't know what I'm saying." Ila looked to Jay. "Do you know what I'm trying to say?"

Jay sat up and leaned toward Ila, resting his arms heavily on the table. "Hell, Ila, whoever knows *what* you're trying to say?" Ila kicked him under the table. "OW! Damn, woman! That hurt." Jay rubbed his shin.

Eve giggled then stopped herself. Jay reached out and took Eve's hand. Her left hand. "You see this hand? This is you, Eve—sensitive, light, confusing. Powerful as hell." He smiled weakly. "You don't even see it; you just feel. But we see that in you." Ila nodded.

"Here's the thing. Ila and I do look different from these people. And there was a time around here when there were more people that looked like us. Not just the few that are speckled around town. Yes, they're part of the community, *we're* part of the community. But it used to be different." Jay looked at Ila. Ila lowered her head. Jay continued.

"There were a few more families at least. We don't know the whole story. Hell, I don't think we even know the story at all. But something happened here in Moira back when we were little. We were what, five, maybe six?" Ila shrugged her shoulders. She didn't look up. "A few years before you moved here. Something around there, anyway." Jay looked around at the busy room.

"No one will talk about it. My parents even brushed me off when I used to ask about it. And they *never* brush me off. All they say is it had something to do with electricity. You know, energy. They said something had been wrong with the infrastructure of the power plant and the lines that brought the electricity to our houses. The plant just said there was a higher demand than they could handle and faulty appliances. All we know about it is some people had too much energy in their houses, too much running through their walls. Things started overloading. There were some small explosions. Low-level appliances— toasters, coffeemakers, TVs, lightbulbs—sparked, exploded. Nothing huge like a stove or refrigerator, as far as I know, but still explosions. Thank God no one was hurt."

Eve looked at Ila then back to Jay. "Oh, my God. How come I never heard about this before?" Jay's house, Zoe on the floor, images from the afternoon flooded her mind. "Was it like your house earlier today?"

Jay shrugged. "No, I think it was different. Huh, I didn't even think about that." Jay stared out across the restaurant, circling his thoughts, trying to remember. "I think it specifically had to do with the wiring somehow. No one's eager to talk about it, I guess. Some of the houses that had 'trouble' were Ila's and mine, though. And some friends of my mom's. They lived around where we do—in the old, original part of town. I think it was a couple of other families. One of them had kids—a mixed couple like Ila's and my parents. That's what my mom said anyway. The kids, I remember playing with them. They were brown-skinned like me. Not all light-skinned like Ila here."

"Pffft, light-skinned." Ila's mouth was pulled to the side in a smirk. "I got your light skin right here." She smiled and threw her thumb over toward Eve's pale hand. Eve giggled.

Ila's wide smile slowly faded. She stared across the room, letting her mind fill with memories. Soft, warm light bathed her face, causing her to look years younger. "Yeah, my dad won't say anything about it at all. I used to ask all the time where they went. God, what were their names? The Rubings?"

Eve giggled again. It was another nervous habit she had trying to lighten situations. "The Rubens? Like the sandwich?"

Jay smiled. "*Rubings.* Yeah, I think those were the kids I knew. Remember Mr. Walters? He didn't have any kids. He used to come over all the time. He was very cool. We used to talk a lot. He talked to me just like he talked to my parents. He never talked down to me like a kid. Remember him, Ila? "

Ila furrowed her brow. "Wait...." She shook her head slowly. "I don't think that's his name ... wait, wasn't it Waters? Remember? Mr. Waters? Yes. Oh, my God. Wait...." Ila's mind floated earlier in the day to Jay's house. The translucent man in Jay's kitchen next to Mave....

"Holy shit." Ila held her hand over her mouth, her stomach suddenly jumpy, flurried with butterflies.

"I had forgotten, but this afternoon, I think I saw him, Jay. In your kitchen. Like a ghost. Isaac Waters. Oh, my God." Ila shivered uncontrollably. Jay wrapped his arm around her and squeezed her tight.

"Ila, he's been gone for a long time—maybe eleven, twelve years." Jay watched her closely. *He's been gone as long as your mother*, he thought to himself. He shook his head, bringing himself back to the current conversation.

"The point is, Eve, people were scared. That's the sense I got about it, anyway. My parents were clearly uncomfortable around that time, extra protective. Because most of the houses that had trouble had people with"—Jay cleared his throat for emphasis—"brown skin. Black. African Americans. I think it got really weird. I remember my dad being irate and slamming around the house about it. I remember my mom not letting him leave the house when he was like that. I was scared. Really scared." Jay shuddered unconsciously. Eve felt him from across the table. Jay lowered his lashes and looked at Ila. His usually bright eyes were both clouded and dark.

Eve watched Jay closely. He let go of Ila and picked up a napkin, twisting it over and over, until it finally reached its end and ripped in half. He raised his eyes and looked at Eve through his thick lashes. His voice was so low Eve had to lean in to hear him.

"I guess that's partly why no one talks about it. I think people were embarrassed in the end how quick they came to be wary of their neighbors. Families who had lived side by side for generations, especially in the old part of town where I live, they distanced themselves from those of us who had houses with those strange surges. I kinda got the impression that the rest of the town felt there was something threatening about the old part of town where we lived. And I think, for a while, they were scared of *us*.

"But when you cracked your hand on Vince's and everyone stopped and stared—that's the same feeling I used to get back then. People do stupid things when they're scared, Eve. And I don't want you or Ila or me caught anywhere close to something like that."

Ila looked out across the yellow glow of the restaurant. Her tight bushy curls shielded her face from Eve. The low murmur of the restaurant faded out as Ila stared blankly across the room at the gently rotating ceiling fans. Light reflected and flashed off the silver blades' every revolution. The edges of the restaurant dissipated, and Ila watched a scene unfold, as if it were in front of her.

A beautiful, brown-skinned woman knelt down and reached out to a young girl. The woman pushed the child's black twisted curls to the side and gathered her small chin lightly in her hand. Ila couldn't hear what they were saying, but she saw that the little girl had been crying. The woman held out her arms.

Eve watched Ila grow silent, the edges of her mouth lowering to a tight line. Eve felt a deep sadness wash over her friend.

Images formed in Ila's mind, pulling her back in time. She saw Jay, young, sitting in a big overstuffed chair, blanket pulled around him, making himself small, listening. She felt his fear. She could hear Edge's deep, angry voice and Zoe's intense voice meeting his, soothing, blocking the door.

The scene shifted—Ila was now watching from a bird's-eye view. She saw a circle of houses, all surrounding Jay's. From within each, a burst of white light flashed simultaneously, filling all the windows at once. She felt the apprehension and unease, the terror and chaos of the families as they scrambled to put out small fires and gather young children. She watched them emerge from their houses and meet in the street, confused and shaking, trying to understand what had happened. From Jay's house, she didn't see any explosions, but she saw a wavy haze only around his house.

Gently, Jay put his hand on Ila's arm. She jumped, startling Eve as well. Ila blinked her eyes, pushed herself up taller in the booth, and shook her head to clear the layered emotions.

"Oh, God, sorry." Ila shook her head once more and stretched her arms out over her head. "I spaced out for a minute."

Ila dropped her hands to the table with a bang, and Eve jumped again.

"So where were we?" Ila rubbed her hands roughly over her face and shot quick glances at Jay and Eve. "Oh, right. All the black folks…." She looked around and lowered her voice. "I mean, all the brown-skinned folks were gone after that. More or less. Except a few, including Jay, Mave, Zoe, and me." Ila smiled at Eve and shrugged her shoulders. Her smile didn't make it to her eyes. Eve looked into her friend's dark eyes, as if searching into her soul. She saw Ila try to mask her pain and felt her own breath forced out of her lungs, leaving her heart wrenching with ache. Eve looked down at her shaking hands. She squeezed one hand around her other fist and brought them to her lips. She pushed hard to hold back the threatening tears. Then she let out a slow breath across the top of her knuckles. She blinked her eyes hard, her heart gripped tight in her chest. She couldn't look at Ila. Eve knew Ila was trying to hold it together. She *felt* the pain that Ila was holding back, the pain Jay and the others had felt back then. She didn't want to be the one to push her friend into that intensity. She was having a hard enough time regulating her own.

"So, that's the story, and we're sticking to it. We're the last of the brown-skinned folks around here, especially in here … right, Jay?" Ila tried to lighten her voice. Jay didn't answer but nodded softly. Eve's brown hair shadowed her face as she looked down. Her eyes focused on the shredded napkin torn by Jay's now relaxed hands.

Jay spoke first.

"Eve, look at us." Eve shook her head, mindfully slowing her breath to keep herself together. "Look at us. Please, Eve." Jay's voice was soft and low. "Please. I've wondered myself how you have felt about us, you know, being different from you and all. Truly. What do you see when you look at us?"

Eve started to wiggle one foot back and forth, slowly at first, then faster and faster so the movement began rocking her whole body. She squeezed her eyelids tight, pushing the heels of her hands into them, until she saw only speckled light in the darkness. Her chest rose shakily. The small points of light behind her closed eyes shifted, darting around recklessly. In one swift move, she swept her elbows to the table and looked out, propping her chin in her hands. For a moment, she was blind. Then the room slowly filled back in, her whole body still jiggling from her furiously wiggling foot. She tapped her teeth together softly and blew quick breaths through her nose.

"What did you just ask?" She met Jay's eyes and squeezed her teeth together.

Jay saw her jaw tighten. He smiled.

"What do you see when you look at us?" Jay asked once more. He held out his arms and looked up and down at himself.

Eve drew in a slow, deep breath. Her foot kept moving, bouncing her slightly in the soft seat of the booth. "What do I see? Okay, what do I see?" Eve looked from Jay to Ila, carefully surveying each of them. "What do I see?" She was talking to herself now. She closed her eyes. "What do I see?" She opened them and looked back to Ila. "Okay, with you, Ila, I see a fierceness. I think that is what I saw first in you—a strength. Lord, how I wanted to be that strong." Eve brought her arms to the table and leaned in. Her foot was still moving furiously, shaking her body from side to side.

"What were we in? Fourth? No, fifth grade I think. And you were different. You know when I realized I loved you, Ila, my sister?" Ila shook her head and waited. "When you colored those silly little frogs from science. It was a silly little flip book, something supposed to teach us something I've long forgotten. Each page had a picture of a frog and you colored each frog multiple colors. Not just green. I realized right then that it had never occurred to me to do that! Frogs were just green up until then, you know? You opened up a world to me with those stupid little multicolored frogs. And I loved you for it." She smiled at Ila. Ila smiled deeply. Her shoulders softened. This time, her smile reached all the way up to her eyes.

"And you, Jersey Lang. You." Eve shook her head slowly. "You." She shifted uncomfortably in her seat. "You, well, let's just say I find you one of the most interesting people on the planet. You've got this wiseness about you." Jay raised his eyebrows. "Oh, don't let it go to your head, mister." Eve sat up taller, smiling, her legs still rocking.

"No, seriously, you have this way of understanding things that you've never experienced before. Like you have read about it or something, and when it shows up in real life, it's like you're familiar with it already, you know? Like Beast today. No big deal for you, like every day you could come across a Cape Buffalo and it's the most normal thing."

Eve paused and looked at him. She studied each of his eyes, the blue and the brown, each sharper, brighter than she had remembered. She moved down to his lips, round and soft next to the stubble that was beginning to form above them. She let her eyes linger a moment then drew them back up to look into his spacious eyes. Jay met her gaze. Eve felt her skin warm. She sat up taller and forced herself not to look away. Jay shifted his seat. Eve held his gaze and studied the soft variation of color and light that swept across his face. Jay shifted once more.

Ila cleared her throat.

Eve tumbled the words out so fast it took a few minutes for either of them to understand.

"Let'sjustsayyou'rethemostbeautifulpersonI'veeverseeninmyentirel ife. I'mgoingtothebathroomnowberightback."

In a flash, Eve pushed herself from the table and disappeared across the dining room.

Jay and Ila looked at each other. "Did you understand that?" he asked.

"Something about the bathroom?"

"Be right back?"

Slowly, Ila's furrowed brow lifted, and her eyes opened wide and large as she deciphered Eve's words. She brought her hand to cover her now open mouth.

"What? Did you figure out what she said?"

Ila was laughing, shaking her head.

"Come on, Ila, tell me!"

"You have to figure it out," she said, pulling herself together.

Moments later, Eve walked back across the room and slid into the booth. Ila started giggling.

"Oh, crap, here you guys go." Jay looked up at the ceiling. "Oh, lord."

Eve looked at Ila and started to giggle, too.

"I knew it." Jay looked from one to the other. Neither could speak. Each time they looked at each other, they laughed even harder. The waitress came over and looked at Jay.

"Are your friends okay?"

"Relatively. Yeah, they get this way. They seem to really crack each other up." The girls were now doubled over in the booth, hysterical. Ila snorted as she tried to catch her breath. Eve's whole body silently shook in response. Jay chuckled. "They're completely certifiable."

The waitress smiled.

"Well, let me know when they pull it together and I'll take your order." She laughed softly. "It *is* contagious." She smiled widely.

Jay nodded. "Indeed."

"Okay, you guys. Pull it together. Our waitress thinks you're both nuts. I do, too, for that matter." Eve and Ila straightened up and looked at Jay. They both bit their lips and tried to keep a straight face. Part of a giggle burst through Eve's lips, and she quickly clamped her hands over her mouth. That's all it took and they were both back in hysterics, laughing so hard, neither made a sound. Tears rolled down both their cheeks.

"Oh, man, we'll never get served at this rate." Jay picked up the menu and hid behind it. Eve and Ila slowly began to putter out. "Thank God," Jay said from behind the menu.

Eve cleared her throat and wiped her eyes. She pulled herself up and grabbed her menu. "Well, that was a little different tonight...."

She studied the menu and settled into her seat.

"Want to share some sweet potato fries, Ila?"

"Why, yes," Ila answered, batting her eyelashes over the top of her menu at Eve. "I do believe they are the most beautiful fries I've ever eaten in my entire life."

Eve widened her eyes and darted a glance at Jay. He was hidden behind his menu. Eve narrowed her eyes to slits, stared at Ila, and nodded her head toward Jay in a silent question. Ila shook her head. With their communication complete, Eve stifled a giggle. Jay looked up. Eve slipped down and hid behind the menu.

"Don't tell me you guys aren't done with that yet."

The waitress approached the table again. "Everyone recovered over here?"

Eve and Ila didn't dare look at each other, or speak. Jay looked from one to the other, then up at the waitress.

"Perhaps, but it's always hard to tell for sure. I'll have a burger, please."

PART II

ILA

Later that night, Ila leaned over her bathroom sink, splashing warm water over her face, rinsing the last remnants of scrub from her glistening skin. She paused to look into her own dark eyes, water dripping leisurely off her chin. She stared into the mirror, turning side to side, trying to see deep into her own depths.

"Girl, who *are* you in there, anyway?" She tried to sound casual, talking softly to herself, yet she knew she was dead serious. "Yeah, I know, you're the girl who doesn't really know *who* she is, huh?" Ila stopped and looked herself straight in the eye. "But you're okay, sister. You really and truly are okay."

Ila stared directly into her eyes and gave herself a small smile, which, for some reason, made her heart swell. She reached over and pulled the hand towel out of the metal holder, wiped it over her wet face, and then hung it back, folding it neatly, patting it into place.

Outside, the night was dark and calm. Her room was steeped in the warm golden glow of her bedside lamp. She loved her room like this, all cozy and half lit. Her light summer covers were pulled up smoothly and neatly, inviting her into comfort and order. As she slid into bed, the crisp, cool sheets evoked a deep, satisfying sigh. She looked around one last time then reached over and clicked off her bedside lamp. Darkness enveloped her.

Ila lay perfectly still and let her eyes adjust. A bright stream of light from outside suddenly appeared through a crack in her curtains, then disappeared just as quickly. Once more, she was bathed in black. Before she got too comfortable, Ila slipped out and adjusted the curtains, pulling them closer, then jumped back into her bed. She gazed out a small crack in her curtains, blowing open then closing again. The curtains gave in and slipped apart once more, leaving a sliver of view out through the open window and into the dark night. In the distance, crickets softly serenaded one another. Coolness swept across Ila's skin as fresh night air slipped through her window. She adjusted her pillow and rolled over onto her side, her ancient bed groaning under her movement. Hugging her second pillow in, she let her eyes find their way through the darkness, past the invisible screen, and into the night sky beyond.

Eve often talked about the stars and the comfort of the night. Ila had never really thought much about it; she had simply listened. She always slept soundly. She didn't have the challenge Eve had of sleep evading her. Once Ila's head hit the pillow, she was swept into a heavy, dream-filled sleep. Even if it was one of those Mave nights, where they met somewhere, somehow, she always felt rested. She had never questioned any of that. She had just gone with it. Tonight, though, she wondered about the stars.

Through the window, Ila's eyes were drawn to the tiny points of light in the black sky, pulsing like heartbeats millions of light-years away. One of them shimmered brighter and pulsed wider, as if calling her attention. Ila smiled to herself, remembering Eve talk about the stars "singing" to her. *That girl has an imagination with a capital I,* Ila thought as her smile widened. Her mind wandered back over the evening, remembering Eve talk about the colored frogs. And the families, the houses, and those who no longer lived in town. Ila's smile faded. The same image she saw at the Roadhouse returned, unbeckoned, filling the canvas of her mind. Once more, she saw the woman and the child. Her brow furrowed as she pushed the scene out, forcing herself to think of something else. The star beyond the window pulsed brighter as the wind swept the thin curtain wide out into the room. Ila's chest squeezed and tightened, compressing her heart.

She exhaled all her air and sealed her eyes shut, consciously squeezing them to match the grip on her heart. Behind her closed eyes, Ila's world brightened, as if it were daylight. Then the light shrank smaller and smaller until it looked just like the distant star outside her window, surrounded by deep, black space. Ila felt a second gust of air sweep over her, the hair on her arms rising up on tiny bumps, alert, sensing for danger. The scent of distant rain filled her room even though there were no clouds in the sky. The star behind her closed eyes pulsed rhythmically, just as the one had in the sky outside, pulling her attention away from the sensations she felt on her body. Ila willed herself to stay with the experience, fighting the urge to open her eyes.

A soft chime echoed faintly in the distance. She softened her ears and strained to hear, but the sound was not from outside. It came from somewhere inside of her head. The soft chime echoed over and over in an easy rhythm, its sound a direct match to the pulsing rhythm of the star.

Another image unfolded in front of her. Fuzzy at first, it gradually formed itself into the shape of a large wooden door. The weathered, light grey wood stood stark and dramatic in the pitch-black surroundings. Ila felt warmth spread over her skin. Her chest gently relaxed the last bit of squeeze it had around her heart. Reflexively, she inhaled deeply. Calm settled into her cells as a sweet, warm scent drifted under her nose. It seemed to come from the door itself.

Eyes still closed, Ila placed her palm wide on the door. It was warm. Her eyes fluttered open, and the large door stood there just the same, its worn wood, grainy and smooth, still under her brown fingers. Gently, she ran her hand across the aging grey. She felt a tug, as if the door were drawing her, gathering her in. Her eyes pooled with tears as a wave of sadness enveloped her, squeezing her in from all sides. Her hand slid to the side and bumped against cool metal, jarring her thoughts back to the door beneath her fingers. Mindfully, she traced the dark metal, feeling the hard bumps of imperfection as her hand moved slowly around the circle. Almost on its own volition, her hand reached into the middle of the metal circle. The firm, grainy wood gave way just a little. Ila paused and her lips curved into a sideways smile. *Oh, here we go*, she thought. Then gently she pushed. The door gave some more. Ila's hand slowly oozed its way into the circle on the door. The hard wood easily morphed around her warm hand, stretching out like a wide, fingerless rubber glove, enveloping her hand completely.

Ila paused for a moment, letting her hand stay in the door, cocooned, as if in warm, inviting water. Then, bit by bit, the door pulled her forward until her arm disappeared into the metal hole. She watched her brown, muscular arm slip out of her sight, the ring expanding to accommodate her whole shoulder up to her neck. Warmth enveloped her arm, but her mind started to panic. Her eyes skipped around, searching for something familiar. Besides the door, there was only darkness. Alarmed, she tried to pull her hand from the door, but it was as if she were caught in the orbit of a benevolent black hole. The harder she pulled, the tighter the door held her. With her heart pounding, her head was flooded with the sound of rushing water. Ila struggled fiercely to free herself. The door would not let her go. Her heart hammered in her chest, threatening overload. She opened her mouth to scream, but no sound arrived.

A warm touch on her unseen hand caused her to freeze. Her chest heaved after her racing pulse. Warmth spread like wildfire through the cells of her body. Ila gradually surrendered to the calmness that followed. A strange, sweet fragrance caught in her nose. Her head became light as she let herself lean into the door. The metal circle widened, and Ila slipped forward. Her eyes fluttered shut as her neck and head slid through. Silence cradled her as she drifted on a wave of lightness. She heard her name being called from far, far away. Her lips curved into the beginning of a full smile. The warm pliable edges of the door closed around her, wrapping her in velvety softness, as she let herself be taken into the darkness.

JAY

J ay bolted upright in bed. Beads of sweat formed on his forehead. Under his soaked t-shirt, a small trickle of moisture zigzagged its way down his amber-brown chest. He rubbed his palms roughly across his sleep-filled eyes, over his head, across his short dark hair.

What the hell was that? he wondered, struggling for the memory.

He stood up and felt his cotton shirt clinging heavily on his back. His floor creaked weakly under his weight as he walked over to his window. Silently, he stripped off his wet shirt and flung it onto his growing pile of laundry. He snatched a clean t-shirt off the back of his chair and slung it over his shoulder, then one-handed, he heaved his window wide open. Tiny bits of paint scattered like rain onto the floor below. He brushed his damp hand over the windowsill, wiping it absently on his shorts before sitting down on the deep ledge. Staring out into the cool night, he shivered as his moist skin met the crisp air. The full moon shone brightly as he gazed out across the southern tree line. Jay couldn't remember what it was he had been dreaming; all he knew was it was bad. He felt it in the pit of his stomach. *There was something about fire*, he thought groggily.

Out his window, the night was unusually still and eerily quiet. His thoughts wove to the previous afternoon. Suddenly, he remembered the heat. Startled into action, he stumbled across the room, wrestling his arms into his t-shirt, then he shot out the door. His feet slapped loudly on the cool tile as he hurried down the stairs. He hadn't seen his parents since they were at Mave's place yesterday. His dad had checked the furnace but found nothing wrong. At Zoe's insistence, he even had the heating and air guys come out to have a look around.

"Nothing here to tell," Edge had told Jay when they spoke earlier that evening. "Strangest damn thing, but not much else to do. It's a strange world we live in, Jersey." His dad had been nonchalant. Jay had imagined him shaking his head across the phone. "Some things just aren't explainable. Looks like it's all okay."

And that was that. But it *wasn't* okay. The house had been hot as hell. *That's just not right,* Jay thought as he hurried room to room, making sure everything was in order. It all seemed fine. Jay stood in the middle of the empty living room. The warmth he felt with Eve earlier rushed in, greeting him, as if it had been patiently waiting for him. He let the glow wash over him once more, his body responding with a deep sense of calm. He shuddered from head to toe.

Jay peeled his feet from the floor and crossed the rest of the room, landing heavily in his favorite chair. The large chair faced the window seat Mave and Zoe had occupied earlier that afternoon. *Ah, good old U chair,* he thought, its soft plush arms cradling him just as it had when he was little. Swinging his legs over one arm and resting his head on the other, he let himself settle in and be comforted.

It's not right, Jay thought again, shaking his head, slinking the soft fleece blanket off the back of the chair and tucking its silky edges tightly around his shoulders. He gazed out the clear window. *Something's definitely not right.*

Jay was used to strange things happening around Moira. Weird and unexplainable things happened often. He was used to weird. Suddenly, he remembered a conversation last week with Shelby, the vibrant, harmless, free spirit who gave psychic readings in the park.

"You are an old soul," she had said when he greeted her. He hadn't asked for a reading; in fact, he had never had one from anyone. *"Your current family,"* she continued, *"they're very tied to you, and to this land."*

When she had said that, a loud ringing had filled his ears. He had missed a lot of what she said after that. He had watched her mouth move, had tried reading her lips, but his eyes had started watering. A fuzziness had grown around her. It had been hard to focus, the resonance in his head had been too loud to hear anything.

"Yes, Jersey," she had finished as the last of the ringing had left his ears. *"You indeed are special."*

He bristled at her words again. His jaw and fists clenched tight, remembering.

"Thanks, Shelby," was all he had said. But that had soured it for him.

Special. Yeah. Isn't that what someone always does—deems one group, one person special? So what does that make everyone else then? Jay tightened his lips, feeling bitter all over again. He flipped roughly to his side. *Why can't people just embrace each other's quirkiness, their differences, without needing to be 'special'! Damn it! It's always the same thing—some kind of 'You're the ONE to save the world' bullshit! Why do they always say it's just ONE?! Damn it! There's no way it can only be only one of us. We're all fucking special!*

"Deal with your self-worth crap on your own time, Shelby," Jay spat out loud, disgusted. "Don't put your bullshit on me."

He jerked the cover tighter around him. *What the hell is wrong with people?* He settled down further. His breathing slowed, and he let himself sink deeply into the warm comfort of the chair.

Ah, U chair, you always got it going on, he thought. *Now, U chair, I can see THAT as something special.* Jay smiled, letting his anger float off. He stared blankly out the clear window into the night sky. A soft glow from the full moon peeked into the dark window. *All bow to the magic that is U chair,* he thought, suddenly sleepy. "I don't know how you do it, U chair," he said groggily, his eyes heavy, his smile still pulling on his lips, "but I'm sure glad you do."

ILA

T he first thing Ila noticed was how incredibly comfortable she was. Her body relaxed as she settled against the soft, fuzzy ground below her. Through her closed eyes, she saw the familiar red of her eyelids. It felt as if a warm mist was lightly dusting her skin. Shapes and lines of colors she had never experienced before began to dance and dart across her screen of red. Her whole body felt as if it were bouncing with animated vibration, although she could tell she was lying still on some kind of ground. In her ears, the dull rushing sound was fading, replaced by utter silence. Beneath her head, her back, her legs and arms, she felt as if each cell was being supported and cradled with attentive care, as if she were a precious package sweetly held by the substance below her.

An easy smile of sheer delight spread across her lips. She exhaled, a barely audible "Aahhh" warming her lips. The sound softly echoed again and again and again, until the sounds rang together into one all-pervasive "Aahhhh" that vibrated through her whole being. Ila let herself be surrounded by the sound. The vibration rang both through her mind and her body, until the last note gently faded into a blissful silence.

EVE

E ve coaxed her eyes open. Everything was blurry in the hazy, diffused light, as if she were looking underwater. *Where am I?* She tried placing her hands on the ground to push herself up, but her arms felt heavy, leaden, like she was moving through tar. She inhaled deeply and felt her chest rise without effort. *Huh, that's strange,* she thought. *Breathing is usually my challenge, not moving my arms.*

Mave appeared in her mind—it was as if she were watching a video clip.

How can anyone forget to breathe? Eve remembered the scene. It had happened just last week.

The video continued—Eve saw herself lying on the ground, surrounded by settling dust in Mave's barn. Mave's face was now directly above hers as the perspective shifted, and she began experiencing the scene as it happened once more.

Child, it's automatic! Mave was scolding, uncomprehending her ability to stop breathing. Eve was both confused and not, having both perspectives—the conversation then and the conversation now. Mave reached out her weathered hand, and Eve met it with her own. Mave hoisted her up so quickly Eve's feet popped off the ground then landed solid. Mave held Eve's chin in her strong hand and turned her head, so she could look into each clear, green eye.

"How on earth can you forget to breathe, Eve?"

Eve felt her head turn away, embarrassed, even as she lay here on the lush ground.

Did I pass out here? she wondered, the old images fading completely from her mind's eye.

Eve was mortified at her lack of control—her lack of mastery of such a primary and necessary function of her own body. How *could* her breathing just cease, until she fell unconscious? Once her mind was out of the picture, though, her body would resume breathing, as if nothing had gone awry. She was not able to stop or control it—the world would simply and slowly begin to fade, her limbs systematically betraying her upright position, crumpling under her like a rag doll.

Her brow furrowed, struggling to remember how she had gotten on the ground this time. She squinted through fuzzy, unfocused eyes. *Where am I?*

Wide washes and soft strokes of color emerged above her, as if someone were painting the sky while she watched. Her brow relaxed slightly as she watched the pleasant images.

That's really cool, she thought, her lips pulling into a smile on their own. *Oh, good,* she thought, *my motor skills are returning. Well done, body.*

Eve moved her lips all around, opening and closing her mouth, pulling her lips wide, shifting them side to side, and then pursing them as far forward as she could. She rolled from one side to the other then planted her hands on the soft, springy ground. Warmth seeped across her palms, out to their edges, then vanished. She pushed her hands into the ground and felt the ground, ever so lightly, push back. She pushed down harder, and this time her hands sprung an inch off the ground. Underneath, the soft, fuzzy blades beneath her hand waved after her, as if blown by the wind. Eve raised her eyebrows and blew out a long, slow whistle.

"Oh, my," she muttered to herself, her eyes clear as she scanned her surroundings. *I must be dreaming ... or something like that.*

"Crap, what do I do now?" Eve had never asked Ila how she and Mave actually moved around in their dreams.

Methodically, Eve placed each foot on the cushiony, green ground and pushed herself upright. The ground daintily launched her, causing her to catch the smallest amount of air, floating her momentarily. She landed knees bent, arms outstretched, balancing herself on the cushiony ground. Around her, the world was absolutely still and silent.

The cloudless sky brightened, reminding her of a pastel-rich desert sunset. The colors shifted and changed, dancing soundlessly across the horizon. Eve smiled at the scene. She felt lightness throughout her whole being, as if her cells were electrified, energetically bumping into each other under her skin.

God, I hope I don't wake up ... or pass out, she thought, slowing her breath, trying to keep her body calm and under control. *All right then, stay together, body. Let's figure this place out!*

GROUND

Ila felt the ground beneath her expand like it was part of her lungs. Her chest filled with something that felt lighter than air. She rolled her eyes open and tried to focus, but all she saw was large swaths of hazy, translucent colors. She squeezed her eyes tightly, small tears gathering under her lids, then opened them again. The air and the world around her was vacantly quiet. She ran her hands over the fuzzy, pale green ground. As she waved over its velvety softness, the color brightened as if by magic. A swirl of golden light accompanied by a sweet and slightly fruity scent fluttered up from the ground. Ila shivered. Soft colors—pinks, golds, greens, and blues—seemed to emerge from under her skin, encircling her and rippling out, as if they were rings of water. Ila's mouth curved into a wide smile.

Ahh, dreaming....

She stood and felt the ground below dip lightly with her movement, as if she were on a trampoline. She waved both hands out in wide circles and spun around, creating a small colorful whirlpool around her. Her vision was improving. The colorful world around her responded to her every move.

"Ila!"

Ila froze midspin.

"Ila!" Her name echoed again into the soundless world around her.

Eve? The voice sure sounded like Eve. She tried to yell back, but her voice was weak and hoarse. A soft croak was all that puffed out of her mouth.

"Ila!" she heard a third time.

Ila squinted in the direction of the voice. She saw a form coming her way, outlined in a swirl of color. She cupped her hands over her eyes and strained to decipher the image moving toward her. It was coming in fast!

Wham!

Ila was hit with a force that took her back down, bouncing her lightly on the soft ground, trapping her beneath the weight.

"Damn," Ila wheezed out, more irritated than frightened. "What the hell?!"

"Language, chica," Eve laughed in her ear. "Sorry about that. I'm just so glad to see you. I have no idea where we are, but you're freakin' here! I can't believe you're here. With me! And I'm here!" She planted a big juicy kiss on Ila's cheek. Like a wave, the sensation smoothed out in all directions and slid over Ila's skin, sinking down in.

Ila hugged Eve back. "Good to see *you*, chica!" The warmth and lightness rose back up and over Eve's skin.

"Whoa, look at that?" Eve said, peeling herself off so Ila could sit up. A field of color had emanated out, surrounding them. Blues and deep violets echoed off their bodies and rippled further and further out in concentric circles.

"Wow, very cool," Ila said, looking at Eve sideways. Eve gave a small approving nod. "Impressive."

"Are we dreaming?" Eve asked as she ran her finger through the morphing colors like they were smoke, shifting the pattern as she drew across the air.

"Yeah, um, I don't know," Ila said. "Sure seems like it, but it's different. I think I came through a door." Ila's memories were murky and far away. She reached into her mind to pull them forward.

Eve stopped drawing and dropped her hand to her side—it was suddenly heavy and leaden once more. She looked at her friend a long while, focusing hard on her familiar face to keep her breathing steady. She spoke slow and low. "What kind of door?"

Ila's smile faded, mirroring Eve's falling expression. Eve's eyebrows almost met across the deep furrow on her forehead. Ila knew the look—Eve's internal struggle to continue breathing.

"Hey," Ila matched Eve's low tone. "Hey, you're fine here, Eve. It was just a door." Ila willed her mind to pull up the image of the door.

Her thoughts felt almost as hazy as this new atmosphere. Finally, it appeared again, clearly, as if it were in front of her.

"Hey, okay." She put her hand on Eve's, instantly warming. "I see it. It was … it *is* … a large wooden door. Grey, weathered…." Ila watched her own brown slender hands slide across the door, the scene unfolding just like it had when she was in bed. But when she looked down, her hand was resting just where she put it on Eve's. She seemed to be seeing two scenes simultaneously. She focused on the vision in her mind. It continued as if she were watching a recording of her recent past. The more she focused, the more detailed the scene became.

"It had a metal circle…," Ila described, watching as her own hand traced the circle in her mind's vision. She felt the cool hard metal beneath her hand. As she watched, her long, slim fingers reached into the middle of the circle. She felt the gentle pull again, just as before, even though she knew her own hand currently resided on Eve's, unmoving.

In a flash, the image altered, and she saw her hand lighten and become Eve's inside the door. She felt the ripple of panic as she watched Eve yank her hand from the door and hold it to her chest. The vision evaporated, and Ila looked at Eve's downturned face, hidden in the shadows of her thick hair.

"You've seen this door, too." It was not a question. Ila reached over and hooked her hand under Eve's chin, lifting it to look into Eve's wide green eyes. Light danced through the colors swirling behind Eve's head. Eve nodded, her eyes flitting around. She tried hard to focus on Ila's calm face. The colors around them began to jump and pulse sporadically in response to Eve's agitation.

"Hey, girl," Ila said, low and calm, her knowing, brown eyes holding Eve's steady. "You are *all right*, I promise." Eve felt a soothing wave of calm wash over her. Her tightly gripped hands relaxed as her breath steadied into an easy rhythm. She nodded slowly, a lock of her coarse brown hair slipping into her eyes. Ila reached up and brushed it behind her ear. Immediately, it sprung free.

"You good?"

Eve nodded again. The surrounding atmosphere, whatever it was, responded with a stream of soft reds, blues, and violets once again, swirling and moving, becoming thicker and more opaque. Their surroundings began to organize as if they were the background colors in a Van Gogh painting.

"This isn't dreaming." Eve's voice was hoarse and low. She gazed steadily at Ila, her eyes finally collected and calm. "Is it?"

Ila shook her head, her long curls bouncing more than usual. They watched the shades of blue around them wrap and curl against each other, morphing and flowing into a filmy background of color.

Ila answered in a slow, mock Southern drawl, eyebrows high on her forehead. "No, darrrrlin', I don't think we are." One side of her mouth curled into her sideways smile. "*This*, my friend, is *different* with a capital D."

CROSSING

"So what happens now?" Eve asked, her voice grew stronger as she regained confidence. She balanced herself on her feet and bounced lightly, her hair waving out around her face. It flopped back down then flew out in a wide circle again as she bounced on the springy ground. Ila took one look at her and cracked up. The sound of her light-filled voice caused the world around them to vibrate and pulse with streams of gold that added themselves to the cooler hues already swirling.

"Feeling better, are we?"

Eve nodded, bouncing higher and higher. Her wild flowing mane circled her head, making her appear weightless.

"Well, I guess we should check this place out." Ila watched the golds weaving themselves through the rest of the moving colors. Across the soundless field of color, Ila noticed a spot on the horizon slightly more radiant than the rest. The swirls of color seemed to be flowing in that direction. "I think we should go this way." Ila stretched her long arm out, pointing the way. Color seemed to stream from her fingertips.

"Okeydoke." Eve slowed down and crouched, bouncing lightly a few times, gaining momentum. Then, without warning, she bounded forward. Landing on one foot, she sprung up and out again and again, leaping across the unfamiliar landscape.

"Just like walking on the moon!" she called over her shoulder as she gained distance between her and Ila. "Come on, woman, hurry up!"

Ila sprung forward, mimicking Eve's movements. She gained confidence with each landing, trying to shorten the distance between herself and Eve. Below her, the landscape whizzed by at dizzying speed; the short, green grass became dotted with delicate, white flowers. The further they went, the taller and more colorful the flowers became.

Ila pulled up beside Eve, and they leapt side by side over a small patch of flowers. As Eve crested the flower patch, the colorful group swayed with her foot, as if blown by the wind. The flowers paused at the end of their reach, as if they were magnetized to Eve's foot. Then, abruptly they let go, springing backward, bouncing back and forth like they were literally on a spring.

"Check that out!"

"What?" Eve slowed herself down. She came to a running stop and leaned over, resting her hands on her thighs. Her rapid breathing was the only sound in their silent, colorful world. Even with all the colors swirling around their heads, they felt no breeze at all.

"Watch." Ila bounced lightly and sprung herself over a large batch of flowers. As Ila began her arc, the flowers hooked into her movement. They swayed over just below her feet. As Ila neared the ground again, the flowers let go in unison and sprung back like a needle on a scale after the weight is taken off.

"Oh, that's very cool. Did that happen with me?"

"Yep." Ila reached down and placed her hand about an inch away from a purple flower.

"I can feel them." Ila's eyes widened, a luminous grin spreading across her face. "Oh, my God." The flowers gently shook in response to Ila's enthusiasm and excitement.

"Look at you—feeling unabashedly!" Eve knelt down next to her and held her own hand next to Ila's. She gave Ila's shoulder a soft, friendly bump.

"Wow, okay, damn." Eve felt a purple and yellow flower pull and turn to her hand, as if receiving light from the sun. "But dang, woman, you! I feel YOU bouncing under my skin!" Eve looked at Ila. "You are literally glowing!"

All around Ila, a golden-white bubble had formed. It expanded as they watched, reaching luminous, fingerlike tendrils out into the blue-and-violet background accompanying them.

"Well, now, that's something." Ila stood and held her arms out to either side of her. "I've got me a light suit." The golden color cocooned her, surrounding her in comfort. She flapped her arms, and the blues and violets swirled like a river in the direction they had been moving. "*This* feeling stuff is very cool."

"As opposed to *other* feeling stuff?" Eve teased, throwing her arms around her friend. Ila stumbled backward, overwhelmed by Eve's sudden contact. Eve caught her and held her upright. "I got you, woman," she said, steadying her friend on her feet. "I got your back, my friend."

Ila looked down, her insides suddenly felt sharp and hard. Even here, her instinct was to push Eve away and handle everything herself. The swell of sharpness moved outward as the colors around her shifted from golden to orange-red. Ila let the sharpness fizzle out from under her skin and steam into the atmosphere around them. Slowly, the hues around her shifted back to violet. Ila looked up, her mouth pulled slightly to the side. Her warm brown eyes were wide open and light, and her brown skin glowed radiantly once more.

Eve nodded and smiled. "Well done, tough girl. You're doing all right."

Ila gave her a wide, proud smile, brightening the colors around them. Without a word, she turned and moved in the direction of the flow.

JAY

J ay woke sweating. Outside it was still dark. The bright, full moon gazed down lazily over the far hill. Nearby trees, washed in the pale moonlight, cast long, dark shadows across the fields.

I don't feel so good, he thought as he reached a quivering hand up and wiped his brow. It was soaked with sweat. He swung his legs off the edge of the chair and put his head between his knees. The whole house seemed tilted and slowly spinning. He steadied himself on his feet and noticed the soft velvet of the chair was soaking wet. It looked as if a shadow of him was still there sleeping.

It's so damn hot in here!

Jay tried to focus his eyes, willing the world to stop spinning around him. He stumbled to the kitchen, using the pieces of furniture for support. *Oh my God, this feels like an earthquake.* He banged hard into the corner of the kitchen doorway. *Damn it!* He leaned into the doorjamb, holding his aching shoulder. The whole kitchen was wobbling and undulated, as if it were underwater. His vision began to shrink, the edges of the room pulling in smaller and smaller. *Window,* he thought. His head began to throb, as if it were being squeezed tight. *I've got to get to that window.*

He willed his eyes to stay steady as he turned and faced the window across the moonlit room. Bumping and stumbling over the stone floor suddenly hot and stinging on his bare feet, he made his way forward. One eye closed, he focused intently through the other as he crossed the last steps to the window. Grabbing hold of the top, sweat biting into eyes, he heaved the large window open. Jay punched through the screen, throwing his body forward, collapsing half in, half out of the wide-open space. His body steamed against the cool night air. Into the cool darkness he stared, unseeing, as his lungs burned, struggling for air. The forms below him were barely discernable in the low light. He blew a forced breath out at the bushes. It floated across his lips in a stream of vapor.

Eve. The name unexpectedly sprung into his head. Jay pushed himself up, swung his long brown legs out, and sat on the windowsill, catching his breath. He gazed off across the moonlit field. The night echoed with the light, airy chirping of the field cricket's symphony. Jay noticed the absence of the cicada's nighttime buzz. It was still early summer, too early for them. He looked back into the house. The noiseless room was swallowed in quiet. He reached a hand back in and felt nothing unusual—the temperature was fine. He swung one leg back into the room and reached a toe for the searing floor. Nothing. He leaned in and placed his whole foot on the floor. It was cool as the night air under his bare foot. He squinted into the quiet room and felt his shirt. *Was I dreaming?* Under his hands, his shirt was cool and wet. *I don't get it.*

The moon above cast his shadow out across the floor. *Eve.* Her name whispered through his head, as if it were calling him from across the blue-grey field. Far off at the distant edge of the field, something moved. He squinted into the night. Two distinct figures shifted on the horizon.

What the hell?

Jay watched the shadowy figures swiftly cross the horizon, a golden white light around them silhouetting their bodies. *Are they bouncing?* Jay blinked his eyes and rubbed his damp hands across them. He leaned forward, holding the ledge, straining to see more clearly.

What the hell is that?

The small dark forms bounced and leaped across the edge of his view. Suddenly, they stopped. They looked human. As he watched, one of them bounced in a long arc, long hair waving up and bouncing lightly as they landed. *Holy crap, that looks like Ila.*

He studied the other one. The slim frame leaned its weight onto one leg and cocked its head, watching the other. *And that's Eve! I'd know that stance anywhere!*

Jay swung his leg back out and launched himself off the ledge, careful not to land in the plants below. His legs stung as he hit the hard ground. He bounced impatiently, waiting for feeling to return. As soon as the tingling stopped, he gently pushed his way out of the bushy foliage and took off at a steady jog toward the field and the figures.

"Eve! Ila!"

Silence answered.

Jay slowed as he reached the fence, then he leapt onto the long wooden planks and threw his legs over the top. He landed with a small thud in a dusty corner of the field, taking his eyes off the horizon only for a second. When he looked up, the figures were gone.

"Where'd they go?" he asked out loud into the night.

He stopped and paused, watching the horizon for signs of movement. The field crickets resumed their chirping one by one, until they were back into a full chorus. Jay caught a glimpse of movement far off to his right. Then, again, they were gone.

Jay flew out across the field, the dew damp grass quickly reminding him he had forgotten his shoes.

"Fuck it."

He ran on, smiling to himself. The damp earth beneath his feet felt cool and invigorating. He crossed the field quickly and reached the edge of the hill. He stopped, his chest rising and falling swiftly, as he surveyed the surrounding fields. Off in the distance, he watched what looked like billowing, misty haze. Then, instead of rising, it began to swirl and curl in on itself and gently flowed to the right, as if blown by the wind. *That's odd.* Jay felt a warm breeze blow across his damp skin, the light, earthy scent of clovers and dandelions from the fields finally catching up with him. He looked down at his bare feet. *Way to be impulsive, Jay,* he silently chastised himself, finally realizing the consequences of his impatience. *I really hope I don't need those shoes.* He looked around at the blue, moonlit field, then turned and gazed back across his foot-trodden path through the sea of shadows. His eyes landed on his house. It sat dark, a silhouette of triangles and squares, dwarfed by the venerable oak beside it. The horses were grazing again, having been stirred awake when he ran past them.

Where's the fence line? He was at the edge of the pasture. *Where the hell is the fence?* Jay's heart quavered in his chest, his jaw tightening as his teeth clenched together. He turned his back to the house. The thought of Eve pulled his attention and he strained to see the edges of the fields. *Eve, Ila, where the hell ARE you?* Jay studied the thin horizon. There was no sign of movement, only the swirl of haze that began to lighten at the far edges of his sight.

STRUCTURES

"**H**ey, look!"
Ila followed Eve's finger out across the hazy, color-swirled sky. Thick, angular stilts sprouted from the distant ground. Eve and Ila slowed, continuing their strange bouncing gait toward the emerging object.

As they rapidly approached, the tall labyrinthine beams expanded across the ground. The structure towered up and plateaued in the swirling haze, the top seen then unseen as the sky moved and changed around it. The formation continued on as far as their eyes could see.

They came to a stop at the base, bouncing lightly on the still springy ground. Ila circled one of the large metal feet, losing sight of Eve completely behind the enormous base. The circular rivets embedded in the metal were as big as her head.

Eve stood between two of the gigantic feet and looked up at the towering metal beams. Two humongous x's braced the feet—one low and one high, the top one barely visible beneath the platform far above. Triangular trusses filled the space between, crossing and supporting the structure with beautifully configured angular designs.

"Holy wow," Eve whispered, circling the width of the foot. "Who could have built this —"

"Out here in the middle of nowhere?" Ila finished Eve's thought.

"What *is* this thing?" Eve asked, backing up and straining to make out the distant skyward platform. "Are those cables?"

Ila cupped her eyes and stared hard.

"I think they are! Power lines?"

"I was just thinking the same thing." Eve looked far off to the distant horizon. "Look, way over there, more feet like these."

Ila followed Eve's gaze then turned around and looked the way they had come.

"It ends here." Ila's own words descended on her like a weight, her heart unexpectedly heavy in her chest.

"Or begins here." Eve wrapped her arm around Ila's shoulder.

Ila studied the grey edges of the structure enveloped in the hazy swirling colors. Far above them, a long swoop of a cable peeked out from the cloudy haze.

"Look," Ila pointed skyward, "Up there … look, see that?"

Eve followed Ila's finger and stared, waiting for an image to appear. The colorful sky had lightened. No longer deep and rich with darker hues; no longer swirling and flowing as it did when they were moving. It was as if the sky had become like a stagnant river, an eddy flowing back on itself. Eve saw the faint curved line Ila was pointing to emerge from the white-grey sky.

"There!" Eve pointed, too. "I see it. There, swooping off this giant leg and following the length. Look, there's lines coming straight down from it, see?"

Ila nodded, bringing her hand up to shield her eyes, as if it would help define the images.

"It's a bridge," Eve said definitively. "I'd bet money on that." She strained her eyes to make out more. "Those cables go as far as I can see. They're suspending it, I think. Yes, it's definitely a bridge."

"Yeah," Ila answered, "I see that. A bridge … but a bridge for what?"

JAY

With Eve and Ila nowhere to be seen, Jay broke back into a steady jog, following the strange swirling haze. It was getting thicker by the minute.

"Eve! Ila!" Jay hollered in vain, his voice echoing on and on into the shrouded landscape. He knew it wouldn't reach them. They had been out of sight for too long, but still he tried. "Wait!"

Jay pumped his arms and legs harder, until he was running at full speed. He felt the hair on the back of his neck prickle and stand on end, his body on full alert. "Please wait," he pleaded softly as he sprinted in the direction they had headed. His whole body prickled with alarm.

BURNING

"How can it just end here?" Eve turned and looked back over the landscape they had crossed. The multicolored flow they had followed was barely visible as the grey-white sky thickened above them, billowing up like threatening thunderclouds.

"This place is creeping me out, Ila." Eve shuddered lightly as she crossed her arms and hugged herself.

"Yeah, this fog … I'm definitely not a fan." Ila shivered, too, and looked up. The cables and far away platform were once again invisible in the dense gathering grey.

Ila sat down heavily on the faded grass. Little by little, the color drained from their surroundings, leaving them beset in a dreary, muted landscape. Ila leaned onto the hard concrete foot of the bridge. "Look, Eve." Ila waved her hand over the green-brown grass. It barely moved under her hand.

"What's wrong with it?"

Ila shook her head. Her own bushy curls barely moved. "I dunno. It's like the sky. It's all lost its vibrancy, its…," Ila's voice trailed off. "This is really different, Eve. I've never been in a place like this. It's like we're in a world in between or something." She shook her head again, her hair listless, her face solemnly contemplating. "I just don't know."

"We're just going to sit here, then?"

"I guess. What do you think?"

Eve paused, her eyebrows knitting together, surveying their situation. She looked around at the encroaching haze. "I think it's a bad idea. But I'm tired. And I have no idea where we would go, anyway." Around them, more and more of the strange world disappeared into the thickening fog.

Ila nodded. Eve plopped down next to her. The lightness that had filled them was gone. Side by side, they gazed out over the clouded landscape. A sliver of pale, reddish-orange was the only color visible along the lowest stretch of the horizon.

"Looks like the sky is on fire over there," Eve said absently, adjusting herself on the ground. She readjusted herself again. Then she squirmed once more.

"Damn. It feels like this ground is on fire. Literally." The grass in front of them instantly turned dark brown. Eve hovered her hand gingerly over the ground. The brown grass turned orange. "Hey, is this ground hot to you?"

Ila touched the ground and immediately recoiled. "Ow! Damn!" She jumped to her feet. "Shit! Eve, it burns!"

Eve jumped up and hopped from one foot to the other as the hot ground heated through her shoes. "What do we do?!"

Ila quickly touched the metal leg they had been leaning against. It was cool. "This way!" She ran under the middle of the tall structure. "Come on, Eve!" The closest rung was a few feet overhead. Ila jumped up and missed. The ground below her hissed and sizzled as she landed. She backed up and took a two-step jog then bounced hard, like she had seen gymnasts do. She sprung up and awkwardly grabbed onto the angular bar, swung one leg up, then hauled her body onto the metal rung.

"Eve, jump!"

Eve followed Ila's lead and jumped, swinging her hand out wildly for the bar. She missed, her feet sizzling on the ground below just as Ila's had. Ila shimmied over to the side of the bar.

"Here, over here! It's lower!"

Eve cried out. "Ila, it burns!"

"I know, I know. Come on, Eve, jump!"

Eve tried again and missed. The ground gave a tiny bounce when she landed.

"Eve—bounce like you did before! Come on, girl! You can do it!"

Eve's eyes were wild. She bent her knees and jumped up, bouncing once then twice, each bounce adding to her momentum. Eve jumped once more, throwing her body higher, flailing her hand toward the metal. She missed again.

"One more and you're on! Eve! Grab it—now!"

Eve bounced hard—eyes narrowed, dripping with sweat—and threw her whole being at the bar, reaching with every ounce she had. Her hand gripped this time. Frantically, she grasped the bar with her other hand. The air around them was thick and motionless.

"I can't hold on!" Eve's moist hands slipped on the angular edge of the bar. "I'm too sweaty!" She squeezed her eyes shut, her face a contorted grimace as gravity threatened to pull her off the bar. Sweat ran down her arms as she poured all her attention into holding on.

"Hold *on*, damn it!" Ila commanded. "Like the flower, Eve! Feel it! Feel the bar! Let it connect to you! Look here! Look right at me." Ila wobbled as she reached out for her friend.

"I can't!" Eve clung desperately to the bar over and over as her hands slipped off the smooth edges.

"Yes, you can. I've seen you do it. This is just one time. Just one more time." Ila's voice was measured and steady.

"Breathe, girl." Mave's voice echoed in both their ears.

"Slow it all down, Eve." Ila's voice was steady and strong. "There you go—that's it. You got it. The feel. The feel. Feel that bar, Eve. Draw it in under your skin. Yes!"

Ila didn't know where the words were coming from, but she steadily gave them to Eve.

Eve peeled her eyes wide open. Her hands were gripping the bar tightly. She felt the metal holding, gently pulling, and keeping her connected.

"Yes!" Ila hooted. "Now get your tail up here, girl!"

Eve shimmied her hands across the bar. The metal let go just enough so that she could move. Ila grabbed her wrist as soon as she came within reach, the connection immediate and sure, and hauled her up. Crouched side by side in the triangular corner, they both felt the pull of the cool metal. The structure held onto them, as if it were some kind of benevolent force tethering to them—somehow keeping them safe. Eve brushed a lock of damp hair behind her ear and finally looked down.

"Oh my God."

Ila held onto the metal beams with both hands and shook her own hair out of her eyes. Beads of perspiration ran down the sides of her face, her warm skin glistening even in the grey mist.

"Yeah, I didn't want you to see that. The ground just disappeared. It fell away, Eve, into that … that lava. It just swallowed it … gone."

"Oh my God." Eve stared at the fierce, bubbling ground beneath them. "Holy shit, I almost died."

"Yeah, well, I was trying not to think about that option."

"Thank you for that." Eve leaned her head on Ila's shoulder and blew out a shaky breath. "Damn, girl. What in the world would I do without you?"

"For starters, you'd be, um, in that bubbling goo that used to be the ground we were sitting on."

"I guess so."

"But you're not."

Eve pulled her head up and watched smoke rise from the incinerating ground below. The dry, burning trail singed their nose and throat.

"But I'm not."

MOVE

J ay stopped in his tracks. Smoke silently snaked and spiraled up over the hill, billowing up like ominous grey clouds rising out of the earth. *Oh, crap.* Like a silent wave, the earth lifted, crested, and then rolled back down, both solid and fluid at the same time. Jay swayed with the earth, arms wide, balancing on the recklessly moving ground. Steam and smoke floated up in huge bulging clouds around him. The thick scent of smoke hit his nose forcefully, instantly burning his eyes. *Shit! That's fire!*

Jay shot one look back for his house and the horses but found no sign of either. *I sure hope they're all okay. Shit, I hope I'm okay,* he thought, his heart skipping at the thought, shooting more adrenaline through his body. He brushed his sweaty hands on his shorts and shot his eyes around him, surveying his threatening surroundings. In all directions, the ground was rising and dropping, moving more and more violently. The ground below him shook hard, almost knocking him off his feet. *Move or die.* Jay instantly turned and ran, responding immediately to his instinctual thought of survival.

Far off in front of him, a light blue layer of color materialized steadily above the wavering horizon. Jay narrowed his eyes and locked his sights onto the steady blue. Jay felt himself pulled in that direction, as if he were now in a swiftly moving stream.

"Okay," he said out loud as the color on the horizon widened. The immediate world around him faded away as he focused all his attention and energy on the widening blue. His arms and legs pumped full tilt as his body flew across the landscape. His nostrils flared, trying to keep pace and fuel his speeding body. No smoke burned in his nostrils—the air was fresh and clear. He felt it energizing his cells, pushing him forward. Around him, lightness emerged from the thick dark clouds of smoke, growing more and more vibrant. It waved and moved, weaving itself into the deepening blue, filling the whole sky. Jay tightened his jaw and gathered a deep breath through his nose, lifting his head slightly, then sped even faster into a breakneck sprint across the land, which was surprisingly steady beneath his pounding feet.

CLIMBING

Ila and Eve assessed their surroundings. Below them, the fiery ground continued to crumble in on itself. Thick smoke spread into the sky, darkening the world as far as they could see. It became harder to breathe. Above them, the metal shaped and arranged itself into various forms, appearing then disappearing into the lighter, grey-white haze above them.

Ila caught Eve's eye and was surprised at the strength she saw in them. Ila gave her friend an apologetic smile, unsure why she suddenly felt completely responsible for their circumstances.

"Nowhere to go but up, I guess," Ila shrugged, her voice more shaky than she wished. Without warning, her shoulders felt burdened, as if an extra weight had just landed on them.

Eve's brow drew closer together as she watched her friend closely. She gave a nervous laugh, trying to sound nonchalant. "I guess."

Ila blew out a heavy sigh. Her sullen voice had caught her off guard. All at once, she felt completely and utterly exhausted. Her whole body felt as shaky as her voice, like it was vibrating imperceptibly. She began to tremble. From deep inside, she felt something give way, as if a part of her had fissured and cracked just then—just as the ground had below them. She reached her trembling hands up and smoothed her curly hair back away from her face. Holding her thick hair back behind her head, she tried to steady herself. As she peered up at the dull, empty sky, the dull ache outside felt like a mirror to the dull ache she felt deep in the recesses of her heart.

What the hell are we doing here? Ila's thoughts seemed to have a life of their own. *Mave, where are you? This is just like my dream.* As each thought crossed her mind, they added their own pressure to her burden. *Jesus, where the hell are we? I don't think we can do this. I'm sorry. I know I'm not supposed to let myself go there. I know I'm supposed to believe ... to be strong. But, Mave, I can't....* Suddenly, Ila felt small and vulnerable and utterly alone. Hot tears pressed up behind her eyes. She wrapped her arms tightly around her as the world loomed menacingly—towering up and dwarfing her. She forced herself not to look at Eve. She stared at a high crossbeam and focused on the large circular rivets while she fought against the tears. Something deep within her was fracturing. She steeled her jaw and fought back, blinking her eyes hard against the threatening inner upheaval.

Eve shuddered, as if a cool breeze had blown over them, watching Ila carefully. The familiar vibrancy of her friend had all but vanished. Before her, Ila seemed almost invisible and terribly small. Without warning, Eve felt a bolt of energy surge through her body, strengthening and invigorating her. Somehow, she knew she was meant to share it with her friend.

"Well, then, Ila. Come on then. Lead us on, sister! What are we waiting for?" Eve sat up taller, buoyed and energized by the surprising burst of strength. She stared at the back of Ila's head until Ila turned and met her piercing gaze. Silently, Eve willed the strength she felt rushing through her veins to be shared with her friend. It seemed to work. Far back, in the center of Ila's eyes, she saw a spark, then watched as if a flame ignited deep within Ila. Her friend expanded back into herself, solid and full once more. Eve's chest relaxed as she blew out a silent breath of relief.

A small tremor shook Ila from head to toe. She blinked long and slow and looked hard into Eve's eyes, her piercing gaze this time reassuring.

"As you wish," Ila finally answered, her voice strong once again. She drew her lips into a half smile and stood, pulling herself up with both hands. She widened her feet, filling the angular space with her presence, and gave a flourish of her hand, adding a small bow as an accent. Ila felt much lighter. She shook her head, her hair cascading gracefully around her shoulders, releasing the last remnants of uncertainty, and surveyed their surroundings with fresh, bright eyes.

The metal beams gleamed even though they were still surrounded by the grey-black smoke. Ila squinted, looking for the source of the light but found none. She focused on the beams again and settled her eyes on a path. With stealth and confidence, she started across the long, straight beams, her slender frame moving easily across the converging shapes and angles that held the immense structure aloft.

With each placement of her hands and feet, Ila felt more and more connected and supported by the beams, the ease and smoothness of this part of their travels heartening her with each step. She paused for a moment gathering herself, then delicately reached one leg around the edge of the structure, gripping the metal tightly with her hands. Again, she felt the pull and connection of the metal under her hands. She shimmied to the outer edge then eased the rest of her weight around, perching on the outside of the framework. She didn't dare look down. Carefully, hand over hand, she began to scale the wide triangular trusses. Eve finally exhaled, realizing she had been holding her breath as she watched her friend navigate the perilous turn. Ila waited a few steps above as Eve made the turn, following Ila's route exactly.

Silently, they picked their way up the huge metal giant. Ila paused to reach back to haul Eve up; Eve hoisted Ila from below as needed. As they climbed, the holds grew closer and closer together, until they formed into neat vertical rungs, one above the other.

Around them, mist gathered thicker then thinned again as the air around them moved ever so slightly. Washes of white began to mingle with pale yellow, shifting the dismal grey tones, yet offering only small glimpses of the world above them. The smell of smoke and charred earth faded the higher they climbed. Occasionally, one of them would sputter and cough crisply against the silent backdrop, the unexpected sound against the stark background startling them both.

"Hey," Eve finally uttered huskily. She cleared her throat and started again.

"Hey, I was just thinking… I heard Mave's voice way back there. When I was jumping for the bar…." Eve's voice trailed off into the mist.

Ila hesitated, her heart skipping a beat. She recovered almost instantly and continued to climb.

"Yeah," she answered finally, "I think I did, too."

"Really? What's that about?"

Ila could barely see the cool metal under the hand right in front of her. Tentatively, she reached up for the next rung. Her hand moved freely through open space. She searched through the mist for metal. Eve bumped into her leg.

"Hold on. I can't find the next rung." Ila fished her hand wide in the air. She took one step, almost losing sight of her secure hand, and reached up further. She found nothing. She stepped back down, rubbed her damp, free hand lightly on her jeans, then gripped the bar and wiped the other one dry.

"Maybe we're at the top," Eve offered. "God, I sure hope so. I'm tired."

"Me, too." Ila leaned and reached forward. Her ribs bumped into something hard. "I can't find any more steps." Her reaching hand felt a flat, bumpy surface. The cool metal extended out in all directions. She noticed her hands were again quivering. "Yep, I think we're there."

Ila leaned as far forward as she could, keeping her feet steady on the bar under them. The mist parted briefly, and she saw a space at least wide enough for them both to sit before it claimed her view again.

"I think we can rest here. It feels solid, like a metal floor or something."

"We'll both fit?"

"I think so. I can't feel any edges. I'm going to climb up and check it out."

"Please, Ila, be careful."

Ila shimmied out on her belly using her forarms to pull her forward. She stayed on her belly and reached her arms and legs out as far as she could in a wide circle, the hard, bumpy surface pressing into her skin. She spun on her belly in a half circle until she was facing Eve.

"It's at least as big as me." She sat up and felt out around her. Her hands bumped into a side rail. As if reading Braille through the mist, she made out a railing. "Yeah, here." She tapped the metal rails, the soft ring loud against the quiet, and made room for Eve. "Here, come on up. There's railings up here, too. Thank goodness." She tapped the metal lightly in a couple of different places so Eve could understand the dimensions better.

Eve crawled around Ila and sat beside her, leaning into her as a soft sigh of relief escaped her lips.

"Eve?"

"Mmmm?" Eve responded dreamily.

"I've been thinking about it. I don't know how we both heard Mave's voice. I heard her say, 'Breathe, girl.' Is that what you heard?"

"Mmmhmmm."

Eve's breathing was light and smooth.

"Eve?"

"Mmm."

"I think we're awake. Fully awake. I can't explain it at all. But I think Mave...," she trailed off, trying to comprehend how she could hear Mave's voice. She felt Eve's warm body gently rise and fall.

"Eve?" she whispered. The low murmur of Eve's breathing was the only sound in the thick void. "Eve, are you sleeping?"

Eve's soft breath was her only answer. Ila smiled. *Lucky.*

The white mist thickened around them, creating a tight cocoon. Ila looked down, searching for a hint of the metal below them. She held her hand out in front of her, but even then, she could not see it. Ila's heart quickened. A soft blanket of pale yellow began to infuse itself into the concealing white clouds. The yellow thickened, swaddling them, and began an airy dance.

"Ila."

Ila froze at the sound of the voice. Eve's slow, steady breathing continued in her ear, unaffected by the sound.

"Ila, it's okay, hon. It's Mave."

BREAKING

S carcely breathing, Ila watched the yellow swirl brighten around her. Eve shifted, her warm body settling heavily as she drifted deeper into a peaceful sleep.

Ila kept her own voice a whisper.

"Mave?"

"Yes, honey, I'm here." Ila heard a light chime that seemed to come from the swirling atmosphere around her.

"Mave." Ila felt tears swell and push at the edges of her eyes. She refused them again, clearing her throat. "Oh, God," she whispered, "I'm so glad to hear you." The strength she harnessed for their ascent was spent. Tears rose against her will, pooling, clouding her sight. Silently, they seeped out and slipped down her warm cheeks. Ila didn't have the energy to fight them any longer, so she finally let them go. "This is so different," she whispered through jagged breaths, laboring to keep the last bits of control on her emotions. "Mave"—Ila inhaled, her chest shaking from her ragged breathing—"I'm really scared. I don't know what to do. It's dangerous here, Mave. Eve, she almost…," Ila trailed off, her chest rising and falling rapidly, tears spilling freely as the full weight of the circumstances became crystal clear in her mind.

"Listen." Mave's voice was soft and kind. "Listen here, Ila. I know, sweetie. It's different. I knew something was up when Beast strolled into our lives." Light chimes rang softly, and pale gold infused itself into the light yellow mist surrounding Ila, causing her heart to flutter in her chest.

"You're not alone, baby. I know Eve is with you, but I also know you, Ila—how it's you against the world—and I want you to truly hear this: you're not alone in this one, honey." Mave paused and she stared

125

off into the darkened, web-filled rafters, waiting, wanting the words to sink in. "And, Ila, I think I know where you are."

"You do?" Ila edged forward. Eve adjusted herself, leaning her weight comfortably onto Ila. Gently, Ila eased herself back into the railing to better support her friend.

"Look, Ila, there are some things that you should have been told. Jay, too. You guys are old enough now. Your dad should have told you, but you know how well he handles things…."

Ila saw an image of her dad, head in hands at their worn kitchen table, his greying hair shielding the rest of his pale, white face. She felt her jaw tighten.

"Yeah, I know." Ila felt heaviness envelope her again. Her voice fell flat. "Yeah," she mumbled. "Coulda, shoulda, woulda," she finished, giving Mave's often-used words back to her.

Far away in the incandescent light of the barn, Mave felt the edges of her mouth turn up. "Touché."

Ila stared blankly at the vibrating mist. The image of her father crashed down on her, making it hard to breathe. *Home*. Her heart filled with heavy emptiness. Fresh tears oozed up, spilled out, and trickled down her cheeks. A deep ache began pulling in the recesses of her heart. *Where the hell is my home?* Ila let herself fall into her aching question, too exhausted to fight it any longer. Soft sobs shook her entire body.

A deep sadness swirled and permeated the shadowed barn, pulling profoundly on Mave's own heart. Across the moonlit pasture, Beast raised his prodigious head and peered out, scrutinizing the timeworn barn. He ambled through the moonlit night to the back gate. Mave glimpsed his long shadow falling across the silvery ground and watched as it grew larger and larger, until it formed into a complete silhouette of the animal just outside the open barn doors.

"Look, baby…," Mave began, her heart tightening. As clear as if in front of her, she saw a young Ila run through the barn, looking for a place to hide. Dust puffed up from each hurried step she took. Giggles tumbled high and sweet out of her young lips. Mave let herself relax, and the scene unfolded as if it were happening again, although she knew for certain it had occurred eleven years ago.

Ellen stood still in the opposite doorway, surrounded by early morning sunshine. Her long, lively curls were animated even as she paused to listen to her daughter.

"Where'd you go, bug?"

Mave smiled as the voice she remembered from long ago echoed richly through her ears. She heard Ila's young giggle from behind the haystack. As Mave watched, Ellen entered the barn, just as she had done a thousand times before, and glided across the wide-open aisle. Her soft, almost elegant steps barely disturbed the dusty floor. Particles danced around her in the sunlight, sending sparkles of illumination across her shadowed figure. Mave's heart warmed seeing her old friend. *My God, I miss you, Ellen.*

Mave felt wetness on her cheeks and let it ooze down her face, sliding over the grooves in her neck, finally disappearing into the fabric of her shirt.

"I'm going to find you, girl!" Ellen's soft teasing elicited a cascade of giggles from the young Ila. Mave watched silently as Ellen walked past her and down the otherwise empty aisle. Her figure faded as it moved further and further away from her. When Ellen reached the golden brown haystack, she disappeared completely. A full and absolute silence settled across the barn. Once Ellen's apparition was gone, Mave found herself looking directly at Beast. Through the darkness, he silently returned her gaze.

Across worlds, Mave heard Ila's low sniffle and instantly understood the vision. *Ellen.*

Ila heard the name ring in her own head as if it had been spoken. *Ellen.* She clenched her jaw tighter. Her breath became rough and uneven again as she steeled herself against this threatening wave of pain, the one she knew for certain she could not bear.

"Ila," Mave began, her voice low and smooth, "Ila, honey, I know things have been tough for you…."

Across the distance, Mave felt Ila stiffen and attempt to pull the walls back up around her breaking heart. "Ila," Mave uttered, soft as silk, "I should have been there for you, child. I should have talked to you more about your mom. I should have been there for you. I knew how bad you were hurting … I know that now, baby." Mave felt Ila's walls crack, the crevices spreading across her vast interior, completely shattering the last of her defenses.

As if she were next to her, Mave felt Ila lean into her. More than anything, Mave wished she could wrap her arms tightly around Ila and hold her while her young heart peeled open and unleashed the pain hidden there.

"I know...," Mave started, her voice catching in her throat as her own heart squeezed in her chest. "I know...," she began a second time. Mave felt a searing pain run across her own heart and pierce her so quickly that it took her breath away. Instinctively, she wrapped her arms tightly across her chest, hugging her shoulders, as if protecting herself from a threatening predator. Mave struggled to steady her own breath. "Ila," Mave finally confessed, "I know exactly what it feels like to be ... alone. To be ... different." Mave let her own long-held tears spill forcefully from her eyes. "I know," she choked out, "what it feels like to be left and have nowhere you feel you truly belong, no true home...." Mave bit her firm lower lip and let the deep sobs rack her own body. Across space and time, Ila's chest rose and fell in a perfectly aligned rhythm with Mave, echoing a pure and sublime heartbreaking harmony.

SECRETS I

Ila fought for air as her whole body quaked. Wave after wave convulsed through and gasped out of her as she tried desperately to pull herself back together.

Next to her, Eve bolted upright. Her head flew left and right, her long, tangled hair waving around her in a disheveled, matted mess. Instantly, she was awake, scanning her surroundings for the cause of her abrupt awakening. The light gold and yellow colors around them were thick and still.

Ila felt her chest tighten. She inhaled in quick sharp bursts. Eve spun to face her friend, grabbed her shoulders, and searched her frantically for the source of her pain.

"Ila, what is it? Oh, God, Ila are you okay? What's wrong?"

Eve knelt on the hard ground in front of Ila. The unmoving air around them began to cool, contrasting the frenetic energy in front of her. Eve leaned in close, searching; Ila's face was scrunched and unreadable, hidden in her long curls. Her arms crossed tightly, holding her chest as if it would burst. Eve lowered herself down and peered up at Ila's eyes squeezed tightly shut. Tears spilled steadily through unseen cracks, trailing down her cheeks and dropping to the ground like rain. Her mouth was open slightly, as if she were about to speak, but no sound emerged. Eve felt her warm breath sputter out so completely she worried Ila would pass out from lack of air. Suddenly, she inhaled sharply, gasping and involuntarily filling her lungs.

"Ila," she whispered urgently, "please tell me what's wrong."

"I....," Ila sputtered finally rocking instinctively, "I...."

Ila's mind and body unleashed every memory she had of her mother, dismantling and pulverizing the defenses she had meticulously built up over the years. Each anguishing memory flashed like a picture.

Each short clip filled with vibrant color, consuming the screen in her mind's eye. She rocked harder and squeezed her eyelids so forcefully that, momentarily, all she saw were masses of color pixels. Rebelliously and methodically, the colors reshaped themselves into the same images—flashing like a slideshow of her early childhood, searing fresh wounds across her heart.

"She's … gone…," Ila spluttered out. "And … she's not … coming … back…." Ila rocked furiously. "Eve, it … hurts…," Ila whimpered through unsteady breaths.

Eve watched her friend helplessly. She searched her mind to make sense of Ila's words. *Who's not coming back? Mave?*

"She doesn't mean me, honey." Mave's voice was strangely tight. Eve furrowed her brow, whipping her head around again, searching the concealing fog for another presence. The yellow mist around them pulsed brighter against the dull grey background. Eve narrowed her eyes, noticing the yellow-gold mist scattered through the light grey fog.

"She means her mother."

Ila rocked harder at the sound of Mave's words.

"Mave, you don't sound like yourself. Is that really you? What's going on?"

"Yes, Eve, it's me." Mave sniffed loudly and roughly wiped her nose with a crumpled tissue. "Eve, honey, she's talking about her mom." Mave let her own soft sobs ease out as quietly as possible, wiping the tears away as soon as they left her eyes. She had cried plenty of tears for Ellen. This time, she realized, the tears were finally for herself. And Isaac.

Eve nodded, as if Mave could see her, finally comprehending. "Are you okay, Mave?"

Mave looked across the empty barn and inhaled shakily, nodding.

"Eve, listen to me. Remember yesterday? In Jay's house when we found Zoe?"

That had all been so long ago. Eve struggled for memories in the recesses of her mind. A vision floated into her awareness: one of Ila bumping into her, shaking.

"Yes," Eve answered, confused.

"We, Ila and I, we saw someone there with Zoe," Mave hesitated. "Actually, I saw two people with her. Ila's mom, Ellen. And Isaac Waters."

Eve felt a surge of energy flash through her, searing under her skin, then disappear. She rubbed her palms on her grimy pants. Slowly, as if it were the rising sun, her mind put Mave's words into a coherent context, and her mind burst into understanding.

"I know who he is." Eve exhaled breathlessly. "Ila and Jay, they just told me about him." Her mind flashed to the families in the street. "And the trouble ... with the families...." She was uncertain how much she should confess knowing. "Mave, how did you see them *there*? In Jay's house?"

"Eve, there is so much we should have told you three. So much. First, though, is Ila okay? She's breaking, child. Her heart is breaking. She has tried all her life to avoid this...," Mave trailed off, rubbing a hand over her own aching chest.

Eve nodded, her eyes scrutinizing Ila as she rocked back and forth in front of her. Ila's tears continued rolling in a steady stream, but she was beginning to settle. "I think so, Mave." Eve felt a weight descend upon her chest. Instantly, she knew it was Mave's.

"What's going on? I can feel all these things, but I don't understand them." Eve pressed her lips together, biting her lower lip. "Mave, you guys are the strong ones. I don't know how to do this. I can't...."

"I guess you have to now, sweetheart." Mave's voice cracked. "Eve, listen," Mave continued in a shaky tone. "Ila, you, too, honey." A warm breeze blew though the barn, fluttering across Mave's bare arms, ruffling Beast's short black fur. Mave pushed herself up, took a step toward the animal, and then stopped. The air around Ila and Eve stirred; the yellow mist glistened, mixing and illuminating the grey fog even more. She backed up, suddenly and completely exhausted, and sat back on the hay bale.

"Listen, Jay is in there with you guys. You have to find him. I think you are between our world, Moira, and a place called Ariom. That world exists very near to ours, but it is not our world. I'm certain Beast is from there. I don't know how I know that—I just do. These worlds, they're beginning to overlap. More ... again...." Ila's rocking eased, and her chest began to rise and fall more calmly. A long, stuttering inhale perked Mave's ears as she listened across worlds. "Ila? Can you hear me?" Ila nodded heavily. Mave nodded in response. "Okay, good." Mave's chest lifted as she inhaled deeply. *Where do I begin?*

Ila opened her eyes, rimmed red with grief, and cleared her throat.

"I think," she suggested definitively, "you should begin at the beginning."

JAY

The cool air swept across Jay's damp skin, his feet barely touching the ground as he sprinted forward. The colors around him sparkled and shined like tiny vibrant jewels, swiftly flowing at his side as he flew across the rolling hills. In the distance, Jay spotted grey white clouds towering upon themselves, growing higher and higher by the second. A faint twinge tugged deep in his chest as his palms suddenly became wet and clammy. Around him, the flow thickened and dulled. The grass under his feet transformed from a vibrant green to a pale field of browning yellow, and the surrounding hills leveled out then flattened entirely into one long stretch of landscape. As he shook the dampness off his hands, Jay felt an urgency he could not explain. He narrowed his eyes and quickened his pace.

Up ahead, the swirling atmosphere around him began to divide to the left and right. On either side of him, small rivulets had begun to back up and spin off in blue-white counterswirls. Jay slowed to a steady jog and surveyed his curiously changing surroundings. In a flash, he realized that the flow was moving back on itself, as if someone had thrown it all in reverse. The copious atmosphere rotated like a building storm of darkening colors, tinted with a smoky grey-white mist.

Out of nowhere, an enormous pylon materialized in front of him, standing definitively and solidly in his path. Jay tried to swerve around the looming obstacle, but it was too wide. He threw his weight backwards, trying to stop, but that, too, was futile as his momentum continued to propel him forward. Preparing for impact, he threw his shoulder forward and braced himself. He hit the grey metal structure with a force that knocked his breath clean out of his lungs.

Jay crumpled to the ground. The grass below him wafted a sweet light scent around his nose, followed by a tinge of smoke. Behind closed eyes, Jay heaved in pain, desperately grasping for a full breath. Around his shoulder and down the whole right side of his body, Jay felt sharp, searing pain. His shoulder felt as if it were on fire.

Alarm rang through Jay's mind as his body called him to high alert. His eyes shot open wide and adrenaline poured into his system. From shoulder to foot, every piece of his body touching the ground stung and burned. Jay sprung from the ground, cradling his throbbing shoulder as his thick-soled feet burned, no match for the scalding ground below. Around him, fissures crackled across the flat land oozing out red-hot molten liquid. Jay's system surged, ready to bolt, drowning out any pain or injury he had only just moments ago. Survival consumed him.

Jay sprang nimbly onto the thick concrete surrounding the metal pylon, his arms swinging wildly to keep him balanced on the thin, hard edge. Smoke billowed up, consuming the world around him. Jay spotted a rung above him that was disappearing rapidly in the thickening air. Jay gathered himself then flung his body recklessly toward the now invisible bar. His fingers found the bar and hung on tight. As the momentum heaved his body forward, he swung his second hand wildly through the mist to find a secure grasp. The ground below hissed and steamed, the rising heat creeping ominously around Jay's entire being. His hands slipped, his sweaty palms grasped and clawed onto the bar repeatedly. His face pulled into a tight painful grimace, every muscle in his neck taut down the length of his arms, willing his body to hold tight. His weight pulled him dangerously away from his only salvation. Again and again he slipped and regained a hold on the bar. Then all at once the bar under his hands began to suction into him, as if it were magnetizing his hands and drawing him in. His grip tightened steadily until he was sure he was connected securely and, for the moment, held safe.

Jay commanded his body into a gentle, even swing and inhaled shakily as he gathered himself again. In one giant thrust, he swung his legs out hard, hurling them up to catch another metal rung a few feet away. Deftly, he twisted his body onto the bar and sat in the triangular space between rungs, his heart pounding in his chest as adrenaline surged through his sweat-coated body. Jay sat perfectly still while the pulsing rush filled his ears. Glistening and clouding his vision, sweat dripped in a small stream off his chin. Jay let it fall, unwilling to let go of the grip he had on the metal scaffolding.

Through clenched white fingers, Jay watched, frozen, while the earth below him disappeared completely as wave after wave of searing lava oozed up and claimed it. The thick, smoky surroundings shifted continually, concealing then revealing the terrifying scene below him. The roaring in his head quieted and was replaced by the roar of the violent land below. The concrete base and tall metal pylon remained intact, but he felt the heat rise and sear the hair on his bare legs.

"Oh, shit!" he said out loud, his voice barely audible over the rumble groaning out of the fracturing ground. "This is just like Ila's dream."

Through squinted eyes, Jay searched above him through speckled openings in the thickening smoke. Bits and pieces of his metal surroundings flashed briefly, as if they were pieces of an unfinished puzzle, then promptly vanished from sight.

Trusses. The word popped into his head. *Trusses.* In his mind, an image of an immense metal bridge, supported with patterns of arched scaffolding, appeared wide and clear. *Ah, yes! A bridge ... maybe ... okay. Good.* Jay's chest rose and fell more and more evenly as his breath leveled out. His mind slowly cleared.

I've got to get out of here. With nowhere to go but up, Jay started to pick his way across the strangely cool metal until he was holding larger pieces of the structure under his determined hands. Even with shaky legs, his bare feet molded easily onto the angular bars. Jay moved slowly at first, making sure his legs wouldn't buckle and betray him. The smoky haze filled his nose and burned his eyes. Jay paused, squeezing his trembling hands tighter against the small beams, and stooped in the cramped space as he searched for a path forward. Slowly and methodically, he began to move. With no choice left, he began his cautious and delicate ascent.

ARIOM

Mave adjusted herself on a prickly bale of hay, strangely grateful for the uncomfortable seat. She didn't feel like she deserved to be comfortable at this moment—she hadn't all night—not when the kids were unsafe themselves. Dark shadows filled the barn behind her, and she found herself shifting to keep that area visible out of the corner of her eye. *Come on, girl, get it together now. This is no time to be spooked.* Mave shook her head, silently chastising herself. A shiver ran down her spine and out across her arms, making the hairs on her arms rise up.

Beast shook his massive head. Mave jumped.

"Oh, my God," she whispered hoarsely as the unexpected jolt through her system settled. One soft note rang and echoed beautifully through the lofty wooden beams. A small smile creeped across her lips. "Thank you, boy." Mave nodded in Beast's direction. This time, Mave was not surprised at all when Beast nodded back.

Across waves of space, Ila and Eve heard the note ring and echo through their own ears, settling into the air around them. The sound blanketed them, transforming the charged atmosphere into a calm cocoon. Ila relaxed her grip across her chest. Eve sat next to her friend, leaned against her once more, and draped her arm heavily across Ila's shoulder.

Mave cleared her throat.

"Okay, the beginning." Mave closed her weary eyes and searched for the beginning. "Well, truly, that I do not know, but my beginning with this world, with Ariom, started very young. My mother introduced me to it. And her mother before her knew it as well. Edge and Isaac are the only men I ever knew to cross over. Zoe has gone with me; both me and your mom. But we don't have time for all that. Let me think, what do you need to know?" Mave's heart lurched and skipped a beat in her chest. *Isaac and Ellen.* The names planted themselves in the center of Mave's thoughts. *All right then, we'll begin there.*

Ila heard Mave's thoughts clearly, as if they were her own. She also felt Mave's grief landing heavily on her own already weighted heart.

"Mave?" Ila's raspy voice called gently. "Mave, you don't have to go there if you don't want to. You don't have to explain now. I didn't know how bad you've been hurting, too. About Isaac. I … I … I didn't know…." She trailed off, not knowing what else to say.

Mave shook her head, her hair casting a spiky shadow behind her.

"No, child, I should have talked to you long ago. I knew what you were going through without your mom. I knew I should have talked to you. Deep down, I knew. But, oh, honey, you had built your walls up, and I just kept waiting for a crack in there, a way in. I should have come straight out with it, but I didn't. Coulda, shoulda, woulda."

A wry smile pulled on Ila's lips.

"I honestly didn't know how to delve into this notion of…," Mave looked up, searching for the word, "of belonging, I guess. I watch you struggling with it—being on the outside of things. Keeping yourself there. I have watched you with it for years. It wrecks me, Ila. Because I haven't figured it out myself. Honey, some days I feel so different and so damn alone on this planet that I think I'm the last person on earth that should be trying to help you through your darkness. You know?"

Ila nodded almost imperceptibly, her eyes glistening, unfocused. Eve stared straight ahead, her eyes wet, too, her chest squeezed tight—listening and feeling both Ila and Mave's anguish.

Mave continued, "This world—some of us just don't fit in here all that easily. But, honey, don't you think for one minute you aren't loved—for whatever reason—because you look different from some of those folks around here, from these folks in town. Because your family looks different. Because your mama left. Because you feel things in ways that others don't. I suspect even if none of those things happened, you would still feel different. Some of us just do, Ila. Some of us just do.

"That's the deal. Yes, your skin is brown and your father's isn't. Yes, there aren't many in this town that look like you. Yes, your mom had to leave—yes, I said *had* to leave—because that's the way she felt about it. It was a choice, Ila. The hardest one she ever had to make. She loves you so very much. I know we didn't tell you that enough. We all avoided it. Your father is broken, Ila, you know that. He cannot function without your mother. He is a shell of a man. And he promised her he would take care of you. He tried, Ila; he really did. But truthfully, I suspect you would have felt alone even if he was able— some of us are just wired that way. We just are. We're all looking for home, kiddo, some place we belong. Some of us just don't know it. And some of us know it from the very moment we're born."

An image appeared in Ila's mind—one of her dad holding a young, flailing version of herself. He was rocking her, trying to get her still just for a minute. Ila watched as her younger self gritted her teeth, closed her eyes, and swung wildly at the forlorn man trying to comfort her. His eyes were red; it was clear he had been crying himself. Ila's young fist connected with his cheek hard enough to knock his head back. Full of blind fury, the young girl continued to kick and punch ferociously, her tangled and matted hair whipping around like her fists, her clothes mismatched and disheveled. She truly was a wild child.

Beaten, the man gently set the uncontrollable child down. Even in the midst of her repeated small-fisted blows, he handled her with the utmost of care. He let her rage and flail on the floor in front of him, helpless to help her. He leaned forward and held his head in his hands, his most familiar pose. The only difference was that his hair was much darker back then. Ila watched as his shoulders shook heavily as his own grief spilled out and joined the chaos of the room. Ila sniffed so lightly Mave almost missed it. Ila did not remember this scene. Mave had known things were bad back then, but she had no idea they had been this bad.

"She had to go, Ila," Mave cut in, ending the vision that had shown itself simultaneously to Mave and Ila. "Not because of anything he did. That's what crushes him. Daily. And not because of anything you did either, honey. Not in the slightest. You are the brightest light in your mother's world. I don't know why we did not tell you this earlier, Ila. I guess we all broke in our own way when your mother left."

Ila sniffed loudly, adjusting herself on the hard ground. Eve sat silently next to her, her faraway, almost-vacant eyes glassy and unreadable as she digested Mave's words. They explained a lot about her friend. Eve squeezed Ila gently then moved her arm off and rubbed her hands together in her own lap. Ila took hold of Eve's left hand. Instantly, Ila felt heat and warmth emanating from Eve's soft skin. It soothed her. Ila leaned her head back against the rail behind them and looked around. The yellow mist was bright and vibrant. The dull grey had lightened and thinned, almost disappearing completely. Ila stretched her long legs out in front of her, feeling much lighter herself, her vision clearing in unison with the atmosphere around them.

"What about Isaac?" Eve asked the questions so quietly she was almost inaudible. "Why did they go, Mave?" Eve felt her heart lurch and skip a beat. Below them, the metal shook infinitesimally. Ila and Eve looked at each other.

What was that? Eve stared at Ila, her chest rising and falling briskly, while her breath moved through her flaring nostrils.

"What was *what*?" Mave's voice rose. "What happened, you guys?"

Ila shook her head. "It's okay. Just a tremor. It's fine." Ila looked steady at Eve through her red-rimmed eyes, the fire still in them. "We're *fine*, Eve. I promise."

Mave looked over at Beast. Moving one foot precisely at a time, he turned and faced away from her. His large head swung back, as if in slow motion, as he peered across the long aisle of the barn one last time. A loud, low chime filled the whole room, vibrating deep into Mave's cells, reverberating off the entire weathered interior. Across space and time, Ila and Eve felt the low and forceful vibration of his sound. Ila pulled herself to her feet. Eve scurried up behind her. Beast slowly and deliberately navigated his way back into the darkness.

"Mave, I think we need to move. What do we need to know?" Energy began to surge through Ila's limbs. Hastily, she wiped her eyes and shifted her weight from one foot to the other, barely able to stand still. She stamped her feet one at a time, the thick metal underneath responding with a muffled ring against the sting on her soles. Eve's eyes darted nervously to Ila then around their surroundings. The sky grew lighter until it was only a vaporous yellow-white haze. In front of them, a clear path materialized. The silvery metal stretched and gleamed out in front of them, gradually rising and arcing in a long, smooth curve.

Mave clasped her clammy palms together and brought her fingers thoughtfully to her lips. "Okay, okay, need to know, shoot." Mave's thoughts raced through her head. "Your mom, Ellen, and Isaac crossed to Ariom to help the Others. I have a feeling that's where you're going, too. The Others—they are energy balancers in Ariom; they monitor and regulate their energy supply. There's a connection between our worlds. I don't understand it. No one fully did. Not completely, although the Others understand it more than anyone. The Others— that's how they're referred to collectively—Ila, this is partly why I couldn't find a way to talk to you about being different. The Others, they truly *are* different, really different. And they are not treated well there, at least not by our standards. They are seen as less than— individuals of service—at least by the surface. There are some in that world who consider them soulless.

"Your mother, she could not bear it. And Isaac, he had ideas, a plan of sorts, to help them. But that was long ago. We lost the connection. The portal that you three slipped into—or portals I should say—they move and shift. And we lost it. I'm sure entry was lost on both sides, or we would have seen or heard from them before yesterday. Ila, that was Isaac you saw in Zoe's kitchen. You did see them, didn't you? Isaac and your mom…."

Ila bounced lightly, jumping up and down on the metal path. Eve paced back and forth like a caged cat, looking up every few seconds, watching Ila for their next move. "Yeah, I saw him"—Ila shook her hands out as she bounced—"but not her. Mave, something's really shifting here." Ila was distracted. "It feels like I want to jump out of my skin."

"Me, too," Eve added, pacing wide from one side of the soaring structure to the other.

"Mave, I feel we need to move out of this spot. But I don't want to. I'm afraid we'll lose you, too."

"Go, child. That's the best way. There, even more than here, you need to follow those nudges you get, those impulses of what to do next. You hear?"

Ila nodded, her eyes darting a quick sideways glance as she skipped forward, then landed into a light jog down the open path. Eve took off, too, and fell into pace beside her. Their strides matched exactly as their long, slim legs beat a steady clang onto the thick metal.

"We're going, Mave." Ila's voice was uneven. A puff of warm air breezed past them, ruffling Ila's hair and drying the last remnants of wetness she had on her face. With it came a faint tinge of smoke. Ila inhaled deeper, making sure it wasn't just in her mind. Eve huffed steadily at her side, surprised how easy it was to keep up.

Back in the barn, Ila's words sounded faraway. Mave had known it was coming. The connection never lasted for long. Her body slumped as she realized they were on their own again. Mave let her eyes fall closed and sent out a silent prayer for their safety. Bright swirls gathered behind her closed eyes, the colors pulsing in vibrant, rolling waves. Mave recognized the otherworldly sky instantly, even though she had not seen it in years.

Isaac? Ellen? You out there? Mave had continued this ritual, this calling across worlds every night since she last saw them eleven years ago. A static-filled void had always answered back.

"Mave?" a gravely, far-off voice rasped into her ears. "Mavel? Honey, is that you?"

Mave's eyes flew open as she hugged her hands over her open mouth. She stood perfectly still, barely daring to breathe. Across time, the voice crackled through the barn, deep and low, as if a radio had been adjusted just right.

"Mavel? You there?"

Mave's heart lurched as she broke into tears for the second time in one night.

"*Isaac?*" she choked out. The barn warped around her as tears clouded her vision, blurring all lines. She wiped them away impatiently, searching the shadowed building for any sign of him.

Like a sigh of relief, his smooth voice breathed out heavily across worlds: "Mavel."

Mave could feel his smile even though he was nowhere to be seen; his warm voice was intimately familiar even after all this time. It surrounded her, melting places in her heart she hadn't even known had hardened.

"Oh my God, Isaac, is that really you?" Mave reached behind her, searching for the hay once again, afraid her unsteady legs might betray her completely.

"Yes, Mavel, it absolutely is."

Mave let the tears roll down her cheeks unchecked, their gentle descent caressing her lifted face as she smiled widely and broadly for the first time all night.

TOGETHER

J ay paused, one hand gripping the smooth metal above his head, and looked out at the vast space surrounding him. Before his eyes, the white mist began to lighten. A soft yellow swirl of color took its place, becoming more and more vibrant as he began his upward ascent. When there were no more rungs above him, Jay shuffled sideways across the structure until he found a suitable foothold. He stepped into it and heaved himself up from below. Towering above him, he could see angular trusses weaving diagonally up to a wide, flat landing. Jay crisscrossed, snaking his way through the beams, then heaved himself out onto the open surface. He stayed there face down on the hard, bumpy metal platform and let the rhythm of his breath comfort him, the metal a welcome respite for his tired body. He stayed there motionless, enjoying the cool metal against his warm skin, until he gathered enough energy to push himself up. He scooted to the edge and leaned his arms onto the thin metal railing, dangling his legs off the edge as if he had just made it to the top of the jungle gym. The colors swirled around him gracefully, as if they were also celebrating his ascent.

Ila slowed her pace then stopped, cupping her hands like binoculars around her eyes, trying to decipher the image that just emerged before her. Eve's feet slapped to a stop next to her and she, too, stared out at the horizon. Eve squinted, one hand shielding her eyes, to see what Ila was searching for. Silently, Ila pointed to a small, dark figure at the side of the bridge. Eve squeezed her eyes tighter as she tried to decipher the image. The form turned in their direction.

"*JAY*?!" Ila and Eve hollered in unison. Wide-eyed, they looked at each other, shocked at their exact timing. Smiles burst across their faces, and they took off down the long stretch of space between them.

145

Jay squinted into the diffused light, his heart recognizing the voices before his mind. Two figures approached swiftly, their forms growing larger and more familiar as they neared. *"EVE! ILA!"* Jay scrambled to his feet. "Ahaha!"

"HEY!" the girls answered in unison just before they slammed into him, squealing out indecipherable sounds. Jay's heart leapt in his chest.

They squeezed him from both sides.

"Oh, thank God." Eve exhaled breathlessly, clutching him tighter. Ila squished him from the other side. Bubbling excitedly, their combined energy smothered him.

"Um, they tell me breathing is good for you," Jay wheezed out. "A little air, please?"

"Oh, sorry." Eve lightened her grip. Ila relaxed, too, but both were reluctant to let him go completely. Jay searched back and forth between their eyes. They were so close he had to pull his head back to see them clearly. Both of their faces were flushed pink, their long hair recklessly framing their brilliant, wide smiles. Around the three of them, magentas, blues, and greens appeared from nowhere, swishing and swirling vibrantly. Jay wrapped his arms around them, and pulled them in tight.

"I can't believe you're here!" he choked out, pulling his hand back in to swipe the wetness from his eyes. "Jesus, you guys scared the crap out of me. I've been chasing you down all night—"

Jay stopped mid sentence as solid metal trembled beneath their feet. Ila threw a glance back down the path where they came. As she watched, the lively, dancing hues converged and blocked the path they had just traveled. Ila shuddered in spite of the enchanting sky.

"Let's keep moving, you guys." Ila spun forward, taking each of their warm hands and intertwining her fingers with theirs. She pulled them forward. A warm wind circled their heads, slithering a charred trail of smoke across their noses. "We need to keep going," Ila asserted, her voice rising slightly. Neither argued. In silent unison, the three of them broke into a run and fell into a quick, steady clip.

Eve looked down at their feet slapping the metal ground, beating a harmonious cadence out into the strange landscape. "Really, Jay? No shoes?"

I'm not even going to dignify that with an answer, Jay thought to himself, his smile pulling mischievously at the corners of his mouth. Eve grinned, catching Ila's hard gaze, and winked at her.

You just did, mister.

PART III

SHREE

F ar underground, Shree—a towering dark figure in his full eight-foot height—leaned forward and ran one of his large, rough hands across a portion of his smooth quartz crystal wall. The brown igneous rock surrounding the crystal was only slightly lighter than his smooth skin. Shree smiled as the clear crystal lit itself from subterranean depths and glowed tangerine-red. His own skin shifted and lightened simultaneously, until it matched the gleaming orange-red light.

"Hello, my friends." His strong baritone voice rang melodically, a complete contrast to his imposing presence. "How is our flow today?" Responding to his greeting, the crystal passageway flickered to life, lighting section by section down the long, dark hallway as far as his eyes could see.

Deep in the hallway, one section of the orange-red crystal dimmed and then turned deep amber brown. It gradually lightened then dimmed again, repeating and quickening the pattern over and over until the surrounding crystal scurried the flashing signal back through the long hall to Shree. He straightened up to his full height as his skin shifted to match the amber brown beacon. He stared at the pulsing light underneath his hand. Inhaling deeply, his muscular chest lifted, shifting his beige vest on his brown skin. With focused presence, his bare feet stood solid and sure on the uneven floor of the deep mine. Shree waited completely still, hand on screen, and braced himself for their imminent entrance.

Across the wide room, a silver door appeared and slid open with a soft *whoosh*. Five men quickly filed through the open door and lined up side by side, their casual clothes betraying their systematic movements.

"Shree," the middle one spoke in a reserved tone, "it would please us if you would accompany us to the middle level."

Shree paused, keeping his back to the men. With the same focused attention, he shrouded his trembling heart, willing his skin to remain unchanged—just as he was taught by Ellen. Then, unnoticed, Shree moved his fingers in a swift pattern, just as Isaac had instructed should he ever be summoned to the middle level of Ariom.

"Of course, gentlemen, I would be honored to accompany you." Shree kept his rich voice smooth and even. "Please, let me clothe myself properly." Shree placed his palm fully on the crystal as a signature then slid his hand down to his side. A thin bead of sweat gathered at the edge of his shorn hairline. Shree held his breath, unsure the crystalline wall would stay dark and quiet, praying his secret message was sent. To his relief, his walls remained mute.

Shree spun gracefully and strode to the opposite wall, placing his hand on the camouflaged keypad. Another sleek metal door appeared and slid open, displaying the contents of his closet. Shree reached for his beige cloak and slipped it on over his thin, sleeveless vest. He ran his fingers over the keypad once more, and the door whisked closed and disappeared completely. Still willing his skin to remain a deep, amber brown, Shree swept his hands over his head, wiping away any trace of perspiration, and turned to face the men.

"Okay, gentlemen, please, show me the way."

MAVE and ISAAC

M ave's chest rose and fell quickly, soft cries of relief rippled through her body.

Across worlds, Isaac leaned his golden brown hands flat onto the dark wooden table, the delicate bronze inlay warming to his touch. His chest wilted as it emptied, as if he had been holding his breath for years. For a moment, he bowed his head in silent, grateful relief. He let his eyes slip closed. A single drop of wetness slid out of the corner of his eye and fell onto the table. He wiped it away with his palm and, leaning forward, he hastily cleared his throat.

"Mavel—oh, thank heavens—I've been searching for you for so long. The portal, we could not find it from here even with all our resources." Isaac's eyes hinted at a smile. "You know what I'm talking about."

Mave wiped her tears, then dabbed her nose with the back of her hand, ignoring her well-used tissue. Her voice was hoarse and full of emotion. "Me, too. Every day. Isaac, what's happening? Something's shifted. The girls, have you seen them? Or Jay? I think they're close. Do you have a fix on them? Oh, damn it, I wish I were there. Why am I not there with them?" *With you,* she finished in her mind.

Isaac chuckled deep and low. "You know I can hear you. *Everything.* Remember? There's nothing more I wish for at this moment than you being here with me, Mavel Harkins." Isaac paused, feeling his heart thump forcefully in his broad chest. He had been praying for this moment for a long, long time. "You know how it goes: the portal pulls through who it wants to pull through. It pulls through who's needed. We're still working on that. Anusha is. She's working with her animal—although, at the moment, she cannot locate her beast. She's close, we think, to figuring out how to cross at will."

Mave's heart skipped a beat. She leaned forward, her hands pushing into the bristly bale of hay. She ignored the poking strands. "Beast … Isaac, wait, her animal is *here*, at my place! I know it. I *feel* it—all the way into my bones."

Isaac furrowed his brow, soaking in, assimilating Mave's words.

"Are you sure?"

"I'm certain of it."

"Can you keep him there?"

"He's in my field as we speak. I don't see how he can go anywhere."

"He seems to have ways. Anusha trusts him completely. I'm not sure how I feel about him. There are parts to this world I still don't understand…." The soft lights around Isaac fluttered, and a cold breeze rippled through the warm, almost-humid room. Isaac shuddered, pulling his hands off the table and rubbing his bare arms absently. The chill disappeared as quickly as it arrived. Isaac glanced around the windowless room as the hair on the back of his neck pricked up.

"Hey, Mave," Isaac's deep voice was imperceptibly strained. Mave's ears perked up, her heart pumping, responding instantly to his shift.

"Yeah?"

"Listen, I think you should stick close to Anusha's animal. I think that might be a way for us to reach you. I need to go check on something. I think something's happened just now, something I've been fearing for some time now."

Mave's eyebrows knit together, trying to follow Isaac's cryptic words. "Isaac, no, wait. Can't you tell me more?"

"I'm sorry, Mave. I need to get to Ellen—she'll know what's going on. I think something just happened here, Mave. And if so, I don't know what the ramifications will be here or in Moira. These people, Mave, you know how it was, and it's not gotten any better. In fact, I think it's gotten worse. I don't understand how they are so blind. They are making choices that will be irreversible." Isaac backed to the door and rested his hand on the ornate knob.

"I'll fill you in as soon as I can. And, Mave, I should have told you this a long time ago…," Isaac paused, inhaling shakily. "Mavel…."

Isaac felt his heart swell in his chest. He wiped his damp palms on his dark pants. "Mave, I love you. And I promise I will find you again as soon as I can." Isaac turned the knob forcefully in his hand and swung the door wide, hurrying through and closing it before he changed his mind. Time was ticking now, he knew it—but he loathed losing his only connection to Mave in such a long, long time. *God damn it!* Isaac gritted his teeth together, his frustration quickly turning to anger then straight into fury. *God damn these people! God damn this world!*

Mave's heart swelled as the words she had longed to hear lingered in her ears then squeezed her heart painfully as the crackle of radio static—infused with one forceful *"Damn it!"*—echoed through the barn. Mave smiled in spite of the barren silence, more empty now than ever before. *Language, Isaac,* she thought sadly. She hesitated only a moment on her scratchy seat then stood and stretched, glancing quickly around the empty barn and out through the wide open doors. Outside, a hint of morning light inched up over the back pasture, accompanied by distant trills and stirrings of the waking world drifting into early morning life. Mave searched the horizon for Beast.

"All right, mister," she called, looking out into the first rays of dawn, her legs awkward and stiff from her long night. Her eyes searched through the shadows. "You and I, we need to have a little chat."

THE BRIDGE

T he immense metal bridge lurched hard to the left. Ila stumbled, smacking her feet loudly, then regained her footing. Ila, Jay, and Eve slowed their run to a light jog as Jay stole a glance over his shoulder. A large black cloud billowed up behind them, breaking through the turbulent swirling hues of blues, magentas, and deep purples. He spun back around and pumped his legs hard, moving into the lead.

"Come on, you guys, we've got to move!"

The air around them banged and echoed as their feet pounded solid, swift rhythms onto the metal road.

Out of nowhere, a deafening *crack* shot through the mottled sky, ripping and splitting the vibrantly colored atmosphere in two. Deep dark reds seeped into the fractured sky, slowly mingling and mixing with the blues and magentas, creating an ominous and foreboding backdrop.

Wordlessly, the three sprinted forward, heaving and pumping their limbs as fast as they could. Sweat flew off them as the air cooled and began to whip threateningly around them. The sky shifted, turning darker and darker, moving faster and faster, until it converged into a chaotic swarm in front of them.

From somewhere far below, the towering bridge groaned menacingly, creaking and grinding in on itself. The thunderous sound filled the air around them, as the screeching metal on metal pierced harsh into their ears. They pulled their heads down, covering their ears, but kept on running.

Don't stop! Jay ordered.

The bridge lurched rebelliously, this time knocking all of them off balance. Without warning, it jerked back to the right. Their legs flew out from under them, sending all three crashing violently to the ground.

Confusion reigned as tumultuous blasts crackled into the air, booming wide across the landscape and out over the dark sky. High above their heads, one long, thick cable snapped, the sound exploding in their ears. It flew like a monstrous whip across the sky and ricocheted back in their direction at tremendous speed. With another earsplitting *CRR-AACK,* it slammed into the bridge directly in front of them

Move! To the side! NOW!

With Jay's words in their heads, they scrambled on hands and knees to the side of the bridge, just as another cable violently crashed onto the metal bridge behind them. The ground beneath them shook fatally, the thunderous clang of metal reverberating under their skin and out across the violent atmosphere.

Jay peered over the edge of the bridge. There was no possible way they would survive the fall. It was miles down, many miles … and down to what? The bottom was hidden, buried in black billowing clouds of smoke. He had seen what the ground below was like. He doubted there was any ground left down there. Surely it had all been swallowed by the angry, festering lava. Jay looked at the girls, eyes frenzied, hands squeezed against their ears, trying desperately to drown out the awful shrieking metal. *We would never survive that fall.* From somewhere deep inside, Jay heard a long chime ring out, its vibration unfaltering even amidst the outer chaos. Ila and Eve turned to Jay, both of them catching a faint hint of the sound, too.

Another cable snapped and swung dangerously close to their heads, slamming ferociously into the bridge and vibrating the metal once more. The air around them was charged with violent chaos, combined with ear-splitting shrieks of metal on metal.

Terror flew through Eve's eyes as she crouched herself into a small ball. Her eyes shot back and forth frantically between Ila and Jay. Ila saw her chest heaving and instantly knew she was having trouble catching her breath.

A nameless and gentle voice rang through their heads. *Let go, you three. You must let go.*

Ila and Jay locked eyes then intertwined their hands. Ila grabbed Eve's hand off the ground and sealed it into her own, weaving her fingers into Eve's. Instantly, Eve squeezed into her. Jay reached for Eve's other hand as the three of them crouched helplessly on the faltering metal. Their hearts slammed madly in their chests.

Eve! Ila's voice commanded its way into Eve's head. *Eve! Slow everything down! Do it on the inside!* Ila's voice was loud and clear. Eve squeezed her eyes shut; tiny tears beading out through their clamped edges. She clenched her jaw and consciously lengthened her breath. Jay watched her chest rise and fall more steadily.

That's it, Eve, keep it nice and slow. Eve squeezed Jay's hand and nodded faintly in response.

Another explosive crack shot across the sky. Eve lost the tiny bit of control she had found and instantly got back to short, quick breaths. Her nostrils flared and her teeth clenched tighter. The bridge screamed and groaned, tilting dangerously to the left. Jay wrenched his hand from Ila and grabbed onto the rail.

The rail! Grab the rail, Ila, and don't let go. No matter what! All the color drained out of Ila's fingers as she gripped Eve unyieldingly. Beneath her viselike grip, Eve's hand went limp.

Jay! Ila captured the rail beneath her free hand and watched helplessly as Eve's legs buckled and she collapsed to the ground.

"No!" Jay lurched forward, powerless to do anything but keep gripping her hand. Eve slumped on herself as his voice was swept away into the deafening roar.

A long groan trembled eerily beneath them. As Jay and Ila watched, a thin crack twisted and snaked its way across the bridge path, the fissure widening as it went, peeling and ripping metal from metal. Then, in a blinding flash, the thick, hard metal ripped apart. Cables snapped and flew like wild whips. Around them, chaos reigned. Ila held Jay with her deep, wide eyes. The sky hovered dark red and black, closing in on them from all sides. Ila and Jay locked eyes, holding onto each other the only way they could as the colossal bridge split, severing itself in two. Ila held up Eve's hand.

Don't let go. Ila's nose flared as she inhaled forcefully. The strange and surreal world around them became distant, as if she were watching someone else's life unfold.

Jay shook his head from side to side. Ila's eyes sealed on him, filling with tears and clouding her sight.

We're not going to make it. Her voice was clear in his head. *We're not going to make it out of here.* She blinked hard, momentarily clearing her eyes, and gave Jay one small sad smile.

Soft and clear, the gentle, melodious voice spoke to them once more, her voice sure and calm in their minds. *You must let go,* she repeated urgently, low and direct. *It is the only way.*

THE FALL

T he bridge howled, crying out one final time, then finally gave up its struggle. The far edge rose and rocked menacingly toward them as their side rolled away, spinning sideways. Slowly and definitely, they began to fall.

"Jay!"

Hold on, Ila. Don't let go! Jay's voice was frantic in her head.

I won't! I won't!

Ila's hair whipped around, covering her eyes, shielding her from the outer world. The bridge remained solid under her feet, then, all of a sudden, she felt it pull at her, as if it were trying to draw her in. She remembered the flowers. Ila focused on the feel of the ground beneath her feet, letting the metal seep and connect deep into her skin.

Jay, Ila searched feverishly for him through wind-whipped hair, *connect to the metal! Let it draw to you, into you!* She didn't know how to explain it. She hoped he would understand.

Ila felt the rail under her hand. The smooth, cool surface seemed to widen under her touch. She softened her grip just a bit, and she let the metal pull her in, as if they were now chemically connected. She felt herself locked on tight, as if she were tethered.

It's working!

What? Jay tried to decipher Ila's words amidst the tumult surrounding them. Across his mind sprung the image of him swinging on the metal rungs. Jay shuddered at the memory and simultaneously felt the metal link into him, both then and now. Suddenly Jay understood, and he felt the connection deepen as the metal once again magnetized and plugged deep into his cells, as if they were now one.

Crippled and broken, their section of bridge spun a full 360 degrees through the darkened sky. Ila spotted Jay just a few feet away, tightly and surely connected to the metal. His feet were solidly on the ground. Between them, Eve was still limp, held and suspended securely by their grip. Ila watched horrified as Eve's feet slowly floated up off the tumbling metal. As they spun through the air, Eve's body sailed out horizontally, floating gracefully, as if she were in a dance, her head and legs swaying in a fluid rhythm. All the while, her hands stayed unwaveringly connected to Ila and Jay.

The bridge righted itself, lurched once more, then plunged swiftly and perilously toward the ground. All sounds faded as the rush of wind filled their ears, blinding and stinging their eyes in their careening descent. A scream caught in Ila's throat as she realized what was happening. They flew downward.

Then, all at once, the bridge slowed, their plummeting somehow altered, and they found themselves tumbling in slow motion. Their downward spiral continued, but the intensity and speed of the fall morphed, as if the bridge and the atmosphere seemed to come into some type of cooperative agreement. Wind floated smoothly and easily across Ila's face, waving sweetly through her hair. Eve floated effortlessly, as if gravity had begun to buoy and hold her up. Silence enveloped them as all sound was siphoned out of the air. Ila watched the pieces of the world around her shift and move. Light gleamed and bounced off each and every surface. The menacing sky was nowhere to be seen. They were completely surrounded by diffused golden sunlight. Ila turned her head slowly to take in her surroundings. It was all so beautiful.

Then, with an unexpected and monumental force, they crashed ferociously into warm water. Instantly, the world sped up, transforming back into real time. The water stripped them from their metal connections and ripped their hands from each other. The force spun them hard, sending all three of them reeling into their own orbits.

The impact knocked Ila breathless. One moment Eve was there, her hand entwined in Ila's, then in a flash she was gone. Ila thrashed and twisted her body in the turbulent water, fighting the downward pull. She kicked furiously, pumping both her arms and legs. It was no use. No matter how hard she fought, she continued to be pulled down.

Nuhuh Nuhuh Nuhuh. Her mind raced with rebellion. *I am not going down! I am not losing this one. You're not taking me here! Not here. Not now.*

You must let go. The same gentle, feminine voice filled her head.

Fuck that! I am not going down!

THE MIDDLE

Water churned and bubbled all around, offering only cloudy grey nothingness to Ila's frantically seeking eyes. She contorted her body, narrowing her eyes against the familiar sting of the salty, turgid waters. Little by little, the churned waters began to settle. Visibility increased, and Ila slowed her thrashing limbs. She continued to hunt through the havoc for Jay and Eve. Above her, she spotted Jay's arm and followed it until she saw his full silhouette floating peacefully, ringed by light. Debris plummeted, descending perilously all around him. *Jay!* She felt his eyes lock onto her.

Stop moving, Ila. Just stop everything right now and let go. Right now, Ila. Be still. Jay's words were firm and serious.

Jay, I don't want to die, Ila pleaded, arms and legs still moving instinctively.

You won't. Look at me. Keep looking at me. It's the only way. Fight and you go down. Look, you're rising right now.

Jay, I'm scared. I can't breathe.

Trust me, Ila, you can. Breathe. Right now. You can do this. His words softened as they continued in her mind. *Trust me, Ila. I promise. You will be okay.*

Ila couldn't hold her breath any longer.

Let it go, child, let it go, a woman's voice, different from before, whispered into her head.

Ila closed her eyes. She kept her lips sealed shut and inhaled deeply through her nose. Instantly, water roared through her ears, and she found herself both in the water and standing, dripping, in a strange, softly lit hallway. Ila popped back and forth as she continued to breathe. Water. Hall. Water. Hall. Waterhallwaterhall. The images flashed back and forth, until she was in both places at the same time.

Jay was in the hall, too. And in the water. She looked up. *Eve!* Ila saw her floating a far distance above; her limp arms were dangling and dancing as the water pushed them through graceful movements. Light streamed around her, encircling her in a vibrant golden glow.

"Eve!" Ila yelled underwater. Immediately, she was fully in the hall. Jay stood in front of her and caught her under her arms.

"Jay," she whispered breathlessly. "Jay. Eve. She's…." The room began to spin. Ila was dizzy, disoriented. She focused on Jay and tried to balance herself on the warm floor. Around her, bright tapestries filled the long hall. More golden light shone from above and below. Everything about the room was warm and inviting. Unfamiliar smells filled her nose—sweetly aromatic and exotic, something she would have expected in an old, faraway market.

Ila heard a familiar voice from behind her.

"What took you guys so long?"

She whirled around. "Eve!" Eve grinned mischieviously from her perch, casually wringing the warm water out of her hair.

"Ahaha!" Ila choked out, relief flooding through her. Her voice rose, and her laughter started to stutter.

Eve rushed over and grabbed onto Ila as she collapsed heavily in Jay's arms. Eve wrapped her arms tightly around Ila as Jay gently released her to her friend. Two other figures gathered around them as they sunk onto the hard golden stone.

Ila, breathe. Eve's words were strong both in Ila's ears and in her head. Ila inhaled as deeply as she could. The warm room slowly righted itself, gradually shifting back into focus.

That's it, breathe. Ila's chest rose and fell, becoming smooth and regular, as life-giving breath streamed in and out. Her head began to clear.

Did you just tell me *to breathe?* Ila pulled back and looked into Eve's sparkling green eyes. Eve smiled proudly, lighting up her whole face. Ila sat up and swept her wet hair out of her eyes. She stared at one luminous spot on the ground by her feet, studying the variations on the uneven, highly polished stone. Tenderly, she ran her hand over the ground, watching as the brightness faintly shifted under her hand.

Ila. Jay's voice was deep and soft. Ila had never heard him speak that softly to her before. An alarm rang somewhere deep inside her.

Ila, turn around. Ila sat stone-still, the hair on the back of her neck rising up. Her cells began to vibrate, twitching and jumping under her skin. She felt energy bump and buzz throughout her entire body, but she sat perfectly still, momentarily frozen on the outside.

Ila. Jay's voice cracked.

Eve looked up at Jay, eyebrows raised, then her eyes moved to the woman beside him. And to the man beside her. The woman stood as tall as Jay and had smooth brown skin that seemed to glow from within. Her hair was swept back, twisted into an elegant, flowing scarf. Her sage green tunic was wrapped around her dark pants, hugging her edges like they were designed expressly for her.

The man was slightly taller, and his skin was slightly darker than the woman's. His short, greying hair was neatly clipped, framing his inviting, smiling eyes. His tunic and pants were the same color as the woman's, but the shirt had different stitching around the edges. His pants, a shade darker than hers, appeared both light and rugged at the same time. Both of them filled the room with their presence. Eve raised her brow. Ila saw Eve out of the corner of her eye. Ila shook her head infinitesimally from side to side.

Ila? Eve leaned over and placed her hand on Ila's knee. Ila stayed focused on a spot on the ground just in front of her. Eve watched Ila's shoulders shakily rise and fall. Her whole body was trembling.

"Ila?" The woman's voice was melodious and light. Eve felt it float over her with an unexplained comfort.

No. Wait. Give me a minute. Ila clenched her teeth together. Labored, she forced air in and out of her nose. Eve could feel the walls forming around her friend. *Ila, don't....* Ila looked into Eve's pleading eyes. A soft chime rang out three times through Ila's head, surrounding and blanketing her heart. Ila blinked her glistening eyes closed, holding her breath as long as she could. Then she let her breath out slowly and peeled her eyes open. She placed her trembling hand on Eve's, then pushed herself up off the golden ground and turned to face the voice that had not called her name for eleven years.

ANUSHA

The thick, golden ceiling shifted dark then light as shadows crossed the room above her head. Anusha sat completely still and followed them with her light blue eyes. The ancient earthen walls around her were unusually dark, save for one airily glowing crystal at the far end of the room. Its white light pulsed down warmly and delicately, whispering a low, almost-inaudible intonation through the chamber as it flickered like a distant, nighttime star.

Anusha's eyes turned reluctantly to the light, already knowing its message. This crystal had been embedded the day she had been born, its matrix intricately linked with her own, just like the few others of her kind. It had helped name her—*Anusha, bright morning star*. Until now, it had always been a comfort to her, whatever information it brought. This latest information, however, changed everything. She knew he was gone. She felt it before any trace of light appeared carrying the message. The smooth, hard seat below her attempted to radiate its own warm energy into the room.

No, Anusha commanded softly. *No, I need a moment. Let me be with this, please.* Her heart sank as her grand frame leaned forward. She rested her pale blue arms on her thick strong legs, her usually incandescent skin alarmingly dull.

Anusha had never commanded the crystals before; until now, there had always been a flowing communication back and forth between them. Her position required it. But, today, everything changed. They came for him. She knew it even before the surrounding stones transmitted the code—the one they had practiced together over and over, hoping never to have to use it. Isaac and Ellen had warned them that this time would come, but Anusha hadn't truly believed it.

Shree ... Anusha's crystalline skin radiated dimly as her heart called for him.

The single crystal star brightened momentarily, responding to his name, already sending a signal throughout the tunneled earth, searching for him. Anusha knew it was useless. The signals only transmitted through the tunnels underground. They did not communicate with the middle level.

MOIRA

Early morning light cast itself across the dark field, briefly and brilliantly illuminating the short grass into a sea of yellow. Songbirds offered their voices earnestly across the wide-open space. Mave ambled down the familiar path from the house to the barn, the "trough" steady in her hand. She headed straight for the corral, pulled out her cellphone, and slid her phone to life. She tapped Zoe's picture and lifted her phone to her ear, taking a sip from her steaming mug while the phone rang.

"What's wrong?" Zoe cut in without a greeting.

Mave smiled as she sidestepped a half-hidden stick that could have caused her to spill her coffee.

"Zoe, okay, I know we do this all the time, but that's just uncanny. And I'm not sure *exactly* what's wrong, but it's something, and it feels monumental. The kids are there. At least the girls, but I feel Jay there, too. What do you guys know?" Her words tumbled out briskly, contrasting her easy, meandering gait.

Mave was always surprised how calm her body and mind were in a crisis. Invariably it was like this, and had been for as long as she could remember. At times like this, it felt as if a larger *something* was guiding and connecting things at this stage. She imagined this was what it felt like in the eye of a hurricane where there's an immensely powerful existence all around you. But, for the moment, everything is mysteriously serene.

"Jay's not here, and one of the downstairs windows was wide open, the screen punched out." Zoe's voice was calm, too, but Mave felt a nervous energy bubbling and building in her friend with each word she spoke. "Are you worried, Mave?"

Mave paused on the path, considering the question. Her eyes landed on the silvery willow tree swaying in the morning breeze. Beast gazed steadily at her from under its lowest branches, his head lifted slightly when she looked at him, as if greeting her. Warmth flooded her body, comforting her in a way she hadn't felt in years. Her mouth pulled into a sideways smile, and, for a reason she could not understand, she thought of Ila. Resuming her trek, Mave padded her weathered boots across the soft dirt.

"Strangely, Zoe, I'm not worried. At least not at this moment ... I didn't tell you guys yesterday, because I wasn't completely sure it happened. But now I'm certain it did. Zoe, I saw Isaac and Ellen in your house yesterday. Very light, barely there, but I saw them. And last night, well, really early this morning, I actually talked to him." Mave's heart raced buoyantly in her chest. She felt lighter than she had in a long time. "You know how long it's been. I don't know ..." Mave shook her head. "I think this fella here is doing some real good." Mave raised her voice so it carried across the corral. "Aren't you, mister?"

Beast's body stayed completely still as he stared across the corral, his large eyes following Mave closely as she traveled the short distance to the fence.

"Isaac told me Anusha and her animal were looking for way to cross. Instantly I knew it was him—Beast. He's Anusha's animal. And he found a way to cross. I think he can help us communicate with Ariom more directly, at least the middle level. I'm assuming that's where Isaac was when I reached him. It seems like the solar winds have pushed our worlds a little closer, for the moment at least," Mave said, remembering the bewildering experience of somehow crossing worlds herself many years back. She still had a hard time believing it some days.

The rest of the horses gathered near the gate, ready to come in for breakfast. Mave stood for a moment, the quiet morning bright and airy around her.

Zoe reached her arm out as Edge walked past, stopping him in his tracks and pulling him close. She moved the phone away from her mouth.

"Mave thinks Jay's there, in Ariom, with the girls. And Ji...." Edge noted her urgent tone and gave her his full attention. His steady eyes met hers squarely, hiding the fact that the name Ariom caused his heart to skip a beat. "She spoke to Isaac last night." Edge kept his eyes steady on Zoe, but his mind flew into action behind them.

"Okay, then, this is what we've been waiting for. I just wish to hell the kids were never a part of it."

Zoe hugged him tightly with one arm then stepped away, pulling the phone back to her ear. "I know, honey, but those kids were linked to that world from the moment they were born."

Across town, Mave nodded in agreement. Reaching out, she placed her mug on the fencepost, then absently rubbed Boss's soft muzzle. She pulled her hand away and reached out for the latch on the gate. Then it dawned on her. Her hand froze in midair. She had never let Beast in from the field last night. And he had stood in the doorway of the barn. Even the fact that she couldn't find him early this morning for 'a little chat' as she had called it had caused no alarm. She had simply thought he had moved to the back field to graze.

Her heart thumped inside her chest as she turned back toward the corral, unsure whether to trust her memory with all that had been happening. Her eyes darted around the empty corral. Beast was nowhere to be seen. A shiver ran down the length of her spine as her mind struggled to register the impossible. She lowered the phone from her ear, her feet leaden, and searched the surrounding fields and yard for any trace of him.

"But I wish they weren't either." Mave barely heard Zoe's words from the phone at her side.

Beast was gone.

MEETING

Ila stood frozen, staring into a face that was instantly familiar and foreign at the same time. Her past wrestled in her, threatening a terrifying storm. Ila fought herself to stay present, to keep her scarred heart open enough to meet the woman who had abandoned her eleven years ago. It was Isaac who came to her first. He crossed the space between them in one long stride and wrapped his robust arms around her, lifting her effortlessly off the ground. Warmth and comfort radiated from him, stabilizing and landing her in a sense of well-being she had never before experienced. *No wonder Mave digs you.* The thought sprung from Ila's mind before she could stop it.

Isaac's body shook with delight as a hearty and genuine laugh tumbled out from his chest, reverberating throughout the polished room. Gently, he set her dangling feet back on the ground and pulled himself away, still chuckling richly. The entire room glowed brighter as his laughter surrounded them. It seemed to ring directly from the walls and floor.

Ila smiled shyly, perplexed at the resonating sound.

"How are you doing that?"

Ellen stepped forward, the floor lighting softly beneath each of her steps.

"It's the acoustics, Ila, the crystal acoustics. This world is full of them. Actually, to be more accurate, this world is run on them." She stood in front of Ila, her hands clasped tightly in front of her. Her clothes seemed to glow brighter, and Ila could feel the strong, animated energy around her. But Ellen waited patiently and respectfully for Ila's response.

Ila's feet were rooted to the ground, while her past pushed at the edges of her consciousness. But she was *here*. Her mother. In front of her. Not an apparition or a dream.

All at once, Ila dropped her defenses and allowed herself to unleash the all-consuming force of her love for this woman standing before her. Her heart unfettered. Instantly she filled and overflowed with true and boundless affection. Ila felt lighter than air. She leapt forward and threw her arms around her mother. Ellen swallowed Ila in her long arms, hugging her fiercely and unreservedly to her chest. Ila melted, letting the last remnants of her protective walls crumble, giving her heart the final bits of room it needed to fully expand into the present. Ila's throat tightened as she clung fervently to her mother, choking out bittersweet tears washed in waves of shifting emotion. Finally she fell into relief. Small indecipherable sounds escaped her lips as she held steadfast to the woman she thought she would never see again. The space around the two women cocooned them in a luminous, golden-orange embrace, mirroring the complete and utter love flowing between them. Ellen let light sobs move through her as she rocked them both ever so lightly.

Eve leaned into Jay, her cheeks flushed beneath her own light tears. Jay wrapped his arm over her shoulder and pulled her close. Eve sniffed raggedly and let the tears flow, burying her face in his warm shirt, still wet from the watery fall. Jay hugged her shaking body tenderly, his chin resting just above her wet hair, and held her as she wept.

Isaac surveyed the room, his own heart divided by the bittersweet reunion—feeling the absence of Mave now more than ever. *Mave, you there?* He reached out, wondering if the kids held a connection to Moira just as Beast held to Ariom. *I have some good news for you.*

Mave clanked the corral gate open, phone still poised at her side.

Mave stood stock-still, straining her ears against the morning sounds. *I have some good news for you.* Isaac's words came to her ears loud and clear.

"Zoe! It's Isaac. Hold on!"

Isaac! Oh my goodness, Isaac—what's going on?

The kids, Mave, they're here with Ellen and me—in the long hall here on the middle level. We're going to need to move pretty quickly, but they're here, safe and sound.

At the other end of the phone line, Zoe heard Isaac's transmission and gasped.

"Edge! It's Isaac! The kids—they're there! They're together. They're all right!"

Edge nodded, jaw set, and began to run over the long-held plan in his head.

"Can the connection hold us all?" Edge moved closer to Zoe.

"Edge! Oh, man, it's good to hear you!" Isaac's voice boomed, startling the others in the room around him.

Ellen lifted her tear-stained face, her heart beating rapidly. She kept her arms wrapped around Ila.

"Edge?" Ellen's voice was simultaneously feminine and strong. "Can you hear me?"

"Ellen!" Zoe and Mave chorused together.

Mave continued, "Girl, you've been M.I.A! My God, is it good to hear your voice!"

Ellen paused. "How long has it been, total?" She held Ila at arm's length, studying her mostly grown face, glancing quickly over at a tearful Eve held tight by Jay; he was only an inch or two shorter than Isaac. "My God, has it been that long?"

Ila hugged her arms around her mother, allowing her heart to savor what she had never allowed herself to imagine. Her head swam dizzily. The room around them was silently buzzing, the energy palpable even across worlds.

Slowly, Zoe finally answered, "It's been eleven years, Ellen, since you and Isaac crossed last."

Ila's eyes glistened as a few wet drops gathered at the corners of her eyes and slid their way down her cheeks. Ellen reached out her slender hand and brushed them away. She leaned in and kissed Ila's forehead, whispering into her, "I'm so, so sorry, bug. I never meant to stay away from you this long. If I would have known it would be like this, I would never have gone…."

The warm lights of the hall dimmed so slight and brief that no one noticed but Isaac. He glanced at the thick golden stone beneath his feet, waiting for it to brighten. But it didn't.

Isaac cleared his throat. "I hate to do this, folks, but I think we need to move. Before the kids arrived, Ellen had just confirmed my fear that they brought Shree here to the middle. They're planning on moving him to the far side of Ariom. We know how unstable that will make the matrix—hell, even *they* do—and how it will isolate him. And no one knows what being away from his original crystal will do. Extracting him … *isolating him*—separating him from Anusha…." Isaac shook his head, frustrated. "These people, they have no idea. Misunderstanding is a colossal understatement—these people, they'll *never* learn. They have no idea what they have here. *No damn idea.* Their ignorance combined with their arrogance is absolutely lethal.

"Shree will not survive isolated away from his home. I feel it as sure as I'm standing here. And Anusha. They should not be separated. It was never in the design. But we all know how much they care about that. Idiots." Isaac squeezed his hands into fists, spread his fingers wide, and shook them out. He ran them roughly over his shaved face. He gritted his last words out through clenched teeth. "Goddamn thick-skulled idiots. Don't listen to a *word* the Others have been telling them about balancing energies all this time. They think they're beyond the need of balance. They're destroying their own world, and they're too goddamn stupid to realize it."

MINES

D irectly below, Anusha huddled motionless on her smooth crystal seat and finally allowed the crystal energy to radiate into the room. The room immediately brightened and warmed. *Thank you,* Anusha answered passively, a heaviness weighing unfamiliarly on her oversized frame. Above her, shadows flickered then disappeared as the light above brightened—unusually intense for this time of day—and cast a warm tangerine glow down into her chamber. The light dimmed again, bathing her world in shadows once more. Anusha sat up taller and studied the ceiling, her eyes narrowing. She focused her attention on the darkened forms above her. She softened the space around her heart and realized she did not recognize all the energies in the room above.

Anusha swept herself off the bench, crossed her chamber and stood next to the only corner of the room. She swiped her hand horizontally across the dark stone, and a clear, rectangular crystal screen illuminated in response. "Hello, my friends," she greeted urgently. "How is our harmony today?" The screen danced immediately and colorfully to life, dispatching vibrations of color rapidly around the perimeter of Anusha's section of the cavernous mine. The screen fluttered, stuttering through spectrums of hues, until it landed on three individually repeating colors. As each one flashed across the screen, a corresponding note rang into the room. Anusha nodded in response and placed her hand over each color. Her blue eyes brightened as the information sifted from the walls into her body then formed into thoughts in her mind. *They're here?* The screen shifted to pure white light and pulsed slowly and steadily, the resounding assertion for yes. The note accompanying this signal was so low it barely whispered in the room. Anusha nodded again, bringing her hands to her chin and rubbing her fingers absently over her lips, contemplating this turn of events.

This ... this just might give us a chance.

Above her, the crowd of shadows swept across the long hall, gathering themselves once more directly above her head. Anusha reached her hand to the right of the screen, punching a code into a hidden keypad. A low hum whirred, manifesting a silver door that silently slid open. Hastily, she grabbed her beige tunic, slipping it over her bare arms, then swiped the pad again, closing the door. She crossed over to the adjoining wall, positioning herself in front of a large wooden door, the only constantly visible door in the large, elliptical room. Deep sepia in color and carved intricately with overlapping serpentine lines, the wooden door towered over Anusha's full eight-foot height. From the bottom section of the door, smoldering copper lights seeped and weaved their way up, lighting the maze of curving lines. The lines converged ceremoniously at the top of the door. Then the light disappeared completely.

Wispy and faint, Anusha's star began to flash steadily above the massive door, pulsing in perfect rhythm with her own heartbeat. Anusha stood absolutely still and waited patiently for the door to open.

Around the rectangular door, the wall lit, fracturing a flash of light through the prism walls, momentarily disclosing the room's enormous depth, then darkened again. The wooden door swished open. On the other side of the opening stood Ellen and Isaac, flanked by Ila, Eve, and Jay. Ellen and Isaac greeted Anusha with a small nod and a bow. Anusha bowed in return then stepped back to let the five of them enter her chamber. The large wooden door slid shut behind them. Anusha stood, her blue hands clasped in front of her, and waited for Ellen and Isaac to speak first.

"Anusha, I am glad to see you. I would very much like to introduce to you my daughter Ila," Ellen gave a quick smile and gestured briefly to Ila. "And these are her friends—Jay and Eve. Jay is the son of Edge and Zoe. Eve, I'm sure you remember, appeared on your walls when she entered Moira—to them, years ago, but for us...," she added, turning to her visitors, "for us it was only six lunar cycles ago."

Eve swallowed hard, finishing the last traces of a breadlike pastry, and stared wide-eyed—astonished that Ellen knew who she was. And how could her presence have registered across worlds? Anusha's skin slowly morphed, darkening before their eyes, until the entirety of her exposed skin smoothed into a rich amber brown, similar to Ila and Ellen's own skin color.

Ila stepped forward, the ground below her pulling and connecting to her feet with each tentative step. It was just like in the field and on the bridge. Under her, the rocklike ground felt alive, as if it were communicating with her on a level she couldn't quite interpret. Ila knelt, examining the space below her feet, running her hand delicately across the surface, just barely touching it. In response, a rolling deluge of harmonious notes lifted through her ears, ringing across octaves and filling the large room.

Anusha watched Ila closely, understanding fully what the crystalline structure was transmitting. Ila shuddered, assimilating the transmission without understanding it, then rose and looked Anusha squarely in her shining, blue eyes. Anusha's skin had shifted with the vibrations Ila had inadvertently conjured, now emitting a pale pink. Ila stared up at the tall, breathtaking woman, her bright blue eyes soft yet unapologetic in their scrutiny. Anusha allowed her current vibration to flow out, seeping the soft pink hue into the space around them.

Ila never left Anusha's gaze, holding onto her with her eyes, searching deeper and deeper—for what she had no idea—until she reached a satisfying level of inner depth. Anusha raised her dark eyebrows. Then, as if opening an inner door, she let Ila in. The vibration of sound Ila had innocently coaxed from the stones beneath them rang out once more. The room brightened as if a switch had been flipped. Instantly, Ila felt her own heart expand, leaving her suspended, as if she were actually floating, in a lightness she had never before experienced. Then almost instantly her heart darkened with shadows, and she felt small and alone again, as she had for most of her life. This time, the feeling was multiplied exponentially. Ila's face contorted as she struggled against the heaviness growing in the center of her chest. It felt as if the cells of her body were imploding. The weight and pain became too much. Ila tore her eyes away from Anusha and the aching pain instantly dissolved. Ila hugged her arms around herself, all at once cold in the humid confines, and absently rubbed the goose bumps that rippled across her flesh. She willed herself back to the present as her body slowly regained equilibrium.

Ellen moved close and draped a warm arm over Ila's shoulder. Ila leaned into her, and, finally steadying on her, lifted her eyes back to Anusha. *My apologies, Ila. I did not mean to overwhelm you with that information.* As the words floated through Ila's head, she felt warmth spread from her heart and out through her extremities. Ila shuddered and pulled her full lips into a half smile. *No apology needed.* Her smile spread across her flushed cheeks as the translucent pink air cocooning them shifted to pale yellow. Ila nodded once, letting her eyes slide shut for a brief savoring moment, confirming to Anusha she had recognized and understood the sharing of her heart.

Anusha turned and stretched her hand out to Eve, who had been silently watching them both closely and feeling a fraction of what Ila had. Anusha took Eve's pale hand between her own, swallowing her hand completely between the large, now coral-brown hands. Anusha's palms were easily twice as big as Eve's. In Anusha's grasp, Eve's hand warmed. The delicate and warm sensation slid up her arm and arrived in the center of her chest. Eve's mouth dropped as she remembered this feeling vividly from the night in her own room when she had first reached into the door.

"You ... you're the one...." Eve whispered hoarsely into the low-lit room. Anusha nodded. Ellen and Isaac glanced at each other, eyebrows lifted, as they pieced together more and more information.

"The star, was that you?" Eve's voice was barely audible.

The star ... Ila's mind reeled, remembering the faraway, beckoning star from her own bedroom. A low, deep note rang above their heads, filling the wide room as the star above the door answered for Anusha, pulsing in a measured rhythm, as if it were breathing. Another note, one step higher, rang in response inside Ila's head. Anusha watched Ila closely, ignoring the beads of sweat she saw forming on her brow. She was interested in something deeper, again, feeling into her heart. Ila spun away from Ellen and faced the large carved door they had just entered. The star was still fluctuating above it. The rest of them watched her in silent curiosity.

Ila took one step toward the door, and the deep grooves responded by shifting to a vivid, luminous green—the exact hue of the grass they encountered as they first crossed worlds. Ila reached out her hand, the tips of her fingers barely brushing against the warm solid wood. A small metal ring appeared at the door's edge.

The dark brown door flashed into the weathered wooden door in front Ila's eyes, then immediately switched back. Ila's cells leapt in recognition; her heart raced. Ila knew it was the same door. She reached out for the metal ring.

"Don't. Please," Anusha warned. "It is not time."

"Ila, that's the door!" Eve whispered breathlessly. Ila nodded. Eve slid her hand from Anusha's and slipped next to Ila. Tentatively, Eve reached out, steadying her trembling fingers, and ran her hand over the polished door A deep sadness washed through her, just as it had when she had touched the weathered door. She pulled her hand off, and the melancholy feeling vanished. Sadness washed over Ila. She stole a glance at Eve, but Eve wouldn't meet her eye.

Ila's mind flooded with information; from where she did not know.

"Your name," Ila began slowly, "Anusha—it means star, doesn't it? And we came through this door. Well, I'm the only one who actually came all the way through it, but it called to Eve, too. And the star, that blinking far-off star, it was this." Ila lifted her finger, surprised at its steadiness, and pointed at the pulsing starlike crystal above the door.

Anusha smiled broadly, pleased her heart could feel this light in spite of all the morning's events.

"Yes, Ila, it was. We have been working on the portal, my animal and I, with this door. It is the only one of its kind here. He seemed to have misplaced himself, at least I thought he had, but now...," Anusha paused, narrowing her eyes and looking from Eve to Jay. "Hmm. I believe that now he is safely in Moira. I believe he is currently with Mave." Anusha looked into Ila's eyes. Ila was surprised how effortless it was to keep her heart open as she met Anusha's penetrating gaze. "Yes"—the sides of Anusha's mouth turned up into a smile once more—"I am certain he is at Mave's … farm? That's what you call it, yes?" Ila nodded emphatically, returning Anusha's contagious smile.

Anusha abruptly turned to Jay. "You, son of Edge, I believe you will be instrumental in the securing of Shree." She gave one decisive nod, satisfied with the prospect. Isaac stepped forward, his mouth half open, ready to speak. But Jay reached out, placed his hand lightly on Isaac's arm, and stopped him in his tracks. Isaac nodded, assenting, used to unseen information and communication shifting their plans. Jay took one step toward Anusha, and the walls around them brightened, illuminating the room, varying the hues and tones of their amber-brown surroundings. The walls and floors were marbled with transparent veins of lighter rock, exposing more of the mine's dimensions. Jay glanced at the walls then down at his bare feet. Under him, the floor gleamed a luminous yellow-orange, heating and animating his soles. Jay had never felt anything like it.

"May I ask what is a Shree?" he inquired, gingerly lifting each foot and setting it back down, leaving his wide damp footprint on the unusually colored ground.

"It is not what, but who. Shree is my…," Anusha paused and raised her eyes, contemplating how to explain their relationship. Then she nodded, as if hearing the words she was reaching for. "Shree and I are in charge of these mines. Together, he and I, along with the Others, provide stabilization for the energy of this world."

Anusha looked down into each of their transfixed faces, watching as they absorbed the words she was speaking, evaluating how her explanation was landing in their hearts. Her skin shifted to a reddish-purple, rich and mottled with light and once again, her presence made the room feel wide and spacious. Anusha's lips parted as she blew out a slow, long breath.

Then she inhaled audibly and began to speak again. "There is one piece I have not shared, even with Shree, although I suspect he has felt it." Anusha looked down, unable to meet their eyes. "There is no way to hide in the mines. I have tried to shroud and even eliminate this piece, because it is forbidden." Anusha kept her eyes down and lowered her voice to a whisper. "I have tried, but I simply cannot."

Ellen gasped audibly, knowing what Anusha was going to say before she spoke. Isaac lifted a hand to her shoulder, quieting her so Anusha could say the words aloud. He knew as well as Ellen what the ramifications were. But somewhere in him, he also knew it was essential that she speak the words aloud. He knew that the surrounding minerals would feel the vibration of her words and pass them through the entire system. And he knew the energy had to reach the entire mine. He wrapped his arm around Ellen and felt her shiver ever so lightly. He gave her shoulder a reassuring squeeze.

"Please, Anusha, continue." Isaac's words were gentle, encouraging. The space in the room seemed to double as his energy infused with the quiet and peaceful calm Anusha had created in the room. Isaac knew that Anusha's words, spoken aloud, would add a new possibility into the mines, and simultaneously the entire system— altering them forever. He wanted to do all he could to keep the system flowing smoothly.

Anusha lifted her head and looked directly at Isaac, fully aware of his desire to assist her. She nodded to him, giving a small, somber smile, then shook her head, her long ringlets of hair rippling down her back. "I cannot help it. I have tried. I … I…." Anusha's voice echoed the struggle inside. She let her eyes close for a brief moment. Her dark lashes delicately bordered her now light blue skin as she drew in a long, shaky breath. Ellen and Isaac glanced nervously at each other, never before seeing Anusha like this. "I wish I did not. But with all my heart, not only do I love Shree, my balancing compliment, but I am very much in love with him."

The walls around them erupted in a blinding white light, burning across the room, causing them all to shield their faces from the harsh brightness. The temperature shot up—the surrounding walls, floors, and even the ceiling, instantly covered in condensation. Then, just as quickly, the lights dimmed, leaving the walls and floors a soft pale blue. Anusha reached out and ran her hands across the screen in a series of movements, instantly cooling their surroundings. The rest of them raised their heads and peeked back into the room. All eyes landed on Anusha, her skin as light and pale blue as the wall behind her. She stood tall once more, reaching her full height. She was noticeably lighter from freeing the words she held inside for so long—forbidden to feel, let alone speak aloud.

Ila crossed the space between them in two steps and threw her arms around the tall stranger, hugging her tightly. She didn't know why, but she felt more freedom in this moment than she had felt her entire life. Anusha gripped Ila in her long arms. Ila's lips pulled unconsciously into her sideways smile in the comfort of the sweetly fragrant room. Anusha began speaking again, keeping her arms warmly wrapped around Ila, speaking to them over her head.

"Moira and Ariom are connected." Anusha freed one hand and pushed Ila's hair away from her mouth and gazed briefly to each of them. "Our worlds, although vastly different, crossed some time ago and are inexplicably linked. We do not know if this will continue. But for the time being, we are most certainly joined. And our world, at this moment, is in a treacherous situation. Shree has been removed from the mines. Today, just before you arrived, it happened—with the intention to be moved far out of reach of these tunnels. He has been taken—to the Middle, I believe—although our systems are not able to track him as they usually do. This has never happened before in our history. No Other has been removed from the mine." Jay gasped as the full weight of Anusha's words hit him like a punch to the gut. He shifted uneasily from one foot to the other as Anusha continued. "We do not know how this will affect our world. And we do not know what the ramifications will be to yours either."

Isaac stepped next to Jay. "Anusha, we had a plan for this. Remember? We knew of the possibility of removing either you or Shree. Ellen and I have heard their conversations many times. They are afraid. They think they can break the bond—both with the mines and between you and Shree—without consequences. Either that or they simply do not care.

"The three of us crafted that plan: Edge, Shree, and I. That was the whole reason we programmed the second code into the crystals, the one that would momentarily redirect the flow of energy to the middle level, purposely reversing it, like we discussed. It is risky, as you of all people know, but it's the best we've got."

"I am sorry, Isaac, but that will not suffice. I'm afraid any small bit of redirection now will be too much for the tenuous circumstances we find ourselves in. Moving the flow back in on itself, with the way the mines are already fluctuating, I fear would be too much stress on the system. It is already sending large proportions of energy into Moira," Anusha looked at the three newcomers, then back to Ellen and Isaac. "And besides, it is not all we have. Not now. There is now a potential that had never before existed." Anusha nodded to Ila, Jay, and Eve. "We have to trust in this new set of circumstances. We have to trust this new unknown. We must let go of the old way ... of the plan." Anusha looked directly at Jay. "You, Jay, you do have an idea, don't you?" Ila and Eve looked at Jay, both of their brows creased, perplexed.

Jay nodded slowly, surprising even himself. He interlaced his fingers and brought his hands up, resting his thumbs under his chin. The air around them hovered still and warm, momentarily tinged with a strange metallic smell. The scent disappeared almost as quickly as it came.

"As a matter of fact," Jay paused, his mouth forming into a thin line above his hands. "I believe I do."

MIXED

A nusha nodded her statuesque head, her soft angular features more pronounced as her skin shifted to a warm, golden hue. Her thick, tight curls draped her shoulders almost regally as she moved gracefully to her solid bench and turned to Jay.

"I believe we need to proceed quickly. Jay, come, tell me, what is it you see?" Anusha beckoned him over in front of her. A semicircle of stone seating rose soundlessly from the ground behind him. Anusha gestured him to sit. The rest of them crowded around and filled in the seats on either side of Jay. The room buzzed.

Jay leaned forward, his hands clasped tightly in front of him. "I don't have a full understanding of this, but I believe it needs to be Ila and I that go up and look for Shree."

Anusha's chest rose and fell in a practiced rhythm. She nodded ever so slightly, her skin shifting—turning violet, infused with a deep mahogany brown. Jay held her gaze, trying hard to keep his focus on her eyes. Inside, he grew more and more tangled as frustration sprouted and grew from deep within.

"Ila and I, we're...," Jay paused for a second, wrestling with the thoughts and feelings filling him. He grew more irritated by the second. "Goddamn it, even across worlds, it's the same! Damnit! Will we ever get beyond this?" Jay ground his teeth together. He didn't even try to calm his field. He spit his words out more harshly than he meant to. "Because we're both mixed, we'll be able to pass through the mines undetected." Eve narrowed her eyes at him, uncomprehending. Jay looked over Eve's shoulder and didn't try to temper his words, not even for Eve. "We're mixed, biracial. Our parents...." He shook his head, frustrated and embarrassed to say it out loud. "Ila and I, look, we're the product of two different races. Race—*Goddamn it!* Still ...

again! It's fucking about *race*!" Jay's eyes burned as he turned back to Anusha. "Look, the whole reason you and your people are treated like this—kept in these mines, serving god knows who—it's because you're different, right?" Jay couldn't keep the contempt from his tone. He ground his jaw together, knowing the answer, immediately feeling the deep-rooted injustice more than he had ever experienced before. The walls around them began to glow and pulse orange, tinged with a deep plum red.

Anusha held him with her eyes. *It's okay, Jay. It's better for you to let it out.* Her nod was barely perceptible. *You cannot un-know the history of your world. It is part of you just as your childhood is.* Anusha shuddered from head to toe as she spoke in his mind. *The unbalanced, unjust history—around people like yourself, people who appear different than the majority surrounding them* .... Anusha gazed thoughtfully at him as if she were gleaning information from him even in his silent rage. She knew they were all simultaneously hearing her. *But to us, this concept is new. Our structure had not held the expression of un-equal before. Our place has always been here, in the mines. We love it here. It is safe here. Or was.* Anusha stole a glance at the dark ceiling above their heads. *For us, it has not been about the surface keeping us here. This was where we belonged. We are part of these mines and they are a part of us. We understand life here.*

But when Ellen first came across with Mave and Zoe, her revulsion set a new series of events into motion. She detested how we were separated from the rest of Ariom. This sent an entirely new tone into our matrix that had not existed before. Anusha finished her thoughts out loud, in her soft, melodic voice. "That is why even though this is for you, for all of you—an aching reminder of injustices suffered by people considered different in your world—for us, it is not that. We had not experienced those feelings here in our world. We do not suffer in our minds or hearts. Not about that expression. We are quite content in the mines. We know this world and are taken care of here. But a new possibility is now set in motion—a possibility that we hadn't thought of before.

"We know the surface is very different from the mines even though none of us have been there. Simply reading the energy on the surface is uncomfortable for us—it is confusing and unclear there, because there is so much obstruction of energy. So many untruths. For us, it is murky and it causes us great pain. We have loved this situation, living below ground with the clear flowing energy." *Love*. Anusha paused while the image of Shree faded from her mind. "That is why there is no point of reference for this suffering. There is not energy and experience built up around it here ... not yet." Anusha's eyes were hidden behind her long lashes as she stared down at the lightly glowing floor. Her violet skin shifted briefly to a deep, dark mahogony.

Jay stared at Anusha wide-eyed, fists clenched at his sides. "You think this ... this ... this servitude of your people is simply a potential for ... *for growth*?! They are using you—you are not free! How can you not see that? How can you not *feel* that?!"

Jay stood furious, the walls glowing dark magenta, casting their ominous hue across each of their faces. He leaned back against the intensely lit wall, an exact match of Anusha's skin. She spoke quietly. "I *do* feel it, Jay. Now. I cannot help but feel it. That is what is happening when my skin shifts. I feel your heart, Ila's heart, Ellen's heart, all of your hearts, the mines ... I feel *everything*. That is part of my matrix, my structure...." Jay's eyes softened from across the room. He felt a coolness settle over his own skin. The walls around them shifted into a deep indigo. "For me, though, I do not become enraged. What I feel is the pain; that is where I go. That is my only suffering, experiencing pain of others. We do not feel anger; we only feel the core essence, what is underneath. We feel the deep and abiding pain.

"On the surface they fear us. We feel their energy, just like we feel the energy of these crystals. We know them, those above, even better than they know themselves. They have spent their lifetime building walls around their hearts." Ila felt a ripple move through her. Eve saw her tremble ever so slightly then felt a wave of heat move through her own body. "And now, the walls are no longer as solid as they once were.

"The energy in the mines is shifting. We do not yet understand it, but we do not turn away from it. On the surface, it frightens them, so they turn away from it. So much so that they began looking further out, into the skies, for new sources of energy."

Anusha paused and bowed her head, remembering the words she spoke aloud for the first time moments ago. "We were not born here the way you were. We were ... *created* ... before we were ever put into human wombs to grow. Mixed to life. Not in the way you were formed. We were created from one cell. All of us. So we are both very different and not so different from you." Anusha felt a ripple run the length of her body as she lifted her hand and waved it gracefully in the direction of her star. "These stars—they hold the same energy that we do. Each of us has a star, a unique vibration, which was added to the mix, from which we each individually grew. That is why we do not know what will happen, to us or them, when we are separated from them."

Anusha studied the faces in front of her, feeling the collision of emotions running through each of their hearts as they tried to make sense of her words.

"Our technology, it is different than yours. Relatively, we are advanced in this field. Our understanding of the nature of elements is quite impressive, even though our understanding, collectively, of the nature of universal energy is not." Anusha smiled sadly. "We were created out of a desire for more. There is nothing wrong with this; it is the very basis and nature of life, this wanting more. But, above, on the surface, their vision is clouded.

"They do not believe that we are truly life—like they are—because they had a hand in creating us. They feel as if a piece is missing from us. They consider us unnatural. The truth is quite the opposite. They thought they were creating Keepers of the Caves to manage and harness the energy of these tunnels for the surface, and that we would be simple—in all ways. They were unprepared for our capacity in many things—one of these being our longevity.

"So their fear is causing them to look for other sources of energy. They are searching, as we speak, for a way to harness the energy from our orbiting moons. They watch them move across the sky, and we have felt their desire to harness the energy of that movement. They are looking to control, but they don't understand flow, and they don't understand balance. That is why they have us. We do understand. That is why love is forbidden. With it, they would lose control of us, their experiments. Ultimately, they believe they would lose control of their world."

Anusha paused and looked back at her lightly pulsing star.

"And that thought completely and utterly terrifies them."

SIGNALS

J ay lowered his head and looked down at the warm stones glowing deep blue under his bare feet. Against his back, the walls were comforting and calming. His chest expanded and lightened. He felt his anger slipping away. He looked questioningly at Isaac, then to Ellen, then back to Isaac. *What's happening?*

Isaac spoke first. "The mine and the crystals in it, they're like a web. The mines weave underneath the entire city." Isaac waved his hand toward the dark end of the room. "And these crystals thread through them. They are constantly balancing any discordant vibration, any 'off-key' note, so to speak. And your vibration, just now, was 'off-key' simply because anger is not a note sounded down here. You see?" Jay nodded mutely. "So the parts of you that were in harmony with the vibration of these mines—*that* vibration became accentuated. It gets complicated. Do you feel more calm? More settled?"

"Absolutely. But I felt something else." Jay shook his head and furrowed his brow, listening deep in the walls of the mine. "Like a signal, a message. Something like that."

Isaac studied the wall behind Jay. "What else did you feel?"

Anusha nodded in agreement, underneath her grand frame, her seat shifted to soft ochre tinged with pink. "Lean back into the wall, Jay. What else do you feel?"

Jay leaned into the hard stone and let his eyes slip closed. His back warmed, along with the whole room. He thought of his dad and Mave in the field with Beast, instantly knowing he was doing the same thing—tuning in. But he didn't need any movement. The walls felt as if they merged immediately with his cells, like there was very little, if any, differentiation between where he ended and where the porous walls began. Around him the wall shimmered light blue, creating a silhouette around his entire frame. The blue widened, shifting to white the more it expanded, bathing the entire room in a rich, pale blue that reminded Ila of evening just after the sun drops beyond the horizon.

In his mind's eye, Jay saw a path of light in the dark tunneled ground. He knew instinctively this was the way for him and Ila to pass without being noticed. He also knew this tunnel was guarded, somehow veiled from the rest of the network of tunnels and information. He didn't know how he knew, but he was certain it was Shree who configured it. And he knew, unequivocally, Eve would not be able to move through this space without sending out signals. He and Ila had to go alone. Only their blended existence, their mixed background, would pass undetected. Jay's mind felt fuzzy and light, as if he might fade out of consciousness. He fought hard to keep himself awake.

Eve watched Jay's eyes fluttering fitfully behind his closed lids. Under her own skin, Eve felt jumpy; the same surge Jay was experiencing was running through her cells, but she wasn't receiving the translated information. Her voice broke into the room low and urgent. "We have to help him." She slipped off her seat and started to move toward Jay. Isaac grasped her arm, stopping her midstride. His grip was light but unyielding.

"No, Eve, he'll be okay. I promise. Wait just for a moment."

Eve turned to Ila, her eyes pleading. Ila darted a glance to her mother and Anusha, unsure what to do. Ellen stayed silent, her eyes intent on Jay, but her steady and calm presence was reassuring. Ila relaxed. Tenderly, she took hold of Eve's cold hand and pulled her close. *Sit here, Eve. I think he's all right. Let's give him a minute, okay?* Ila wrapped her arm around Eve's agitated body, pulled her closer and held fast to Eve's shaking frame.

Eve shook her head, her wet eyes reflecting the blue from the wall. Her body trembled on the hard stone seat. *No, it's not okay. None of this is okay right now, Ila. I'm seriously really, really scared.*

SHREE

A round him, the middle level felt cold and harsh. Shree knew his own dwelling was directly below the thick, translucently veined stone floor he stood on, but it offered little comfort. He stood silent and still, staying as close as possible to the metal door through which they entered just moments ago. Shree waited patiently, his eyes focused on a small, yellow-white vein embedded deep within the thick floor. The five men accompanying him huddled across the room, speaking in sharp, hushed tones. He knew they were worried and having second thoughts about their plan. He could feel their fear, their uncertainty; it prickled through the air around him like static. And he knew they wanted to be as far away from him as possible. Shree almost felt sorry for them. Then he thought of Anusha and the rest of the Others below. Quickly his thoughts shifted to Isaac and Ellen, then widened without influence to the world above them and to Moira. He steeled his hands into fists and shook his head to clear his thoughts.

If I leave this room, we don't know what will happen. If you put enough stress on a polarized system, the system will eventually switch its flow. The instant this thought came to Shree's mind, his heart cinched in his chest, leaving him momentarily breathless. He clenched his teeth, willing his skin to stay the amber-brown hue it had been when they found him.

Ellen had warned him that the shifting of color was one of the features of the Others that most frightened those from the surface. Only a handful of people from the surface had ever encountered the Others in the crystalline mines, and even those instances were rare. The attendants, those who cared for the Others, were the only ones who stayed in constant communication with them—delivering food, drink, or anything they might need for comfort and happiness.

Happiness ... Shree thought of Anusha the last time he saw her. That day, she had been truly lighthearted, and for the first time that he had ever seen, she seemed utterly happy. The thought of her pressed a smile behind his lips, but Shree didn't let that move to the surface either. He was surprised how easy it was becoming to shroud himself here on the middle level. He glanced around the room and shivered involuntarily in the artificial light.

Shree focused his thoughts on his dilemma at hand, the one that affected *him* and *his* world. This was a direct contradiction of his training. For the whole of his life, he had been instructed to think of how each action, and the energy of that action, would affect the world around him, and then how those actions harmonize and balance. It had always been easy with Anusha at the other end of the mines. They were linked, and had been, for all of their lives. Their matrix crystals balanced each other perfectly. They had been designed that way. But up here, he could barely feel her calm and reassuring presence. And obscuring his own energy like this, it was causing him problems of another sort. Shree was beginning to feel very uncomfortable, like he was tangling on the inside. An unfamiliar torrent, a strange searing flow, began pulsing inside his veins. And the sensation was coming dangerously close to his heart. When he looked at the men across the room, the realization slowly came to him.

This is what Ellen and Isaac had talked about, he thought as understanding dawned in his mind. *This is the irritation they spoke of when a system doesn't flow as it should and it reverses, returning in on itself.* Shree slowed his breath, searching for a smoother flow inside to focus on. Isaac had taught him to do that. Isaac understood a lot about irritation ... and anger, for that matter.

Ellen and Isaac had predicted that this exact scenario would come to pass. Shree and Anusha had known about the possibility, too—from the mines themselves. The mines had been shifting as of late, as if it were trying to integrate a new type energy. As a result, there had been unexpected surges of energies, both below and on the surface. It was as if the energies in the mines were mixing with something unfamiliar and searching for a new, undefined path to house these new currents.

Some of these energies the Others below were able to redirect, but not all of it. Shree and Anusha knew that these energies, these surges, were also felt in Moira. Not only had they received information about them from the mines, but they had felt the warm bursts of energy move between worlds. The surges had been too voluminous to contain, and they had flooded through whatever paths were available, no matter how Shree and Anusha had attempted to harmonize it below ground. The bursts were simply too big. And the link to Moira had become much stronger over the brief time Ellen and Isaac had inhabited Ariom. Shree had spent a lot of time contemplating this new energy.

Shree closed and rested his eyes for a heavy moment, then silently interlaced his large fingers in front of him, glancing down to ensure his skin stayed the same amber-brown hue. He was tired of waiting but stood perfectly still, keeping his light blue eyes focused on the floor in an attempt to make himself smaller. Instinctively, he knew his full essence would affect them much too strongly.

The men were still huddled around their self-appointed leader as he talked through a device he placed to his ear. *Phone.* The name of the device arrived in Shree's head, and its function and purpose immediately followed. *How odd,* Shree thought to himself, *that they need a device to communicate.* One of the men stole a glance in Shree's direction. From the corner of his eye, Shree noticed his brow glistening with perspiration. All at once, Shree felt the man's fear—the clenched grip around the man's heart. Then he felt something else. Inside the man, he felt a genuine kindness and concern for Shree's safety. Shree closed his eyes and pulled in the cloaking around him closer, willing it to thicken. He could not risk connecting to one of these men—for any reason. It was too dangerous.

These people, they were very different from the kindhearted attendants. The attendants were transparent, genuine. These people were foreign to him. He felt vulnerable and unprepared for their kind. He wasn't sure his system would be able to manage and integrate these new experiences and information sufficiently. The more he thought about it, the more fragile his own system felt, like it was barely holding together. Shree slowed his breath and again searched for a smooth flow inside, but on the interior, he was becoming more tangled.

He had a hard time finding a smooth flowing area to focus on. *Please, I must keep it together,* Shree thought as a sharp pain flashed in his chest, knocking the wind from him again. He turned away from the men and focused on the ground below his feet, pleading with the thick stones to stay darkened but support him nonetheless.

Shree imagined his cavelike room below, and, instantly, his heart softened and widened. He wondered what was happening in the mines. He missed the warm comfort of the clear flowing surroundings. He let his eyes slip closed again, and his cavernous room appeared around him. Instantly, he felt the signal he had sent streaming through the system. *Good.*

Shree prayed that his plan would work. It had been almost impossible to shroud the template he uploaded into the crystal mines. Like always, the crystals only allow what they were in agreement with; only what is in alignment with its flow. Shree had breathed a heavy sigh of relief when the code agreed to stay hidden—from everyone in the mines, including the Others—until the arrival of the two. He didn't completely understand how they would make it through, but he knew it had something to do with the blending of energies. And he didn't know what they would do once they arrived—or if they even would.

Through closed eyes, Shree felt his own heart beating rapidly in his chest. He thought his own name. *Shree.* He had been told once what his name had meant— *pure and radiant.* He did not feel that so much now, but as he focused on his room, he could feel the crystals, the pureness of their connection and all that they touched; and he could feel … home.

Shree kept his eyes closed and let himself link into his chamber. Under his feet and all the way across the room, the subdued stone floor began to lighten, growing brighter and brighter. The men at the far side of the room turned their attention to Shree and collectively gasped. Encircling Shree was a luminous field of light blue, slowly expanding and filling his whole side of the room. The tangle of energy inside him dissipated, and Shree began to feel more like himself.

Across the room, the men retreated further, moving to the far corner of the warmed room, away from the soft blue field emanating around Shree. The man with the kind heart stepped forward, the pull of the blue field sparking something deep inside him—a longing, a *feeling*—the pull unlike anything he had ever felt. It was the most comfortable and soothing sensation he had ever known. In his mind, he heard a low, deep chime followed by a one-word whisper through his own mind. *Home.* The man froze midstep. His breath came uneven and awkwardly, synching with a strange squeeze and release of heart, as if his chest were massaging his heart back to life.

Until today, none of the men had actually seen an Other. Shree's attendant had advised against it, but they had sent him away. Now, they were unsure of what to do. The man in charge stole a look at his colleagues. Their faces, the ones he could see, were unreadable. All except Firros, who stood in front of Shree, as if drawn magnetically toward the strange creature. The leader, Kam, turned to Shree, his brow stern and hardened.

"You there! Enough! What do you think you are you doing? Stop that at once!"

Shree heard the man speak, but he sounded far away. The connection he was experiencing was incredibly comforting and rebalancing. He tried to pull himself back to the middle level, but he was having a hard time unraveling the connection—it was taking longer than usual.

Kam shot a glance at his colleagues and steeled his jaw, pressing his lips so tightly together all color drained from them. He stalked his pale frame stiffly across the room, pushing Firros roughly aside as he passed, and stopped at the edge of Shree's glowing circle. The light-blue hue emanating from Shree reflected unnaturally off his menacing face.

"You," Kam ordered through gritted teeth, "stop this right now."

Firros felt Kam's full fury and was shocked at the intensity in which he felt the other man's emotions. Firros wiped his sleeve hastily across his own eyes, removing any hint of wetness, and stepped cautiously next to Kam, resting his hand lightly on his shoulder.

Shree pulled with all his focus to let go of his chamber, but the flowing energy would not detach from him.

Furious at Shree's perceived defiance, Kam, bathed in a luminous blue, growled as he flung both his hands with all his might toward Shree's glowing chest. Firros, knocked off balance, flew to the hard floor just before Kam's hands penetrated the glowing blue cloud. Instantly, the shimmering light pulled him in, and the man was bound, momentarily unable to move either forward or backward. Then, all at once, a burst of light exploded at his fingertips, hurling both the man and Shree backwards, showering the entire room in blinding, white-hot sparks of light. Kam thudded to the ground hard and lay there, unmoving.

Shree scurried back and huddled against the cool wall as the light withdrew from around him. Frantically, he attempted to shroud and contain his heart once more.

ILA and JAY

Ila sprung up into the quiet room, suddenly enlivened, almost knocking Eve off her seat.

"We have to go." She knew it was urgent. Alarmingly urgent. "We have to go now. Shree. The men. Something's happened...," Ila paused, looking up and to the right, like she was listening beyond the room. The blue light surrounding Jay shimmered onto her intent face, softening her features, making her look younger than her age. Above them, the ceiling was errily quiet.

"They're ... clashing." Ila shrugged her shoulders and shook her head, unsure what her own words meant. She slipped next to Jay, his eyes still closed, the light blue encircling him completely. Ila slowly and carefully reached her hand into the blue light and placed it gingerly on Jay's shoulder. As the light penetrated her skin, she shuddered hard, shaking to the core, then went completely still. In her mind, she saw the route through the tunnels, her hand linking her instantly into Jay's vision. *Jay.* She squeezed his shoulder, drawing his attention back to the outer world. *Jay, we have to go. Now.*

Jay trembled visibly and slowly blinked his eyes open. The vast room was much darker than the images inside his mind. He felt Ila's hand loosen its connection on his shoulder while he searched, unseeing, across the room, waiting for his eyes to adjust. When his vision returned, he was staring straight into Eve's wide green eyes.

Eve, I have to go. I promise, I'll be back.

Eve started to get up. *Wait, you guys, I'm going, too.* Isaac moved next to Eve, and Anusha came up on her other side.

"They have to go alone, Eve. The way they're going, it wouldn't be safe for you; you'd be seen."

Eve's eyes blazed as her chest forcefully pushed warm air out of her flared nostrils.

Eve—Jay's voice was low and gentle—*I promise, I'll be back for you. We'll be back. We have to trust this.*

I'm sick of trusting this! Damn it, you guys! Don't leave me here! Eve's voice in their heads matched her pleading eyes.

Eve's breathing quickened. Ila glanced down and saw Eve's hands shaking. Looking up, she caught Eve's eyes darting anxiously around the room. She knew Eve was close to losing control. Her own heart stumbled, gripping in her chest as she pleaded silently across the room. *Eve, breathe, girl. You can do this. I know you can. We have to go ... I'm sorry....* Ila's eyes brimmed with tears. She wiped them harshly off her face. Her heart tore as she turned away from her friend and wiped the remaining wetness from her face. She kept her back to everyone, but through the quiet tension, her words fell easily into their ears.

"The door," she said, low and determined. "Jay, put your hand on the wooden door."

TUNNELS

J ay glanced back over his shoulder as he approached the massive
door. Eve's unstable eyes no longer focused on anything. She was
clinging desperately to her breath, trying not to lose command of her
faculties. She was losing the battle. Anusha moved closer and rested
her wide hand on Eve's shoulder. Eve began to shake. *Go,* Anusha
nodded them on. *We will keep her here. She'll be safe. Go.* Anusha
turned all her attention to Eve. Ellen inched around Isaac and stood in
front of Eve, blocking her view of Jay and Ila.

Put your hand on the door, Jay. Ila's tone was abrupt and
commanding.

Ila, I don't know about this. I don't think we should leave her. Jay
craned his neck, searching for another glimpse of Eve. Ellen squeezed
her hands around Eve's, while Anusha and Isaac each rested a hand
gently on one of her shoulders. Eve's eyes were closed, her whole
body rising and falling with each labored breath, but she was no longer
shaking. Jay turned back to Ila's intense eyes, the force of them
propelling him into agreement.

*We've got this, Jay. I get it now. We're not of a single world, you
and I. We belong to both. We're the link—between—and they need
our ...* Ila paused, her eyes drifting up and to the right, searching for
the word. *They need our possibility. Their worlds here, they're
separate, right? The mines down here, the middle, the surface. Even
though Anusha spoke about being mixed, they don't have the
biological merging that we do. Their world is already shifting. The
energy is moving, but it's not blending. They need our ... matrix, our
blueprint. The system needs our biology to see how it's done.
Understand? Shree, he set this up, you see?*

Jay nodded slightly then narrowed his eyes, staring into Ila's fierce gaze for a long moment. His jaw set as he reached out and placed his damp palm firmly on the large wooden door next to Ila's. The door instantly flared to life. Jay and Ila kept their hands on the door as they ducked against the sudden glare. The light dimmed a little and Ila quickly scanned the fiery lines and curves creeping across the door. One pattern caught her eye above the rest, and she hovered her other hand over it until she felt a pull. Then she placed her palm firmly into its center. All the other inscriptions darkened while the lines under Ila's hand blazed. The door grew progressively warmer until Ila and Jay could no longer bear to touch it. At the same moment, they tore their hands away, shaking the scald off their hands before it settled in. Immediately, the door slid open.

Ila and Jay shot out the door, neither daring to look back, and the door whooshed closed. They spun around in the shadowy hall, just in time to see its outline fading then disappearing. The space filled in with smooth stone walls, as if the door had never existed. The hall they found themselves in was different from the room they had just exited. The ceiling was lower and the walls were smooth, no longer bumpy and earthen like the walls of Anusha's room. Ila and Jay waited quietly for a signal. They looked left and right, contemplating which long hall to travel down. Then the path to the right flashed mildly to life, maintaining a steady pale-yellow glow that brightened one single vein of stone along the length of the crystal floor.

Jay and Ila turned and took off down the hall, following the dimly lit trail. The ground under their feet was uneven, just like Anusha's ceiling. As they sprinted down the corridor, the entire floor below shifted and glowed milky green, and the thin yellow line morphed into white, racing out just in front of them. Jay nodded to himself, completely focused on the task, and followed the continually emerging line.

The corridors twisted and turned as the smooth walls curved off to the left and right. Jay and Ila slowed at each turn just enough to avoid hitting the walls, their feet slapping noisily on the hard ground, then sprinted off again after the racing white line. Each section they flew past brightened—both the walls and the floor. As they ventured deeper into the tunnels, the walls became more and more transparent. Behind the translucent walls, shadowed figures sporadically appeared through the blurred thick stone—sometimes on one side of the corridor, sometimes on the other. Each time they passed one, the wall brightened then dimmed again. Ila shuddered as they passed the ominous figures. *It's the Others, Ila,* Jay reassured her as they turned a tight corner. *They can feel us.* Somehow, Jay knew the Others were not getting signals and information about them through their screens.

Ila understood immediately, the thoughts appearing easily in her mind. *This path, this tunnel, I don't think anyone else knows about it, at least until now—not the Others or the Attendants. Especially not on the surface.* Ila felt a surge of energy from the ground below her feet. She smiled broadly, feeling the encouragement of the path, knowing it was Shree who had set this path specifically for them. For an instant, every surface—walls, ceiling, and the floor—all had the same continuously speeding line of light. Ila felt the light translate in her head, as if the words came from a deep, kind voice. *Excellent—you have found the way.*

Ila and Jay flew around one sharp corner then stopped abruptly, their feet slapping the floor hard and stinging up their legs. They threw their arms out in front of them to cushion their stop. They had reached a dead end. In front of them stood a coarse grotto wall similar in texture to Anusha's chamber. The white light below their feet dashed repeatedly down the hall, ending at the dead end, disappearing completely then shooting light from far off down the hall back toward them.

Overhead, the tunnel curved creating an arched passage instead of the flat, hard ceiling they had seen throughout the mines. Ila and Jay doubled over, chests heaving, and tried to catch their breath. Beads of perspiration dripped from their temples as they wandered back and forth wordlessly, giving their systems time to recover.

SECRETS II

Ila paused as her labored breathing overlapped Jay's ragged breaths. She surveyed back and forth down the tunneled walls. Between flashes of light, she noted an abrupt difference between the shape and texture of the tunnels they had been running through and this final section of the wall at the end. Something in this section felt distinctly different. The air was charged, like a quickly approaching electric storm. The small area she was standing in felt as wide and spacious as if she were standing in one of Mave's rolling green fields. She closed her eyes and inhaled deeply. A cool breeze washed over her arms, and the light scent of damp morning grass drifted under her nose. Ila knew she was still in the tunnels, but the feel of being in Mave's field was strong and convincing.

"Do you smell that?" she asked, eyes closed, her brown face lifted, reaching and searching for more of the comforting scent. Jay inhaled deeply himself, his chest widening and filling as he caught a light whiff of the warming meadow. His eyes slid closed as his mouth curved up at the corners. He let the fresh scent wash over him.

"God, I wish I were there right now," Jay muttered more to himself than Ila. The more he remembered being in the field, the more he felt the spacious outdoors around him. Far in the distance he heard the whispering of leaves—hundreds of them—rustling delicately. The sound echoed longer than any breeze he had experienced. Jay's heart felt lighter than it had been all morning. "This feels like Mave's place, doesn't it?" Through his closed eyes, Jay felt the farm all around him.

Ila fluttered her eyes open and looked at Jay. His body was so filmy and sheer that she could see the wall right through him. She reached out and touched his vapor-thin arm and was relieved when she felt his solid flesh under her hand.

"Jay!" Ila's anxious voice was harsh. Jay's eyes popped opened. His arm became more and more brown by the second—more and more solid. "What are you doing?" Ila's voice was softer now, clearly tinged with worry. "You were almost gone." Ila's wide eyes stared hard at Jay, willing him, all of him, to be here with her.

He blinked his eyes, bringing Ila into focus, and smiled sheepishly. "I'm sorry…I didn't realize…I don't know how.…It just felt so good. Like home."

"Don't leave me here, Jay." Ila's voice was barely a whisper. "Promise me."

Jay's smile vanished, and he was instantly serious. "I won't. I promise." A smile crept back across his lips. "How could I leave my sister from another mister, anyway?" Ila nodded as she pulled her own lips sideways.

"What do we do now?"

Ila shrugged, momentarily at a loss. This section of the corridor was disorienting. She pulled her mind back to their task of finding Shree. Ila stared blankly at the emerald-green stone glowing both faint and luminous beneath their feet. The light seemed to be coming from somewhere down deep. Ila bent down and ran her hand across the floor. The path of her hand brightened into a trail. Ila peered intently into the stone, noticing a repeating pattern in the translucent green. The more she looked, the more a recognizable structure appeared, organized perfectly and spreading out as far as she could see in all directions.

"Jay," she asked quietly, "what do you remember about crystals?"

Jay tilted his head sideways, his forehead wrinkled in thought. He shrugged his shoulders, empty of an answer.

"I don't know, Ila. That was a few months ago. Mr. Abrams went on and on about them, though." He peered up at the curved brown ceiling and followed it back to where it turned smooth and flat. In that short time, one memory slipped into his awareness.

"Actually, I do remember one thing. Mr. Abrams was adamant about us learning that a crystal had to be *'charge balanced'*— remember?" Jay's words came more quickly. "Yeah, it's coming back to me. The amount of negative charge had to be balanced with the amount of positive charge. It had something to do with ions that form when atoms gain or lose electrons...." Jay paused for a second, his different-colored eyes glancing up without seeing, then he continued, "These crystals, the whole tunnel system, they're like a humongous battery with a positive and a negative side. If you stress crystals a certain way, like squeezing, electricity flows easily through it—just like a clock or a battery. But continually stress a crystal—or even a battery for that matter—with too much pressure, and it will reverse its charge and become switched. The charge will switch directions and flow in the opposite way." Jay turned to Ila, his brow furrowed, serious. "Ila, I think Anusha and Shree are the poles on the opposite sides of the crystal. Moving Shree is disrupting the charge of the mines and threatening to reverse the polarity of the whole system." Jay paused and smiled to himself, raising his eyebrows high on his damp forehead.

"Where the hell did that come from? Damn, guess I did learn something in junior year." He softened his brow and knelt down next to Ila, squinting into the floor. "Do you know what it means?"

Ila shook her head, feeling the answer too far away to understand completely. "I'm not sure. But here, look, the line we followed, it was somehow embedded in the stones, right? And here...," Ila gently ran her hand over the uneven floor. The ground illuminated from murky depths, revealing a refracted and repeated symmetry as far as their eyes could see. "Look here, see the organized arrangement in there?" Jay nodded. "This line, it disrupts the arrangement; it interrupts the organized design, see?"

"Yeah, so?"

"So, I think Shree knew the whole system was changing and that the mines are receiving added amounts of pressure and energy. I bet he knew the whole structure is shifting, just like you said." Ila nodded to herself and placed her moist palm flat on the ground. The terrain around it illuminated pale blue. Deep inside, she saw the geometric shapes embedded in the stone shift ever so slightly, pulling the symmetrical design irregular, similar to the way fabric stretches when it's pulled on, Then it realigned itself back into a new, slightly bigger arrangement. Jay leaned in closer and placed his hands on space between them. As they watched, an edge of the design pulled on the rest of the shape, creating a new form deep within the structure. It turned pale blue as well. *It looks like what happens when cells divide,* Ila thought to herself. "Yeah, that's exactly what I was thinking." Jay answered in a low voice. The realm between thoughts and words was no longer distinct. Ila smiled. She kept her hand on the light-filled ground and received more and more understanding, as if the light was transmitting information.

Once the newly expanded piece of the structure settled into its altered organization, the structure around it reorganized, too, rippling out into the surrounding structures. Jay's brown forehead creased, bathed in fading pale blue light, as his mind spun furiously, trying to understand what they were seeing. The ground beneath Ila's hand shifted back to pale green.

Ila spoke again, breaking the agitated silence. "Pulling Shree out of the mines will create instability to the system. Shree and Anusha knew this change was already happening. Just like we saw here." Ila nodded to the floor where her motionless hand lay. "I think Shree has found a way to focus the shifting energy. But he couldn't tell anyone, because he didn't want the surface to find out. They're already suspect of the Others. But hiding information in the mine—it's not possible, right? That's what they said anyway. But somehow, Shree was able to do it. Shree found a way to shroud energy down there, deep within the crystals. And I don't think he told the Others about it. I don't think he even told Anusha. She turned to you to help find Shree, to us, right? - And I don't think she even knows about these tunnels we traveled through—with this emerging path. Hell, she didn't even know we were in Ariom." Ila paused, staring deep into the ground as she let herself sit with the information pouring out of her mouth.

After a silent moment, she inhaled deeply, lifting her brown eyes to meet Jay, and continued, "I think Shree understood how the Others were designed." Ila's face softened as understanding slowly dawned in her. "He figured out how to influence the elements, just like the surface had when creating the Others. Shree taught the mines how to 'grow' and create new passages; he found a way to create another structure, another set of tunnels…," Ila's eyebrows creased until they almost touched at the bridge of her nose, the final words of explanation disturbing her so deeply that she whispered them to Jay, "should the original one ... falter."

"Falter?" Jay narrowed his eyes at Ila, then slowly raised his furrowed brow high on his forehead. "You think they really could be affected... the mines—seriously affected? I don't know, Ila. They're so solid. So deep." Jay shook his head unconsciously and peered down around Ila's hand. The stone matrix seemed so substantial; it was hard to believe they could be damaged.

"I do. I think they already are." Ila looked Jay square in the eyes. "Here, put your hands right here."

Jay paused, remembering the way the door ignited last time Ila told him to place his hand. "What if we activate something? Like in Anusha's chamber?"

Jay felt a pull from the ground below and glanced nervously at Ila. She nodded, her curly hair crimped and kinky in the warm air of the tunnel. "I think that's exactly what we're meant to do. These mines, they're...." Ila couldn't find the word she was searching for. Then, all at once, it popped into her mind: "They're evolving. They're ... intelligent. Not the way you and I are, of course ... but they communicate with this flow, and the mines need both the positive and negative—as in charge—like a battery. And I think it's meant to react to us. Shree, he's somehow infused our signature into the matrix. I don't know how, but this mine, it responds—to us."

Suddenly, a burst of bright light filled the room, blinding them. Ila and Jay shielded their eyes instinctively as a blast of warm air surrounded them. It was gone as quickly as it came.

"What the hell was that?" Jay asked, peeking out from under his glistening arm.

"Shree." Ila dropped her hands heavily into her lap and sat motionless, her kinky hair even frizzier from the warm blast.

"What about him?"

"He's letting us know we're on the right track. I just know. *I feel it.*"

"And you're trusting it?"

"Yeah, I am."

"Wait a minute, Ila, hold up. You do realize you don't trust anything, right? You, Ila my friend, you are an eternal skeptic."

"Look, Jay, you of all people should get it. You have been telling me 'It's all about the feel' for as long as I can remember. Well, finally I get it. Finally, I trust myself enough. I *believe* in myself enough to lean into what I feel. It just so happens that this burst of wisdom came at the weirdest possible time." Ila shook her head at the impossibility of the events.

"I don't care, Jay. You know my story. You know how I've kicked and screamed, fought and built up barriers my whole entire life just trying not to be hurt. But here's the deal: All that time, *that was the hurt*. That was the pain. I love you guys, all of you. But I kept a space, a distance, between myself and the rest of the world—because I felt damaged and unwanted. And even though your family and Mave and Eve, even though you all love me, I wouldn't let it in—not fully—because I was always afraid that it would be pulled away ... at any given moment." Ila looked down, unable to look at Jay, her dark lashes hiding her wet eyes.

"So I wouldn't *let* myself belong." Ila spoke quietly. "I stayed on the outside, like I was watching the world through a window." She stole a glance at Jay, his own head bowed as he listened to Ila.

"But with this, this...," Ila pursed her lips and scanned the walls around her, "this whatever the hell this is we're doing—this crazy-assed journey—it's cracked those hard edges. And I don't want to repair them. I *like* feeling deeply, Jay. Who'd have thought...." Ila paused again, looking up at the curved ceiling, gazing to where it met the more uniform and smooth part of the corridor. "And I feel like we should get moving."

STARS

J ay's heart swelled. Without warning, he threw his arms around Ila and hugged her tightly. "Damn, Ila," he whispered into her thick hair, "that's some serious shit you've got going on."

Ila's whole body shook as her laughter tumbled into the air around them. The room brightened, as if responding to her once more. The soft ringing of chimes echoed off in the distance.

Fuck, this place is weird. Jay squeezed Ila once more, then let go and sat back on the ground. Ila giggled as she scooched close to him on the hard stone. Once more, distant melodic chimes filled the corridor.

"Okay, okay, I get it. We need to move. Where did you say to put my hand?"

Ila crouched down and studied the milky green ground below them, searching for the line that ran down the middle, the one that led them through the tunnels. Finally, she found the spot, the same one that had shifted before their eyes.

"Here, place one here." Ila pointed to the spot on the ground, then she stepped directly across the line and faced Jay. "And your other hand on the opposite side of the line, here. And I'll do the same."

They locked eyes and held their hands hovering above the ground. Jay felt a pull on his hands and nodded to Ila. She felt it, too. Without speaking, they lowered their hands simultaneously onto the warm, softly lit floor.

Once their hands landed on solid stone—just as on the wooden door—lines and curves appeared, burning bright orange-red, swirling and expanding from their hands in meandering wavy lines away from the middle of the floor. Rolling and snaking up the walls, they gracefully made their way to the middle of the arched ceiling. As the lines reached the center of the dark ceiling, one orange-red line shot down the hall away from them, flying across the ceiling and lighting up the entire corridor for as far as they could see. The ground below their hands heated fast, threatening to sear their skin, and then cooled abruptly. They both kept their damp palms steadily pressed onto the floor. More intricate, red-orange swirls and curves slithered onto the walls on either side of them. Then all at once, the fiery glowing lines dimmed and turned jet black on the brown ceiling and walls. Still, they kept their hands on the floor. A breeze swept back down the hall toward them, bringing both warmth and the aroma of damp earth with it. *Stay connected, Jay. Don't let go.*

Jay nodded as the black lines all around began to sway and dance almost serpentlike, then slipped off the ceiling and walls and back onto the floor. Slowly they began to form themselves into inky shapes deep within the ground. Before their eyes, a delicately lined animation unfolded. Thin black lines grew into two figures. One they instantly recognized as Anusha, with her long, curled hair tumbling down around her shoulders. The other was as tall as Anusha but broad and masculine. *Shree.* They nodded together in agreement.

As they watched, the two figures slid away from each other, climbing up opposite walls. They paused halfway up and waited. Another series of lines scurried from the ground and wove their way to the ceiling. The thin black lines drew themselves into a bridge connecting one wall to the other across the ceiling. As soon as the image finished, it exploded in all directions. Jay and Ila ducked instinctively. Dark, broken lines showered down walls around them, and disappeared back into the floor. The two simple figures began to move, walking parallel on the walls to the dead end of the tunnel. They met there, in the middle of the darkened wall at the end of the tunnel.

The animations' wispy hands reached out toward each other then entwined on the makeshift screen. Their essence felt much more real than the simple line drawing they saw before them.

Movement began one more time from the ground below their hands, as more dark lines materialized, drawing themselves into more figures. These new figures migrated down the walls and floor, gathering themselves around Shree and Anusha, some intertwining their hands, some not. After the last figure crawled into its place on the wall, the whole room darkened completely.

Ila gasped. The room was so dark she couldn't see her warm hand still resting on the floor. *I'm right here, Ila. Don't let go yet.*

Little by little, the figures reemerged from the pitch-black background, each lightly glowing in a rainbow of various hues and tones. Around them, the walls remained black and void of color. Slowly and definitely, small points of white light began to shine just above the heads of each of the soft-hued figures. The points of light floated up the wall, away from each of the figures multiplying and filling the entire ceiling above them. Each light pulsed bright then dimmed in varying degrees of rhythms. All around them the vast, sparkling night sky shimmered celestially.

It's gorgeous. Ila gazed around at the lustrous, pulsating sky.

This is amazing. Jay soaked in the images, committing them to memory, letting them settle deep in his heart.

Slowly, the wide, starry sky drew in from its farthest edges, shrinking down evenly into the middle, until it became a singular white pulsing star. Immediately, it floated across the ceiling to the wall at the end of the corridor and embedded itself at the top, directly in the center. From here, the white star continued its graceful pulsating rhythm above the soft rainbow of animated figures below.

Ready? Ila asked after the room had settled into stillness.

For what?

To let go.

RISING

The star above the door shimmered intermittently, sending light across Jay's hesitant face, placing him in equal amounts of light and shadow. Finally, he blinked his eyes and turned to the warmly lit wall. He gave Ila a short, quick nod. Under their hands, the gentle pull released and together, they lifted their hands away from the dark floor. The figures disappeared. In their place another wooden door appeared, carved with the same mazelike lines in Anusha's chamber.

The door slid open. The slick, light sound contrasted the heaviness of the dark, mahogany door. The noise cut through the silence. Ila and Jay both jumped at the sound. Ila crawled, her heart beating hard in her chest, into the doorway and peeked cautiously inside. The pulsating light from above the door shifted to a luminous red-orange. Inside the room, all they saw were two pieces of clothing hanging neatly on the long wall. Ila and Jay scrambled to their feet and hurried into the small room. The door immediately whooshed shut behind them.

Inside, the light above the door continued to oscillate in an easy tangerine rhythm, casting a pale orange light across them and spreading their shadows eerily onto the opposite wall. Again, Ila caught an undeniably airy, damp, and earthy scent. *Mave's fields*. Ila knew that smell anywhere. She inhaled deeply and caught a pungent and musky scent mingled in. Ila cocked her head to the side, trying to place the second smell. It vanished as quickly as it came.

Both Ila and Jay surveyed the only contents of the room. Hanging side by side on the wall were two long shirts, each a light sage green, embellished with beautifully decorative stitching around the collars and sleeves. The only differences between them were their sizes and one tied at the side, while the other had a simple v in the neckline. Jay looked down at his disheveled t-shirt and dingy shorts.

"I think we're supposed to wear these." Jay reached for the larger tunic and ran it through his fingers. Its soft fibers felt fine and luxurious under his touch. He ran his hands across the stitching, the decorated edges intricate and flawless. He noticed the design was similar to the flowing curved lines they had seen on both wooden doors. "These are really well made," Jay commented as he slid the tunic off the hook. He turned his back to Ila and shed his bedraggled shirt in one quick motion. The new shirt slipped gracefully over his shoulders, draping and complimenting his shape, as if it were made for him.

Ila removed the other piece of clothing. "This is so soft. Huh, I wouldn't have guessed. It looks more … rugged." She turned from Jay and contemplated wrapping the cloth over her dingy blouse or discarding her worn shirt altogether. She favored the former and slipped her long arms into the fabric, covering up her own shirt fully. She tied the embroidered tunic off at the side. It concealed her own smudged shirt completely and even hung low enough to cover half of her disheveled pants. She ran her hands over the fabric once more. *It's like everything down here—light and comforting.*

Jay smiled, nodding his approval, then turned to examine the rest of the small room. To the left of the door was a smooth rectangular crystal, a little bigger than the size of their hands. *Keypad?*

Ila nodded. *You or me?* she asked.

You. Definitely.

Jay took a step back. Ila stood in front of the keypad, unsure what to do. She reached her hand out, pausing before contact.

Ready?

As I'll ever be.

Ila placed her flat hand on the cool stone. Instantly, it sprung to life.

"Yes, Ellen, how can we assist you?"

Ila raised her eyebrows, hesitating only a moment, then assumed the role.

"To the middle, please." Her voice sounded confident. Ila held her breath.

"Right away."

Ila let out a long, slow breath. The last wisps crossed her lips just as the wooden door slid open. This time it revealed a harshly lit room. The room smelled of singed hair and smoke under the fluorescent light. Ila and Jay darted their eyes quickly around the hazy room. Directly in front of them stood three men, their backs wet with sweat through their dark shirts. They spun at the sound, facing Ila and Jay, their faces each pulled tight. Their eyes were as harsh as the penetrating light. Across the room, Jay saw another man in a matching dark shirt sprawled on the floor and a fifth man with the same dark shirt struggling back to his feet.

Recoiled in the corner was a much-taller man wearing a tunic just like Jay's, only his was the color of golden sand. His skin was a faded, listless grey. Jay felt his own heart cool and a shiver ran out across his entire body. The tension in the room was palpable. Jay lifted his chin as he held the gaze of the clearly shaken man. *Shree?*

Yes.

Shree straightened, regaining some of his composure. His skin warmed and mutated into amber brown. The three men directly in front of them looked silently from Ila to Jay. Ila felt their fear ripple through her.

She broke the silence. "What has happened here?" she spoke quickly, attempting to sound authoritative.

"Your man ... he ... he...," the man closest to them stammered, his hands clenched tightly at his sides. Quickly he ran his arm across the side of his face. "There was an explosion."

Firros stood shakily on his feet using the wall for support. "Wait." His voice was hoarse and raspy. "Wait a minute." The three other men turned, their gaze direct and intent at Firros. They made no motion toward him or the man on the floor. Shree pushed himself up and stood tall, clasping his hands in front of him. He towered above everyone in the room. He looked over the men's heads and to Jay and Eve. The two of them glanced around the room then back to Shree, uncertain what to do next.

"Permission?" Shree asked, nodding to Ila. Ila lifted her chest and took a step forward, taking up as much space as she could.

"Of course." Ila furrowed her brow, unclear what she had just answered. *Did he just ask permission to speak?* Ila's frame stayed steady and sure, but inside, Shree's simple word had shaken her.

I think so. Jay stepped up next to her, feeling her wobble, and steadied her with his presence.

Shree spoke directly to Firros. "I can help him—your friend. May I?" He stayed still, his hands unmoving, waiting with practiced patience. Firros looked at his colleagues, his brow damp and furrowed. His hands quivered lightly by his sides.

"Why would you want to help him?" Firros stared defiantly at his colleagues, daring them to challenge him. "He attacked you."

"Because I know he means a great deal to you." Shree let the words land softly in the room, no hint of malice or vengeance in his offer. His eyes met Ila directly. As she searched into their amber-blue depths, she felt no bitterness from him toward the man on the floor. His wish was clear. He only wanted to help. His skin shifted to a golden reddish-brown. The area just around his skin shifted to a pale blue.

"Your man is taking great liberties to speak to us directly," one of the other men spoke. His voice was laced with disdain.

Ila turned and faced the man directly. "It seems he is not the only one taking liberties." Ila's eyes blazed at him accusingly. The man shrunk back under her words, clearly afraid of her.

Ila felt him recoil as if she would actually harm him. His reaction puzzled her. Her mind raced as she searched for a way to connect with him. Her eyes softened as she lowered her tone. "Why did you send his attendant away?"

The three men stared at Ila, but none of them spoke. Ila felt their fear rising in spite of their disciplined training. "Who told you to take this man from the mines?" Ila spoke clearly and authoritatively. She steadied her gaze and stood up taller, taking full command of the room. Inside she wasn't so confident. All she truly wanted to do was to grab Shree and run. The stark room was confining, as if it were squeezing life out from between her cells.

The men stared at her, unmoving, unspeaking. She felt their aversion grow, along with their agitation. Ila felt her own irriatation grow. She clenched her fists and leaned forward infinitesimally. "Where I come from," she said, annunciating each word slowly, "it is not polite to ignore a direct question."

Ila felt Shree's gaze on her, soft and open, encouraging her to shift her growing hostility. *Ila,* Shree's words settled into Ila's mind, easing her tension and softening her eyes, then the center of her heart. *You're letting their signature dominate. You have other choices.*

Ila paused and delicately shook out her fisted hands. She nodded her head and turned her attention to Firros. "Let my man help your friend…," Ila paused, knowing the man's name would appear in her mind. "Kam. Your friend's name is Kam." Shree glanced quickly at Ila, then back at the motionless man on the floor.

"He needs assistance," Ila spoke directly to Firros. "That is my job as an attendant—to assist. And you know his purpose"—Ila nodded to Shree—"to balance. Let us help him." Ila paused, narrowing her eyes again as she waited for his name to appear in her mind. "*Firros.*" She nodded. "Let us help him, Firros." Firros widened his eyes as his three colleagues inched toward the open door. Jay placed his hand on the rectangle pad, and the door whooshed shut. The men were trapped. Jay eyed their waist and hands for signs of weapons.

There are no weapons here in Ariom. Jay heard Shree's voice clearly in his head. *The only thing they consider weapons are what Ila did just now—to receive and understand information from the world around her—what we do all the time in the mines.* Shree suppressed a hint of a smile and stepped toward the man on the floor. He knelt delicately beside Kam and waited respectfully for permission once more. Firros shifted his eyes back and forth between Ila, Jay, and Shree for a long moment. He remembered the comforting sensations he felt when Shree was surrounded by blue light. He had felt safe.

"Okay," he said finally, kneeling next to Shree and leaning back on his black-heeled boots. "Please. Help him."

Shree, ever so slightly, softened the guard he had placed around his heart so he could connect once more to the flow of the mines. Instantly, his skin morphed, adding more light to the golden brown of his body. He tried to lessen the intensity—an attempt to quell the men's fear—but it only caused the glow to widen. He shook his head, unable to connect with the man. *I am unsafe with him; my biology, it is responding to our interchange and simply will not allow it. Ila, it will have to be you. Will you help him, Ila?*

Me? I have no idea what you were going to do.

You can do it. He needs to be connected to the flow of the mines. You become the link between. It is a lot like plugging into an electric socket. Shree smiled lightly. *Your mother, she taught us about the way energy moves in your world and up there.* Shree nodded toward the harshly lit ceiling. *Above the mines.*

Ila moved across the room eyeing the men suspiciously. *We should leave here, Shree. Now, while we have a chance.*

It is necessary. There are ramifications from this, Ila. There are always ramifications. Shree bowed his head, his color draining and shifting to a dull grey. *I never meant to injure him. I ... I tried to find balance when he entered my field—a balance between our energies— but his fury restricted the flow. It came back on him amplified from my connection into the energy of the mines.*

Ila placed a hand on Shree's shoulder and felt the anguish bubbling under his skin. All of a sudden, she realized Shree had never encountered something like this before, being a participant rather than an observer of life. Her heart squeezed in her chest as she witnessed a part of his innocence slipping away. Ila knelt down beside him, smoothing her long tunic under her knees. She held a trembling hand over Kam.

When her hand hovered directly over his heart, she felt the pull drawing her in. But this time was different. There was a pull and a resistance, as if her hand were connected and repelled at the same time. Shree felt it, too. Kam's system wasn't used to being open. Throughout his entire life, he had allowed only small amount of his heart to participate in the world. Even lying here unconscious, his biology wasn't allowing himself to be open and vulnerable. Shree glanced across to Jay, now standing between the three other men and himself. Shree was grateful for Jay's calm presence. He nodded once to Jay. He didn't know what would happen if they tried to move closer.

All of a sudden, Kam heaved forward, coughing and sputtering as he gasped for air. The dull grey floor under them lightened, revealing its veined and varied structure through the pale blue stone. Kam sat up and pressed his hands flat on the floor. Directly beneath his hands, the floor grew brighter. Kam's heart pounded in his chest. Blood rushed through his ears. The bright room around him slowly came back into focus.

Easy, Ila sent him the thought, not realizing he hadn't communicated this way before. *Easy, Kam, you just had quite a jolt. Your body, it's still recovering. You'll be fine.* Ila turned her head away from him and pressed her lips together. She wished she hadn't given him so much information.

Kam looked at Ila, his eyes wide and blue, almost as light as Anusha's. Ila returned his gaze and saw a light spark deep within the blue. *You're talking in my head.*

Ila smiled, warming the stark, sterile room. *Yeah, I guess I am.*

"Excuse me." Shree knelt beside them, resting his own large hands on the blue glow of the floor. "Please, tell me about this water. You came up choking. Have you any idea where you were? What was happening?"

The entire floor of the room shifted and shimmered blue-green. Ila saw a faint line appear deep inside the stone and glide across the middle of the floor.

"I … I'm not sure." Kam looked through Shree, as if his eyes were seeing something else. Shree could feel the confusion and chaos the man had just experienced. Ila felt it, too. "I think I was just in my home on the surface." Kam looked across the room at his colleagues who were gathered next to Jay. "And it was underwater."

GOOD-BYE

S hree's eyes softened and became mysteriously still and spacious. He reached his mind and energy back into the mines. His hands and the ground below shifted to an orange-red glow. As the group around him watched, the entire floor became more and more translucent. Gradually it changed itself into a spectrum of colors ranging from light sandstone to a deep coral orange. The men across the room stepped back as far as they could until their backs pressed hard against the plain white wall. They were trying to get as far away from Shree as possible. They glanced down and saw into the depths of the stone for the first time. Wide-eyed, they were both terrified and riveted by the morphing stone under their feet. The entire room buzzed with energy. The three men clenched their hands at their sides and began to shake uncontrollably. Their breathing became labored and shallow.

Shree. Ila reached for his shoulder, but the air around him seemed to push her away. *Shree, what are you doing?* Ila moved her hand over his, hovering above the wavy, flamelike energy rising from his trembling hands. Ila followed Shree's flow into the mines, as if she were walking behind him. He was reaching far into the tunnels, scanning the perimeter, sending and receiving signals from far below them.

Ila understood. He was communicating with the Others below. Over and over, the message was the same. The far edges of the mines were unstable. Ila realized this instablility was very close to where they stood directly above Shree's chamber. Ila felt the distress and confusion as the Others struggled for a way to stabilize the faltering mines. Never before had they faced such disastrous circumstances.

Ila placed her hand on Shree's, adding herself to the conversation flying through the crystal framework of the mine. *Shree, they must all move to the other side of the mine. Far away from this side—to Anusha's area. They must go now.*

Shree kept his hand still and turned his head to stare into Ila's obsidian eyes. *What are you doing?* His words sounded far away in her mind.

Ila held his gaze. *The mine is unstable. The poles are no longer balanced. You know this, Shree. I know you know! Tell them! Stay connected to each other.* Ila spoke directly into the mines, ignoring Shree's invisible protests. *Hold the structure, the form of the mine inside you. Keep it alive with you as you move—connect to it—and bring the energy along with you. Keep it linked. Help it flow. It needs a direction. The flow needs a direction. Help each other now. It is time for you to help each other.*

Ila watched Shree's angular face fall as the tangerine orange faded from around his limp hand. He dropped it heavily to his side. *Ila, what have I done?* His eyes darted to Kam then circled the small room, looking at each of their faces still recovering from the intense energy that had just filled the room. Ila knew exactly what he was thinking.

This is not your fault, Shree. You did not start this. It was happening long before today, and you know that. Ila placed her small hand tenderly on Shree's broad shoulder. *Shree, we have to move. We have to leave this spot. We're not safe here.*

Shree dropped his head and gave one small nod. Ila felt his heart widen in his chest, as if he were suddenly three times as immense as the man standing before her. The room grew so bright they had to shield their eyes from the radiant, dazzling light once more. Shree sent a message through the mines—one that had never before been imagined, let alone transmitted.

You all are my heart of hearts, and it is with deep sadness—more than I've ever before felt—that I send you this message of farewell. I am leaving my home now, and I am going to the surface. Good-bye my loves.

As the final bit of communication departed, Shree's radiance vanished, and he drained of color until he became the dull grey they had seen upon entering. Ila kept her hand on top of his, but she felt him go cold as ice. Beneath their hands, the floor glowed a faint milky-white.

Jay stood at the door, his hand poised next to the keypad flashing its orange-red glow.

Shree, Jay spoke slow and calm, *Shree, we have to leave now. You need to get up. Ila, do you know where to go?*

The only thing I know for sure is we can't go back down. At least not here. Ila's jaw set as she eyed the ground below.

But ... Jay stopped himself, realizing Eve was still in the mines. His blood ran cold as a picture of Eve, her brown hair framing her light, smiling face, flashed through his mind. His nostrils flared as he fought for breath, steeling his mind to the task at hand. Blinking the sting from behind his eyes, Jay shook the thought of Eve from his head and clenched his teeth tightly in his mouth. He forced his breath in and out slowly and methodically. He reached out his raised arm and placed his dark hand firmly in the middle of the keypad.

PART IV

SECRETS III

A nusha spun toward the wide rectangle screen, causing a ripple of energy to vibrate through the already uneasy room. Her skin turned yellow-orange, responding to the call of alarm before the crystals even transmitted it. Her sudden movement startled Eve and Ellen, their own systems already on high alert. They both felt a trail of goose bumps ripple across their skin. Isaac spun toward the screen, ready to spring into action. All three of them waited silently for Anusha to translate what had happened in the seemingly quiet mine.

"Shree," she whispered, her voice catching in her throat as she stood in front of her large dark screen. "Where is he?"

The screen sprung to life, flashing with a tremendous array of lines and colors, crossing and changing so quickly that it took Anusha a moment to translate what was happening.

"This is … it is … a possibility we had feared. The west end of the mine is highly unstable—the place where it meets the sea—Shree's end." Anusha's words were as heavy as rocks. Ellen and Isaac silently moved to Anusha's side. Eve edged in close to Ellen, trying to escape the chaos she suddenly felt filling the room. In the silent room, Eve felt as if hundreds, if not thousands, of people were screaming in panic. She wedged in against Ellen's slim frame and buried her head in the softness of Ellen's tunic, covering her assaulted ears and trying desperately to silence the screams. Almost immediately, Eve realized the noise was not echoing through the room but was raging on the inside of her mind.

"Make it stop!" Eve screamed above the din in her ears. "Please," she pleaded, her eyes pressed shut against the harsh torment. "Please," she whimpered.

Ellen wrapped her arm around Eve and looked at Isaac and Anusha through her creased brow, not understanding.

"The mines." Anusha waved her hand down the edge of the screen. "She's hearing the possibility." Anusha breathed the words into the room, but her focused eyes were searching for something else. Her hands widened the view on the confusing screen. "Here." Anusha pointed to a particularly chaotic section of the grid. "This is from the west edge of the mines. The Others are sending reports. This is happening now." Anusha zoomed in as her hands flew around the screen, making order out of the chaos. "The west end, Shree's end of the mine; it's still there, but the land beyond, out to sea, is failing. And the water, the sea, the temperature is much higher than normal, hot and bubbling. The ground beneath the water—they say it is sizzling liquid, as if it's on fire. The mines are threatened. The west edge is the oldest part of the mine—most of it resides underwater already. If the mines should falter, then it is a very real possibility the surface above it will, too…. That is what Eve is hearing—the possibility." Anusha's skin turned scarlet magenta, her broad shoulders tense, as her hand smoothed down the side of the screen. She began to comprehend the magnitude and horrific outcome if the events came to pass.

"The sound—it's gone," Eve sighed, warily dropping her hands from her ears, unsure if they would resume at any moment.

"I turned it down." Anusha fought to keep her voice steady, keeping her eyes on the turbulent screen. "It is most certainly not gone. But what you are hearing is not yet a reality. It is only a possibility at this point." Anusha cocked her head to the side, both feeling and listening as a new, louder message streamed its transmission into the system. It was being relayed repeatedly, amplified through the entire mine. She hesitated only a moment, and then placed her hand decisively on top of it to bring the vibrating, dark red line to life inside her head. A deep familiar voice filled her ears, causing her heart to skip a beat in her chest. *You all are my heart of hearts, and it is with deep sadness—more than I've ever before felt—that I send you this message of farewell. I am leaving my home now, and I am going to the surface. Good-bye my loves.*

Anusha flashed completely black for one split second, then shifted to darker shade of burgundy. "He's...." Anusha lost her words and froze with fear, her mind filling with images of Shree. Her eyes glazed over as she searched frantically through the mines, trying to reach Shree. Ellen, Isaac, and Eve felt cold flash through the room. Ellen gently placed her hand on Anusha's arm, pulling her consciousness back to the room. Anusha looked at Ellen, blinking her clouded eyes repeatedly. Slowly she recognized her surroundings. "Shree"—she exhaled, emptying herself—"he's going to the surface."

"What? Are you certain?" Ellen leaned toward the board, peering at the messages as if she could interpret them herself, willing them to be different. "You're positive that's what he said?"

Anusha reached to the side of the screen and gracefully ran her hand in a series of strokes that only she understood. The board roared to life. Eve threw her hands on her ears anticipating more devastating cries, but this sound was different. The main stream of sound was a man's deep voice, low and void of all expression. Anusha played it over and over, letting the words sink in to her own cells. Eve understood instantly that it was Shree.

"You all are my heart of hearts, and it is with deep sadness—more than I've ever before felt—that I send you this message of farewell. I am leaving my home now, and I am going to the surface. Good-bye my loves."

Finally, Anusha let the words fade out and dissolve, leaving behind a low howling and wailing in the background. Listlessly, she reversed the code and silenced the wide chaotic screen once more. She turned to face them. Smooth currents of wetness rolled down her dark cheeks in clear rivers, landing one drop at a time on the floor, each with a whispered golden chime. "This—this was not how it should be." Anusha's frame darkened even more, making her appear as a shadow of her former self. She turned to Isaac. "I do not know what to do. This was not the plan. The Others, they are coming to this side of the mine—here."

"Will they be safe on this side?" Isaac's voice was calm and sure. "Anusha, listen to me: this is where we are. This is simply where we are, no matter how we think it should be. It doesn't mean this is where we'll stay. You hear?" He reached out and placed his hands on her rounded shoulders, her light-colored tunic a complete contrast to the obsidian hue of her bare skin. Isaac pulled her in and wrapped her tight in his arms, holding her, as if she were a small, vulnerable child. For a brief moment, Anusha let herself rest, leaning into Isaac's head, her long curls spilling down his shoulders, as her tears fell in quiet streams. Isaac felt her heart fall as the room cooled and transformed into a deep violet red—lighter in some places, jet black in others—until the entire room was awash with deep, shadowed tones.

Eve felt as if a flood were looming somewhere deep inside of her. Then slowly and definitively, one deep, heart-wrenching gong peeled across the room, ringing through each of them and shifting the nebulous surroundings to a diffused tangerine-red shimmer.

Beast! Eve suddenly felt his grand presence, as if he were standing right next to her.

Beast? Anusha raised her head as well, her skin morphing lighter as her blue eyes searched around the room. Her eyes landed on the large wooden door. "Jantu?" One thin line traced itself around the wide perimeter of the door, then moved in concentric circles, spiraling from a large oval then circling smaller and smaller until it ended at a point in the very center of the door. Anusha pulled herself from Isaac's hold and floated to the door in one fluid step. The scent of a summer-warmed afternoon filled the cavernous room, as if it came directly through a wide-open window.

As Eve glanced over her shoulder scanning the room, she caught Isaac and Ellen exchanging confused looks. Eve interwove her fingers into Ellen's hand and held her tight, feeling buoyed by the scent lingering around them. *That's Mave's farm. Remember that smell?* She held Ellen's hand tighter as Anusha placed her hand flat onto the orange glow in the center of the wooden door. Without hesitation, the door whooshed open, and in front of Anusha stood the rest of her kind—thirty-one Others, each about as large as she, each emitting the same tangerine-red radiance as the door. Behind Anusha the room shifted, as did her own skin, to instantly match the group standing at the door.

"Is this everyone?" Anusha gave a breathless bow, pulling each of them into a strong embrace before she ushered them one by one into the room. Sixteen women and fifteen men entered and shifted to their own distinct and unique hue as they gathered next to the fluttering screen. They stood exquisitely still, robed in the same refined sand-colored tunic and tailored trousers as Anusha.

The Others looked to the smallest of their group, her sturdy frame still larger than Isaac, and waited for her answer. Her voice echoed sweetly as she spoke, her long silver hair hanging straight around her lineless, olive brown face. "I am not certain how we came here exactly, but yes, this is all of us."

"Varsa." The wooden door slid shut behind Anusha, her light blue eyes rimmed with red, as she shifted to her own signature blue color. Silently she stood in front of the silver-haired woman and interlaced her fingers into her almost translucent hands. She lifted them to her own dark blue lips and kissed them tenderly. "You found a way."

"I only followed." Varsa lowered her voice along with her eyes. "I only followed the message Shree left embedded within my chamber walls. I ... I don't know how he was able to hide it there, Anusha. And how did it emerge just at the time we needed? My screen, it showed me there was a path, one that would lead us here. It spread out from the floor of my chamber and guided us here, emerging before us as we moved."

Varsa lifted her clouded eyes and spoke earnestly. "I was told your chamber would show us the next step. How can these mines have secrets, Anusha? How could there be anything hidden in them? That is impossible ... *was* impossible." Varsa corrected herself as she looked up to the ceiling of Anusha's chamber. "Shree must have found a way into my matrix from his chamber. But how could he do it? How could he get in—without my signature? Without my permission?" Varsa paused and caught her breath as her mind spun. "And now? He's going to the surface? Oh, Anusha...." Varsa shook her head, her long silver hair gliding like a wave as she let her eyes fall, her long lashes concealing their anguish. "Varsa," Anusha spoke her name softly. Varsa lifted her dark eyes.

"I do not fully understand. It does seem Shree found a way to imbed messages into the mines. I do not know how he has done this cloaking." She hugged her friend tightly, then pulled back and kissed her on both her cheeks, leaving a trail of blue across Varsa's smooth pale skin.

Anusha looked at the group, her blue skin shifting to a deep violet-red as her words draped and fell across them like a velvet breeze. "The mines have clearly changed. Shree seems to have found a way to shroud messages into our system. I think he may have found a way to keep secrets—the one thing that our mines are not supposed to ever be able to do." A light, midrange chime rang quietly in Anusha's ear; she cocked her head sideways as her eyes were drawn into the distant darkened hallway. "I think he may have been able to keep secrets even from me." Anusha paused again, her mind turning, trying to piece it all together. "I suspect...." Anusha felt a wave of flutter down the dark hall and wash across her skin. Her insides danced vividly, shifting her appearance to a pale, golden glow. "Strangely enough, I believe that these secrets are creating circumstances that might be able to reverse this current trajectory of events."

BEAST

The late afternoon sun descended casually through the clear blue sky. Edge turned his truck onto Mave's drive and snuck a look at her out of the corner of his tired eyes. Mave sat silently, staring out the dusty windshield across the fields, her head bobbing gracefully as the truck rambled over the rough gravel. Edge looked past her to Zoe. Even without seeing her face, Edge could tell she was worried; the telltale sign was the light drumming of her long fingers on the door panel. He was worried, too. For five days, they had been looking for Beast.

Edge cleared his throat, breaking the sullen silence. "I know it seems bad here, but I just can't help but feel we haven't seen the last of him. I keep feeling there's something we've overlooked."

"We haven't overlooked anything, Edge. We've checked everywhere." Mave's deflated answer landed with a sense of finality. Shadows fell across the truck as it entered the tunnel of trees lining the lane, casting Mave's face into darkness. They hadn't heard from Ariom. These last five days had stretched on longer than any she could remember. Mave let her weary eyes fall shut. *This can't be it. Where the hell are you, Beast?*

Soft and quiet, rising bit by bit into their awareness, a series of high-pitched chimes rang through the cab of the truck. Edge, Mave, and Zoe looked at each other as Edge slowed the truck down to a crawl. The chimes varied in tone and continued to ring longer than Mave had heard before.

"What *is* that sound?" Edge's throaty voice whispered as he rolled the truck to a complete stop. Edge and Zoe leaned their heads out of their open windows and searched for the sound's source. The chimes rang dreamily all around them.

"You hear it, right?" Zoe looked at each of them, letting out her held breath. Edge and Mave both nodded in agreement.

Mave peered through the dust-covered window at the flowering trees waving their delicate blossoms through the air.

"Hey, Zoe," Mave's words came slowly. "Do you feel any breeze out of that window?" Edge reached his hand out of the window, too, and followed Mave's gaze up to the higher branches.

"No, I don't feel anything." Zoe looked up, following their gazes. Her eyes widened as she noticed the undulating tops of the trees. "Is that possible?" she asked, inspecting the entire line of trees. Both sides of the lane were swaying, as if a substantial breeze were blowing, waving both lines of trees in the direction of Mave's house. But no one felt the slightest bit of air moving around the truck.

Edge's door groaned as he opened it and climbed down, leaving it wide for Mave. The women slid out either side of the truck, each landing with a small, gravelly thud on the hard ground below. They held out their hands in the warm afternoon air, searching for the breeze. Edge picked up a stray leaf, climbed onto his bumper, and lifted his arm as high as he could, bringing his hand even with the lowest of the swaying branches. But when he released the leaf, it came fluttering down to the ground next to the truck, completely unaffected by any wind. The melodic chimes continued to float around them in hushed tones.

Mave glanced down the symmetrically lined road and caught a glimpse of something dark at the end of the lane. "What's that?" She pointed to the last of the trees a few hundred feet down the road.

"All I see is shadows." Edge stopped and faced her, his seasoned face softening. "We could all use some rest, Mavel."

"There! Wait. I see something, too!" Zoe pointed to the left side of the road. "There, something just moved down low in between the trunks of those trees." Edge leaned forward, resting his hands on his thighs as he strained his eyes to see what Zoe and Mave were seeing.

"Ah, there! I see it, too. Shoot, is that a tail?"

Mave and Zoe both shrugged their shoulders, their intent eyes locked on the distant moving form.

"Maybe...." Mave shuffled forward. Three chimes sounded, low and long, and traveled vibrantly up the gravel road to where they stood. Mave straightened up as the notes sang across her skin.

"Yeah, I think it just might be a tail. And I believe I know who it belongs to."

SURFACE

A s Jay's hand landed on the keypad, the entire room went dark, leaving only the milky-white crystals of the floor grimly illuminating them from below. In the corner next to Jay, the men shuffled closer to one another. Other than the sound of their hard-soled boots scraping on the floor, the room was quiet. Resigned and expressionless, Shree pushed himself to his feet and took hold of Ila's hand. In his hand, hers felt small, yet she could barely feel anything else emanating from him. It was as if he had pulled all his energy back inside, and it had disappeared into a mysterious black hole somewhere in the middle of his heart.

Firros pulled Kam to his feet and followed Shree and Ila over to the dark door. Jay held his hand firmly against the keypad, waiting for something to happen. He squeezed his eyes closed, but felt nothing beneath his hand. *Please*, he pursed his lips tightly against his teeth. *Please let them be okay.* Jay felt his aching heart squeeze then expand and heat up. He opened his eyes just in time to see his entire arm, from his chest to his fingertips, emit a soft pale-green light into the wall he was touching. Jay let his hand drop to his side, suddenly exhausted, and turned to face Shree and Ila. *I'm sorry, Ila,* he began, but Ila shook her head and pointed at the wall behind him. Before he turned around, Jay felt a cool breeze float across his warm skin, sending a shiver through his body. He hugged his arms across his chest as the chill moved through him. Slowly he turned around.

In front of him the door had disappeared, and he found himself looking into a clear night sky filled with bright, shimmering stars. Firros stepped through the doorway and into the darkness. Methodically he surveyed their position. He turned back to the group and waved briskly for the rest of them to follow him out onto the dusty path.

"Please," he called to them, encouraging them to follow him out the door. "There is no one out here. It is late. Our second moon rising just to the west."

Jay squinted out the door, unable to see anything but a dark sky. "Where are we?" he asked, his voice steady in spite of his shivering. He squeezed his arms into his body in an attempt to quiet them.

Kam stepped through the open door and studied the horizon. "We are on the east side of Ariom." He turned back toward the light of the room. "This mesa is where I work. We are on one of the fingers of this piece of land. There"—Kam pointed to the eastern sky—"there is our first moon. Both moons are full tonight. This is very rare for them both to be full on the same night." Kam paused and held his chest as a dull ache flashed into his heart, vanishing as quickly as it came. He massaged his arm absently and continued, "Tonight is the night we planned to unveil our new technology."

Jay followed Kam's line of sight. Out across the large mesa, at the rim of the land, stood a large metal structure that looked like a massive telescope. "That's quite a structure," Jay said, gazing warily at the design. "What did you say you were going to do with it?"

"I didn't say," Kam answered more sharply than he meant. He softened his tone. "But it's arranged to gather energy. We intend to pull energy from the orbit of both our moons."

Jay stared at the man as every cell in his body screamed in protest of Kam's words. "Why in the world would you do something like that?" he asked.

The rest of the guards stepped out onto the mesa, their dark shirts and pants blending them neatly into the landscape around them. None of them could find a suitable answer, at least one they were comfortable to speak in front of Shree.

Shree squeezed Ila's hand once then gently slid his fingers from hers. He felt a flicker of life fan deep within his heart, but it didn't make it to his edges. His legs were heavy and slow as they moved across the last steps of the room to the doorway. As if slogging through tar, his legs resisted as he tried to lift his foot to step out of the room. Shree felt the spark of light in his heart again; this time, the light traveled its way back into the rest of his body. He looked at the milky white crystal ground beneath his feet, then out onto the dirt-filled mesa where the men were standing. He felt the pull of the mines into his cells, pleading with him not to exit into this other world. Shree paused and let the crystals under his feet hold him tightly to the ground. Ila watched the ground below Shree's bare feet faintly brighten and begin to fill him—his feet, then his legs, and finally turning the rest of his skin to a rich sepia brown. Shree raised his face to meet Ila, his amber-blue eyes bright once again as the brown seeped into his face.

Ila, Shree's voice called tenderly in Ila's head. *Ila, remember my star, no matter what—understand? No matter what happens, you must remember my star.*

Fear flashed across Ila's heart, and she leapt forward, gripping his large hand in hers. Shree let his full connection with the mines move out through his fingers and into Ila's hand. *Remember how you got here. Remember what was needed—what to let go and what to hold onto.* Ila wiped her free hand roughly across her face as she tried to understand. *What does...?* Suddenly Ila was blinded by light, her entire surroundings consumed with a brightness she had never before experienced. She pressed her eyes together, squeezing her whole face, feeling as if the light were pulling at the very fabric of her cells, threatening to pull her apart.

Breathe, Ila. Shree's voice was smooth and ethereal in her head. She felt as if her feet were no longer touching the hard floor, as if she were floating on air, completely supported and lifted by the light. Directly in the middle of her forehead, she felt a warm pulsation that abruptly cooled then spread down her spine and into her arms and legs. Through closed eyes, Ila felt the solid ground below her feet once more. The bright light shrunk, drawing back into a single pulse behind her eyes. Her head began to throb. *Let it go, Ila. Don't try to hold onto it.*

Ila felt hot tears pool behind her eyes as she watched the light shrink, then disappear completely. Confused and shaken, she let her eyes stay closed while she wrestled with her senses. *Shree ... I don't understand.*

Shree squeezed her hand one more time, then, just as before, untangled his fingers from hers, gently letting her hand fall back to her side. Ila tried to open her eyes, but they were heavy and slow to respond. *Shree, please, wait....*

Ila, it's okay. I promise. It is all going to be okay.

Ila peeled her eyelids apart just in time to watch Shree step, almost effortlessly this time, across the threshold.

Ila squeezed her hands into fists then followed, stepping quickly through the doorway before she could change her mind. Immediately, the wooden door whooshed shut. Ila spun around and threw her hands against the smooth, sealed surface. There was no hint of light or carvings anywhere. She searched fervently, running her hands all around the door and wall for any way back into the mines. Beneath her hands, nothing appeared. It was a smooth, plain wooden door. And they were on the wrong side.

Jay took Ila by the hand, squeezing her moist palm into his, and pulled her away from the door. *It's okay, Ila.* Ila shook her head from side to side.

Shree crossed the short distance between himself and the men."I'll tell you why they are readying their machine. They are searching for other ways to harness energy." Shree looked directly at Kam, his eight-foot height strangely appearing much larger out of the doors. "Because they knew, just like we did, that the mines were shifting." Shree took a tentative step forward, unsure how the atmosphere would respond to his body. Without effort, his skin stayed deep brown, and he felt a strange distance from the environment around him. Shree smiled to himself, glad the mines had been able to predict how his biology would be affected once he reached the surface. "Nothing would please them more than seeing the mines destroyed. This is correct, isn't it, Kam?" Shree's voice sounded sharp in the clear night air. He took a step toward the man in dark clothes.

Firros shook his head. "No. No, that isn't correct, that isn't correct at all. Tell him, Kam. Our energy supplies, they were overloaded." Firros's anxious voice rose as he hurriedly tried to explain and help Shree understand. "The systems, our systems, they've been irregular. We are only looking to supplement, because it was felt the surface was taxing the mines too much. It had become clear that we were a burden to the current system, that we were burdening you and your people." Firros looked at each of the guards, but their faces were unreadable in the darkness. "Kam? Isn't that right?" Firros's voice was almost frantic. "Kam. Tell them!"

Kam's voice was low in the quiet night. "No, he's right, Firros. Our orders were to unbalance the system." Kam studied Shree bathed in the light of two moons, his eyes seeing the man before him as if for the first time. "I'm sorry"—he shook his head, trying to clear it, as if waking himself from a deep dream—"our orders were to untangle Ariom from the energy of the mines. And the beginning of that was our order to extract you and let the system, the mines, crumble from within." Kam hung his head, ashamed of the truth as he confessed aloud.

Firros's heart sank. "No, we wouldn't—"

"Unfortunately, they would." Shree's voice was strong and sure across the space between them. "Men commit all sorts of transgressions when they're afraid. But *you* did not succeed. *You* did not extract me from the mines as *he* commanded." Shree stifled the lightness that tugged from within him, keeping his face still and unreadable. "No, you did not complete your mission at all." Shree turned to Jay and let a small smile erupt across his lips, unseen by anyone in the darkness. "It was not you who brought me here. It was Jay who showed me the way to *this* spot ... on the surface."

SURFACE II

E ve felt warmth under her feet even before Anusha's chamber floor shifted from its tangerine glow. The flat screen next to them went dark and silent. Eve felt the room fill with agitated, jittery energy, and begin to glow a milky, light green color. Below her feet the ground rumbled and rolled, then heaved side to side in one quick and powerful shake. Eve wobbled, almost losing her balance completely. Ellen grabbed her arm and steadied her on her feet. Adrenaline shot through her body, tingling to the far edges of her fingertips. She waited a moment for the sensations to subside then spoke quietly, "What the hell was that?"

Ellen looked closely at Eve. "What was what?"

Eve surveyed the half circle of beings surrounding her, each of them watching her curiously.

"Didn't you feel that? That shaking? The ground, it just...." Eve raised her eyebrows and looked at each of their inquisitive faces. She turned to Ellen. "You didn't feel the ground shake just now?"

Ellen shook her head.

Shit. Eve inhaled loud and deep through her nose, clenching her jaw and her teeth tightly together, then forced air out in a long, low growl. *I am not losing it on this one, damn it,* she commanded herself through her gritted teeth. Her eyes narrowed, fierce and determined, and stared at the light-orange point in the middle of the wooden door. Eve leaned forward as the glow shifted before her eyes, methodically reversing the circle and spiraling back outwardly. Eve steeled her body, willing it steady and calm. It responded immediately, aligning and agreeing with her determined mind. Without a look, gesture, or sign from anyone, Eve knew undoubtedly she was meant to move to the door.

Thank you, Eve. Anusha's voice was sweet and melodious in Eve's head, sounding exactly like it did in their first conversation when the door had first appeared in her room. That night seemed very far away. Eve's mouth pulled up at the corners, and she nodded imperceptibly, keeping her eyes focused on the door, afraid that at any moment, she might lose her newfound confidence.

The spiral grew and filled the door. Perpendicular lines emerged and spread out in all directions from the outermost circle, like rays of the sun. These lines then all turned right and joined together, drawing a border around the perimeter of the door. All the lines of the design, from the center to the edges, turned and glowed the same milky light green as the floor below their feet.

Eve firmly placed her hand on the door. The sturdy wood felt cool and inviting, melding gently and immediately with her hand. An image of Jay appeared in her mind with his dimpled smile, wearing a shirt just like Isaac's. Then he was gone. Under her hand, she felt energy flowing, soothing her down to her cells. All at once, the door went dark— its glowing lines disappearing completely. Eve's heart skipped a beat, but still she kept her breath steady and under control. The wooden door lost its inviting draw as the smooth grains gradually released their pull on her. She was left with a quiet void. Eve kept her hand planted securely, but inside she was quaking, unsure of her bold instincts. The room was silent and still. Dim white light emanated from the ground below as the Others stood and watched with reserved discipline.

Suddenly, the dark door under her hand softened and began to literally pull her in. Eve watched a small circle appear around her hand, becoming more and more solid, forming itself into a wide metal ring. Eve gasped audibly as the cool metal bumped into her wrist. Eve's heartbeat was even and measured, as if the door had reached directly into her nervous system and flipped a switch. As she pulled her hand out of the solid circle, she traced the cool metal ring in a featherlight circle that sent shivers cascading down her spine. The world around her settled into full silence, causing her to wonder if she had transported herself somewhere else. With a relaxed ease,

Eve dropped her hand, and it floated unnaturally to her side. Instantly, the door slid open.

A burst of dry air blew in, desperate for moisture. Eve gasped as the air hit her lungs. She inhaled quickly, then without thinking, she stepped one foot across the doorway of the chamber—standing half in, half out of the room. She stared out into the cloudless night. Blurred yellow lights flickered and waved in the far distance. Above her head, stars filled the jet-black sky, sparkling silently far above their heads. A bright full moon descended in the east. The sheer enormity of the sweeping view made Eve want to crouch down and slink back into the comfort of the warm, familiar room. She stayed put and held her ground. She knew if she moved from the doorway, it would disappear completely. Ellen and Isaac joined her. Ellen turned, her face ghostly in the light of the silver moon, and stared back, disbelieving, into the warmth of the cozy room.

Ellen pushed her hair out of her face with a trembling hand. She held it there, visibly shaking as she grasped a lock of her own hair in an attempt to quell her rising panic and steady her trembling hand. The warm breeze picked up, as if challenging her attempt at order. With wide eyes, she cleared her throat and spoke into the watchful room. "We are on the surface."

BEAST

E dge hurried back to the truck, with Mave and Zoe following closely on his heels. They heaved themselves onto the worn seat, and Edge sped the truck down the rest of the lane as fast as he could without churning the gravel below his tires. He eased in next to the dark trees, and the three of them scanned the area for any trace of Beast. In between the dark trunks of the trees, they found nothing but shadows.

Zoe scanned the pasture and caught a glimpse of a large, slow-moving object just past the last of the grazing horses.

Beast? The thought in her head was followed immediately by the word *Jantu.* "Jantu?" she repeated aloud, shielding her eyes and squinting into the fading afternoon light. The form stopped moving. "Jan-tu," Zoe annunciated each syllable, as if the sound of the word had as much meaning as the word itself. Edge and Mave followed her gaze out into the field. "Beast," she breathed his name out like a sigh, as the large animal let himself be fully seen.

Edge and Mave stared at the dark form as Zoe's words echoed in their ears.

"There you are, mister," Zoe said as the animal slowly spun to face them. As the three of them watched, his dark form began to fade, moving from solid to transparent, then finally disappeared right before their eyes.

"Jantu," Edge repeated, keeping his eyes on the edge of the field. "Where the hell did you go?"

"Come on," Mave said calmly, "pull up to the barn, Edge. I think I know exactly where he's going."

NIGHT

E llen stepped outside into the night, the ground below her feet dense, hard, and distant. The flickering city lights waved from far away, and she thought she caught a whiff of smoke in the dry night air. In the pale moonlight, she crossed the small plateau until she was a silhouette on the edge of the high cliff. She looked back at the metallic, windowless building from which she had emerged. It was almost as wide as the mesa it sat upon. Ellen peered down over the edge of the cliff into the darkness. It was a sheer drop. Ellen glanced silently up at the sky, wondering what they should do now. *Mave? You there?* Out of habit, Ellen interlaced her hands in front of her while she patiently waited for an answer. Nothing came.

Isaac shuffled aimlessly around the small ledge, while Eve stood in the doorway, waiting for Ellen to return.

"What do you think?" Isaac's grave voice cut across the rustling wind, too impatient to wait for her to cross the last few steps.

Ellen stood beside the open door, unsure exactly what to do. Her job was to keep Anusha safe. Now she and Isaac were suddenly responsible for thirty-two of the thirty-three Others as well. Where were their attendants? What would happen if they left the mine? And their stars, their connections—what will happen with that? And what about the mines themselves? Ellen leaned her face against the cool metal on the side of the building and stared out at the blinking lights. The cold felt good against her skin. This was all going terribly off track. And Ila and Jay, she had no idea where they were. Her heart sank, feeling weighed down by all of it.

Ellen felt a broad hand land gently on her shoulder. "Give me a moment, Isaac, will you please?"

"It's me, Ellen," Anusha's voice was tentative as she contended with her brand new surroundings. She felt uncomfortably empty, the trodden ground below her feet quiet and hollow. Eve took Anusha's hand in hers and wrapped it in between her own.

"Anusha, Ellen, I think they're here." Eve's assured voice surprised even herself. She squeezed Anusha's cold hand in hers and felt the warmth from her hands flowing into Anusha, just as she had done with Vince back at the Roadhouse.

"Someone needs to stay here with the Others. We cannot abandon the mine entirely, right?" Eve nodded to the group standing eerily still behind Anusha, squeezing her hand for emphasis.

"I do not know what will happen." Anusha looked at the gathering. She had to fight the urge to run back and find her place beside them in the safe, familiar comfort. But it was no more safe in the mines than it was out here. Out here, at least, they had a chance to change things. Inside, she had felt it, the possibilities were quickly diminishing.

"Jay and Ila … and Shree—I feel them; they're close to here." Eve lifted her chest and chin high. Her eyes slid closed momentarily, and her young face shone in the soft light of the moon. "You have to go this way"—she nodded her head to the left of the building—"around the edge of the building. That way. You'll find them there, on the other side of this building. I'm sure of it."

Eve glanced back into the mine, her long brown hair falling haphazard across one of her eyes. She shook it impatiently out of her face, still holding tightly to Anusha's hand. Anusha's voice whispered in her head. *I do not know what will happen in the mines, Eve. How can I leave them? I can't help up here and in there.* Anusha was torn between two worlds. Her eyebrows shaped into a sharp V as she tried to feel the most balanced way forward. The world around her seemed quiet and vacant.

"I will stay with them." Eve's whispered words were not a question. She squeezed Anusha once more, then dropped her hand and turned away before she could change her mind.

CURRENTS

S hree ran his brown hands across his eyes then briskly down the front of his tunic. He looked at his hands, realizing that they hadn't changed once since he stepped onto the surface. It had been easier than he imagined. He peered across the distance to the metal, telescope-like structure pointed to the east. He knew he needed to get closer.

Jay moved to one side of Shree, and Ila scurried to his other side. Shree looked from one to the other, his heart swelling with pride at their accomplished escape. He beamed down at each of them. *We have to get over there.* Shree's deep voice was light in their heads. Ila and Jay followed his eyes to the machine glistening in the light of the moon.

Ila furrowed her brow. *I think you should stay as far away from that thing as possible, Shree.* Ila shot a look at Jay. He stayed silent, carefully surveying their spot on the high plateau.

Across the wide-open space, the silent machine suddenly whirred to life. Ila's heart thudded in her chest. *Shree ... Jay, we shouldn't be here. I feel it.* Her voice rose louder in their heads. *That thing is dangerous—especially for you, Shree.* Jay studied the machine as if he could see inside it. Its hum grew louder in the quiet night. Kam, Firros, and the other guards gathered around them.

"It's beginning," Kam said quietly.

Shree nodded. "It is just a magnet, you know, this machine of yours."

"Yes, of course." Firros wrinkled his forehead. "We are using the charge, just as we do from the mines...." Firros studied Shree intently, sure he was giving him some kind of message, only Firros didn't understand.

Jay walked slowly toward the machine. *Do you think they can hear me?* He spoke directly to Ila and Shree. Ila glanced at the men. They seemed unaffected as they watched Jay casually shortening the distance between himself and the magnet.

No, I don't think so. Why?

Because, Ila, start walking this way, too. We need to each be the poles of the magnet, to keep it balanced. Jay nodded toward the metal shining and humming in the moonlight.

Ila skipped forward and hurried next to Jay. *What are you doing?*

I'm not entirely sure, but remember those crystals in the tunnel? How they shifted and changed their shape? I think Shree has an idea of how to shift this energy here on the surface. Jay nodded toward the large structure. Ila glanced up at the smooth side of the building, sure someone would see them walking. *There's no one around, Ila. They think it's too unsafe. I can feel it.* Ila's chest tightened, feeling Jay's agitation. *They're all hiding on the middle level. They're too cowardly to stay on the surface to see what they do to their own people. Ila, if this works, and they pull on that moon, it will be destroyed. You can't pull on a moon's orbit without having catastrophic consequences. They think they can "tap into" that flow of energy, but they will shift it the moment they come in contact. I don't know how they don't know that.*

They do know that. Shree's words stopped them both in their tracks.

Who? Ila looked at the ground beneath her dirty shoes, pretending they were not having this conversation.

He does, Shree responded, nudging Ila's gaze up to a small, almost invisible circular window high up on the side of the building. It faced directly over the large machine. Ila and Jay darted to the side of the building.

What if he saw us? Ila glared in Shree's direction, the pulsing adrenaline momentarily blocking out all sound. As the whoosh in her head quieted, she cut into Shree. *Damn it, Shree, why didn't you tell us someone was there?*

Jay looked up at the high window then back to Shree. All the guards backed away without a sound and stood by the open doorway.

Shree stood alone in the open, his imposing figure only an outline in the moonlight. *Trust me, Ila. This is very simple mechanics. You will be fine. He does not see you. He is too concerned with his precious machine. He thinks he can use the charge of the mines to reverse any damage he creates. He believes he has this all under control. I have been receiving this information in the mine for a long time. I know his plan completely. Just because he created part of the system doesn't mean he owns the system and can do with it as he pleases.*

Ila felt the heat and anger brewing in Shree. Jay did, too. It made them both nervous.

ABOVE

S hree stood in the pale light of the rising second moon with his back to the open doorway. Out of the corner of his eye, he noticed the first moon was beginning to creep around the east side of the building in its continued descent across the star-filled sky. The light of both moons reflected off the shiny metal building, causing the half-circled courtyard to be unusually bright for this time of night.

The machine hummed a short distance away. It whirred faster and faster, sending long, deep vibrations across the plateau. Shree felt his insides jumble and tighten against the invisible assult. He realized his body was keeping a barrier between his outer and inner worlds. The vibrating energy bounced off his brown skin. *It must be this anger, this irritation that is keeping it out. Good,* Shree thought defiantly.

Shree! Ila's voice cut into Shree, surprising him. *What do we do now?* Ila silently noted Shree's reaction. The vibrations coming from the machine were shaking her entire body. Her teeth chattered uncontrollably inside her closed mouth. She did not want to be here. She did not want any of them to be here. This machine was strong. She felt it pulling at her insides, pulling on her cells. It was the same as when Shree held onto her hand earlier. She didn't know how long or how much more of this she could take.

Ila, you move to the far side of the generator. Jay you stay on this side. That's it, on either end of that wall.

Ila's hair drifted up and out, lifting sideways as she scooted past the machine. Impatiently, she brushed her floating hair back down, but it was no use. It rose again and again. Jay pressed his hands together, cracking his knuckles nervously. *Shree, this doesn't feel right.* Jay shifted his weight from one foot to the other, his clothes pulling toward the now rapidly spinning machine. From the outside, the machine looked calm, but both Ila and Jay could feel the energy it was generating. But what was Shree going to do?

"Jay," Ila whispered sharply in his direction, trying to get his attention. The surface was affecting Shree, and Ila was scared. Whatever the plan was, Shree obviously had thought a lot about this, but Ila wasn't sure how things were changing as his irritation rose.

"Jay!" she whispered louder as she threw a small pebble in his direction. It bounced against Jay's bare leg. He whipped around, clearly anxious. Ila held her finger up to her lips, her curly hair rising all around her face. Jay stifled a laugh. *Really?* Ila shot at him accusingly. Jay held his hands up, silently asking her forgiveness.

The machine whirred faster, then suddenly pierced the night air with a high-pitched squeal. Jay and Ila threw their hands to their ears and instinctively fell down low. Ila pressed firmly against her head, but it was no use, the deafening noise screamed in her ears. Ila felt as if her insides were heating up, threatening to explode. The sound, combined with the pull on her body, was too much. She tucked herself into a tight ball, unable to move. Through tiny slits, she saw Jay's mouth moving, calling for her, but she couldn't answer.

All at once, the piercing stopped, and the machine hummed higher and faster, until the gathering energy shot a single white beam from the tip of the machine's long scope into the eastern sky. Ila clenched her jaw as the beam increased the pull on everything around it, including her. It was vacuuming everything in proximity toward itself. Rocks and brush swept past Ila, bouncing and flying across the short distance between her and the machine—each landing with a solid thud on the shiny metal base. Ila felt herself being pulled, too, caught in the force that was slowly dragging her in. She dug her shoes into the dirt, clawing and bracing herself against the ruthless pull. Her thick hair covered her eyes, blinding her as she slowly slid across the dusty ground.

Ila! Jay threw himself toward her, but the force that pulled Ila forward repelled him backward. He tried to move toward her, but the force stopped him, as if he were bumping up against an invisible field.

Shree! Jay pleaded, *Help her!*

Shree turned and saw Ila being dragged across the ground. Instantly, his mind cleared as he realized Ila's body could not handle the pull of the machine. He widened his feet on the shadowed ground and focused all of his attention on the machine, feeling and linking himself to the colossal force of the beam. Shree stumbled on the hard dirt as the machine latched onto him and heaved him forward. Shree searched down through the hard clay, reaching for the familiar light-green comfort of his chamber. He caught a glimmer of the line of milky-green light pulsing deep in the mine and he let it draw him in. Instantly, he felt the tangled shield inside him melt away. The connection under his feet strengthened, and a surge of energy entered his body, rocking him backwards, pulling him from far below.

Hold on, Ila!

Ila heard Shree's voice faint in her head, the roar of the machine was pulling so strongly on the insides of her mind.

Shree, I can't! I feel like I'm being pulled apart....

Don't let go! Ila, focus into the mines, remember them, the star—find your way down—find the current! Shree steeled his body against the rising force from the machine drawing him closer, straining and dragging it backward with every ounce of his being. *Don't. Let. Go!...*

The familiar green crystals miles below secured Shree's energy further into the mines, grounding and tethering him, as if he were actually standing with his feet embedded up to his ankles in their solid mass. The magnetic beam from the machine pulled relentlessly, but it was no match to the clear and familiar link from below that lit him like a radiant, glowing sun. His consciousness found its way to his own chamber, and Shree's confidence grew. He doubled his efforts. He threw his awareness back to the machine, grabbing onto the streamlined bolt of energy still flying toward the setting east moon. In one great effort, he heaved it back toward him. Instantly, a thread of the beam broke off and ricocheted dangerously close to Jay's head as it flashed across the courtyard. It embedded itself like razor sharp teeth into Shree's flesh. His entire body recoiled as he flew backward, reeled from the sweltering impact. Teeth clenched, his face contorted until it was almost unrecognizable, Shree wrestled furiously with the wild thread no longer part of the larger beam and finally hooked it firmly into the energy of the mine. The thin beam of white hot heat immediately siphoned down into the tunnel walls, adding its forceful torrent into the landscape of the mines.

Ila's skin settled onto her body as the machine's deadly magnetism lessened. Digging her heels frantically into the packed dirt, she willed her cells to reach down and find the riverlike force of energy she knew was present in the mines. The pull of the generator was still too strong. She couldn't find a path into the flow, and she could not free herself from the clutches of the determined machine.

Help me! Ila's panicked cry pleaded through both Jay and Shree's minds.

Shree continued to reel in more and more, pulling one thread of energy at a time from the beam into his own body. The more he pulled, the more Ila's body became free, until finally she was able to shuffle backward and scurry as far away from the machine as she could, finally thudding hard into the metal building behind her. Ila leaned into the cool surface, afraid to move in any direction.

Firros, Kam, and the guards stared, frozen, watching the terrifying scene in front of them. Firros had no idea what to do. He feared that any movement would distract Shree and quite possibly overload the delicate balance he seemed to be straddling, sending them all careening into destruction. He could feel the tenuous balance Shree was struggling to hold. How? He did not know.

Kam placed a light hand on his shoulder. Firros jumped. All five men held their breath as Shree's body wavered, the ripple in Firros's energy felt instantly across the space between them. Kam moved a trembling finger ever so slowly into Firros's line of sight. Firros, with only his eyes, followed it up to the high window on the metallic building. Inside, a shadow stood, watching the scene unfold from above.

BELOW

Deep inside the mines, Ila's scream crashed into Eve, as if she were standing next to her, leaving her blood chilled and her hair standing on end.

"Did you hear that?!" Eve hollered to her companions over the rising chaos in her head. "Listen!"

Varsa's golden hands shifted to light blue as she planted them firmly on Anusha's dark screen, calling it to life. Lines and shapes flashed colorfully around the screen, telling an imageless story that only the Others could discern. Varsa's hands flew from one pulsing shape to another, reading and listening to the strange communication.

"There!" she claimed triumphantly. "I've got her. She's outside of the mines." Her brow furrowed, creasing her entire forehead as she concentrated, "But the mines, they're gathering energy—it's foreign, this force that's coming in; it's from outside." Varsa's voice was urgent as she widened her stance, her hands flying over the entire surface of the screen. "The mines—the balance is off. Shree and Anusha hold the poles, the opposite ends. They create space for the energy to flow optimally. This new energy, it's crossing our lines down here, and we don't have them to stabilize and balance this current. It's changing and confusing the established flow." The Others instinctively began putting their hands on the wall, one by one, spreading out around the room and tapping into the mines directly. "This is too much." Varsa shook her head, her straight hair waving out around her face. Our system can't handle this much additional voltage. We're overloading. We've got to find a way to smooth out this flow! We've got to harmonize it or it will override the entire system!"

"Here, I found it!" Varsa had full command of the room. "The source. Above us, here, above us—on the east side." Heads nodded as the Others tapped in and found the powerful link leading them to the voltage beaming far above them.

Suddenly, Varsa felt Shree. The force knocked her off balance, and she fought to keep her feet planted on the darkening floor. "I've got Shree! He's there." Her furrowed brow rose then contorted again as she tried to interpret his location. The thin, light hair on her arms began to rise as she felt how much energy he was siphoning through himself and into the mine. "He won't be able to hold all of this. It's too much—it needs to be balanced!"

Varsa's body straightened as she sent the new line of energy into a smooth current already flowing in the mine. "He's out of the mine, like Ila. They're above." Varsa felt a light wind cool her brow. She paused for a split second as an image gathered in her mind. "The surface." Her voice was just above a whisper. "He's on the surface." Eve felt a wave of energy ripple across her skin. "It's pulling her, too." Varsa's voice rose as she steadied herself against another wave of foreign energy. "It's too much! Someone, find her—quickly!—and tether her to the mine as well. We need to dissipate this intensity—it's pulling them apart! There's a charge...." Varsa felt the unusual mix of energy coming from this artificial source. Her eyes flashed as an unknown sensation twisted and turned inside her. Her voice was quiet and disbelieving. "Someone has designed this charge very deliberately. The only thing a charge like this could be for is pulling things apart." Varsa brought her fingers to her lips, rubbing them absently as she began to understand. The knot in her chest began to soften. "It has to be harmonized. There is no other way. If we don't succeed, this will certainly be the end of the mines. We must find a way!!"

Eve felt helpless. She searched frantically around the room; her heart pounded irregularly, but her feet stayed solidly on the ground. All at once, she felt a deep red energy rising from beneath her feet, momentarily blocking out the room as its force merged with her body. She felt as if she were being pulled down through the ground below. The energy felt like cool, clear water. She fought to keep her mind in the room with the Others. Suddenly, space opened up around her, and she felt herself fading into it.

Varsa! Eve's voice was barely a gasp in Varsa's ear. Everyone in the room whipped their heads around to Eve. She was barely there. *Eve!*

The Others locked onto the deep red stream rising around Eve and widened it, pulling the entire stream of energy toward them little-by-little, linking this deep red space solidly into the room in which they were standing. It was as if they were anchoring a ship to harbor. Eve felt herself becoming more solid. She leaned her back into the warm wall, spent. The room they were in felt suddenly wider and bigger, like an invisible second chamber had just merged with their solid room.

Pull the energy from Shree and connect it here, into this space Eve created! We can work with it from there! Varsa's command shifted the room's attention immediately to the surface. The group of Others listened far into the walls, each finding their own way to connect to the energy above and draw it deep into the ground.

ANUSHA

A nusha felt the hard ground below her feet waver for a split second as a strong, invisible gust rippled across the three of them. She grabbed Ellen's shoulder, stopping her in her tracks. The tangled brush below their feet crackled as Isaac continued forward. *Isaac.* Anusha's voice was a sharp whisper. Isaac halted and swung around. The three of them heard and felt a low hum vibrating through the still air. Anusha searched the perimeter and saw nothing but the dry brush flanking the building, reaching all the way to the cliff's edge about a hundred feet away. The second moon of Ariom rising in the western sky bathed them and the faraway city in its silvery light.

Wait. Anusha felt something else ripple through her, drawing on the cells of her heart, its familiar pull bringing a small smile to her brown face. *It's him! Shree. He's close.* The hum grew louder, filling the air around them. Anusha's hands trembled as she felt the vibration reverberate through her, pulling firmly on her cells. She squeezed her large hands into fists. *Something's wrong. Something's pulling.* Anusha's eyes narrowed as the hum erupted into sound, shrieking loudly into the dark night. The three of them ducked, adrenaline instantly pumping through their bodies, preparing them to move. *This way,* Anusha commanded. Ellen shot a furtive glance at Isaac, then followed Anusha's large frame to the corner of the building. Isaac squeezed one of his jittery hands into the other, and quietly cracked his knuckles as he followed the two women.

At the corner of the building, a strong blast blew her long hair almost horizontally. *It's Shree.* Anusha leaned back into the metallic building, feeling into it with her palms, searching both the air and the structure for information. *There are more.* Ellen and Isaac waited, unaware they were holding their breath. *Ila ...* Anusha murmured. *I feel Ila.* Ellen's hands flew to her mouth as she exhaled audibly. *And Jay,* Anusha added, nodding. Her bare feet glowed ever so slightly, and Ellen realized she had found a way to hook into the mines even from this distance.

I'm going around. You stay here. It's not safe. Anusha's voice had turned harsh and cold.

Anusha, let us help you. Isaac's voice smoothed itself across their minds; it was light and kind, coaxing Anusha back from the sharpness she was emanating. Anusha paused as Isaac's gentle energy settled around her, and realized for the first time how uncomfortable she felt on the inside. She softened her skin, and her light blue eyes brightened visibly even in the low light. The menacing pull of the machine instantly yanked Anusha forward.

Anusha! Ellen grabbed hold of her arm. In a split second, Anusha snapped her head clear as if she were shaking off the invisible irritation, then steeled herself from the inside out, as if she were donning armor. *I have to go. Now! He is in danger. They all are. This energy, I have never felt anything like this before. I do not know what will happen.* Anusha's shook her head again, this time more gently. *Please, if you come, please be careful,* she pleaded. She met both of their eyes one brief last time.

Anusha turned, inhaled deeply, and braced her fists at her side. In one quick movement, she slipped around the corner and out of sight.

TOGETHER

E ve felt Ila through the wall, as if they were sitting back to back. Ila's torment decended from above and filled Eve, oscillating in her from head to toe, as if she, too was in front of the machine.

Varsa, Eve whispered, afraid to lose the connection with Ila. *What do I do?* Eve blinked her eyes hastily to clear the wetness gathering behind them. She wasn't sure if it was relief or fear, but she had no time for either of them. She placed both palms against the wall to steady herself.

Varsa surveyed the Others stationed equal distances around the room. All eyes were on her now, their unanimously elected leader, looking for instruction. Varsa paused, momentarily at a loss of what to do. Deep red filled the entire floor and seeped up across the walls. Varsa turned to Eve, her long silver hair beginning to tangle around her damp, alabaster face. *I ... I'm not sure.* Varsa's heart fluttered uncontrollably in her chest. She knew that time was paramount, but it was as if her mind went blank. She searched Eve's bright green eyes.

It's okay, Varsa. Eve's eyes moistened, stinging her nose as they gathered. She let the thin drops fall. *It's okay.* Eve pressed her pale lips together and gently bit into her lower lip. She nodded to herself, tears weeping off her chin as she choked back their full force. She pushed on the wall and inhaled. Her eyes lifted with her rising chest and landed on the thick, glowing ceiling.

Ila ... Eve sent a call gently through the walls, from her heart to Ila's.

From out of nowhere, images of Ila and Jay in Anusha's chamber appeared as clearly as if they were in front of her. The scene was from earlier. She could feel her own agaitation from back then, coupled on top of her current state. As if it were happening now, she heard the words Ila expressed to Jay earlier *"Their worlds here, they're separate, right? The mines down here, the middle, the surface. Even though Anusha spoke about being mixed, they don't have the biological merging that we do. Their world is already shifting. The energy is moving, but it's not blending. They need our ... matrix, our blueprint. The system needs our biology to see how it's done. Understand? Shree, he set this up, you see?"* Eve had been too upset to hear them before.

All at once Eve understood. She squeezed the last bits of the wetness from her eyes and sniffed loudly as her mind played one word over and over in her head—*blending*. The Others heard it, too. Eve gave one great shake from head to toe, then more words filled her head; they were simply there. She had no idea where they came from. She relayed them to the rest of her companions, speaking directly into their minds. *We cannot keep this energy separate. It needs to be blended and diffused—mixed together to create something new—not just flowed side-by-side in harmony. If we don't, it will pull everything apart. We need to blend our own energy together to show the system how to do it.*

Varsa's brow creased into tight lines as she shook her head. *This is directly against the code of the mines. The energies are to stay separate. This is the only way to balance them. Each of the Others are trained to harmonize with their matching line of energy, the one most compatible to their own signature matrix, and flow it in the same direction as all the rest.* Varsa's penetrating eyes stayed fixed on Eve.

Eve felt Varsa's struggle. Her heart ached for her. *Varsa, things are changing. These mines, they're shifting. The mine won't be able to hold this new energy. It can't be streamed with yours—it's too different. It needs to be infused together and turned into something else. All of it. Shree has thought of this, I promise.* Eve didn't know how she knew that, but as the words left her mind, she was certain it was true. *We have to combine our energy here in this room.* Varsa lifted her hand to her temple, then rubbed her palm gently back and forth across her forhead. She shot a nervous glance around the room. The Others looked from Eve to Varsa, one after another nodding, until the entire room was in full agreement.

Varsa smiled weakly at Eve. *Okay, then, together. On three. We soften our edges and merge our energy—agreed? And we need a more direct route to bring the energy through.*

Eve nodded and returned her smile warmly.

One ... two ... three!

As soon as the words left her mind, each of them pooled their signature stream of energy and focused it into the center of Anusha's deep red chamber, mixing and merging their individual currents into one vibrant ball of bright white light.

ABOVE and BELOW

A gainst her back, the cool building warmed, drawing Ila's attention away from the chaotic events in front of her eyes. Beneath her, she felt the ground surge, then softly and solidly weave its way into her biology. Ila shook her touseled stray hairs out of her eyes and looked down. Beneath her feet the ground glowed faintly, warming as much as the beam firing its way across the dark sky.

A sob escaped her lips. Ila's face contorted as she saw Jay lying face down on the ground. He was surrounded by jagged streams of light shooting over him, each landing sharply in Shree's body. They kept coming, like ragged bolts of lightning, one after the other. Ila knew he couldn't hold much more. And she knew, no matter what, he would keep trying.

Ila! I'm here. Eve's voice broke into the hopeless scene. *We're here. We're ready. We can help. The Others, they will blend the energy into the mines and shift it completely ... you know, blending it with theirs. Can you open the door? We need to have a more direct route.*

There is no door!

There is. Beside you. Varsa can see it on the screen down here. It's just not visible to you. It's there. Ila, you have to find the keypad.

Ila glanced up at the smooth wall. Sparks flashed in the reflective metal. She saw no trace of door; nothing but smooth, shiny wall. Ila's voice rose, desperate, verging on frantic. *There's no keypad, Eve, help us! Shree—he can't hold this energy much longer!*

Down below, the energy continued to mix and build in the center of the room. The screen under Varsa's hands flashed light blue, dancing spastically around the board. *Anusha!* Eve and Varsa both recognized the signature and called her name simultaneously.

She's not here! Ila screamed desperately in her head. Another beam shot off the machine in front of her and hit Shree in the shoulder, reeling him backward. A scream wailed out of her before she clamped both her hands over her mouth. A wave of scorching heat blasted out across her as the machine wobbled critically on top of its metal dome. *Eve! Help us!*

Ila's panic throbbed through the wall, warming the room of the mine dangerously fast. The Others stood exceptionally still and focused holding the threatening energy in balance. This new blend of energy was unfamiliar. It had more space to it, which made it unpredictable. They focused their attention wider, holding all the vibrations they could find in their awareness.

A pale green flash shot into the pulsing blue light on the screen down below. The intense green light shocked Varsa like a jolt of electricity. She shook her silver hair out of her face, inhaled deeply, and sent a stream of her own into the walls. It took all her strength and focus to keep her hands on the screen and flow calm steadiness into the system. Chaotic energy from above came twisting and barreling into the mine system. Varsa widened her range of connection and listened beneath the chaos. *Ila, she's coming! Hold on!*

Ila felt the ground beneath her shudder. Another sob escaped her quivering lips as she smashed herself harder against the solid wall.

Jay caught Ila's eyes and held them tight. *Ila, I hear them. You hear them?*

Ila nodded anxiously, her eyes as wild as her hair recklessly circling her face. Jay whirled back to Shree. Behind the guards, pressed against the wall, a towering form slipped stealthily around the corner. Jay's heart skipped a beat. *Ila!* His own voice caught. *There! Behind the guards.*

Ila kept her head plastered against the wall, her breath pulling in sharply. *Eve—She's here, we see her! Anusha!*

Behind Anusha, Ellen and Isaac crept around the corner.

Shree's body glowed, dissolving the edges of his being into a widening, white hot circle of sizzling light. It grew larger and larger as more and more beams sparked off the machine and sunk into him like arrows.

Shree felt Anusha, her familiar and comforting lightness penetrating his icy hot body. He turned to her. A stray beam followed Shree's attention and shot toward Anusha. He caught it midstream and growled aloud as he dragged it back toward him. With one final yank, he reversed the rogue stream, rocketing it back in his direction. It hit his body so hard he flipped through the air and landed with a bone-chilling thud on the dirt. Bright sparks exploded in all directions, sizzling and burning a wide circle around him as he lost hold of some of the stream.

Shree struggled to his hands and knees.

Shree. Anusha closed her eyes and tried to link in and draw some of the force from Shree. "NO!" Shree's howl filled the night air as he energetically pushed her away hard. More white hot sparks showered out into the courtyard, flying off the metallic building and raining down around them, sizzling all the way to the ground.

Eve scanned the faces in the cavernous mine as the growing ball of blending energy below lurched and shook in response to the scene above ground. "We've got to do something. Now! Ila can't find the opening! We need to help him!"

Varsa closed her eyes for a brief moment, her hands still firmly on the smooth screen. Eve felt the temperature cool around them. Varsa opened her eyes and stared beyond Eve's shoulder. "There's always a keypad when one is needed. Eve, I understand now. We have to work together. You three have to be connected and activate the pads—Anusha, Ila, and you—all at the same time. You have to activate this door. That is what the screen has been communicating with the green flash. It is you—it cannot be one of us. It has to be another type of energy—yours."

"But Ila doesn't know where the keypad is!"

"She'll have to feel for it. We only have one shot at this; Shree is barely holding together. We have to move now." Varsa's intense gaze caused Eve to shift her position. *I know you can do this. You both can.* Varsa's confidence buoyed Eve. She closed her eyes, her long wavy hair falling haphazardly around her.

Ila ... Eve inhaled deeply and held her breath for a long moment. She blew it quietly across her lips, as her chest fell. *Listen, you have to press the pad at the same time as Anusha. I know.* Eve cut Ila off before she could protest. *You have to feel for it. It's there. There is always a pad. Once you open the doors, move out of the way quickly, you hear?* Ila nodded. *Jay, too. Jay? You there?*

I'm here, Eve. Jay's voice caressed Eve's mind, cascading down her spine and sending shivers out across her skin. The walls around them brightened briefly to a light pink then settled back into deep red, shimmering and reflecting the bright glowing ball of light in the center of the room.

Anusha! You there? Eve called to her. Anusha nodded.

Yes, she said softly, her voice flat as she watched Shree struggling inside the bright white glow, unable to help him. *I'm here.* Anusha ran her hand listlessly across the smooth wall until she felt the pull of the invisible keypad under her hand. Ila squinted across the courtyard and nodded as she watched Anusha locate her pad.

Ila pushed her back up the smooth wall and stood tall. She reached one hand out, palm down, and searched for the pad. Almost instantly, she felt a pull. Below, Eve felt Ila's hand, as if it were poised and hovering directly over her own. She nodded to Varsa. "They have the pads. They're ready."

"Okay, this might get rough. Remember where you are and stay *here*. We're all right here, in this room with you. Don't let anything pull you away." Varsa looked solemnly from one face to another. "Above all, remember, you are not alone. We are all here together—understand? Whatever happens, do not let go of this room we created together. Do not forget that." Everyone in the room nodded silently in the shifting light. They each turned and repositioned themselves to feel the strongest connection to the crystalline mine around them.

RADIANT LIGHT

Varsa nodded to Eve. As she did, her long silvery hair slipped out and covered her face. Impatiently, she tossed her head back to clear her view and waited for Eve to give the signal. The room flared brighter as the Others tapped in stronger and prepared for the unknown.

Okay, Ila, Anusha, here we go. Ready? Eve's words came fast and clear. Ila and Anusha nodded mutely.

"NOW!" Eve's voice echoed out into both worlds.

Ila and Anusha slapped their hands fast and hard against their invisible keypads. In front of Eve, the large wooden door filled with deep magenta red that rose from the bottom, until it glowed red hot in the center. Eve threw her hands instinctively into the firery center of the door, and bit her lip against the sting. The ground below them rumbled violently.

Ila squeezed her eyes shut against the searing pain under her hand. The entire wall shook. Tears stung her eyes as she blinked hard, trying to see back into the courtyard. The machine wobbled in front of her eyes. Then the laserlike tube pitched upward and spun around, shooting its full fury directly into Shree. He flew off his feet and skidded backward across the dusty surface.

Shree! Let me help you! Anusha searched her way through the chaotic mines, feeling the wide and spacious current of her chamber, blended with something wide and unfamiliar. A small stream from below began to seep into her hand and fill her entire arm, creating a funnel. Anusha threw her other hand toward Shree, stretching herself, fingertip to fingertip, and willed some of the energy around him to come to her. A fiery bolt shot off Shree and hit her with a force that knocked the air out of her lungs, swaying her backward on her feet.

Anusha whipped her heavy curls back behind her shoulders and steeled her body between the two worlds above and below. She pulled hard, drawing more of the stream into her own body. Shree struggled back to his feet, swaying recklessly, sparking off more and more searing beams. The machine lurched menacingly toward Ila. She plastered herself against the wall with her hand still on the pad, afraid to breathe, and waited for Eve's next command. Jay scurried under the electric air sizzling above him and flung himself against the building. He searched for an escape from the squealing generator. Sparks and beams flew menacingly around the yard.

The machine shook hard on its foundation, clanging and screaming louder and louder. Smoke snaked through the air around them, laced with a sharp, acrid smell.

Eve! What now?

"Let go!" Shree's deep, baritone voice roared through the din, grabbing all of their attention.

The bright room below ground buzzed electric, humming and ringing as it blended more and more of the Other's energy, mixing into the charge already coming through the mine's walls. The door under Eve's hands glowed milky green as Shree's signature hue spread and filled the entire door. Eve sounded the alarm: "NOW!"

Anusha, Ila, and Eve ripped their hands from the walls and door simultaneously. Three doors flew open. The metal generator in front of Ila lurched hard on its foundation, leaning grievously toward the open door beside her. Blinding white light mixed with a low harmonious tone, streaked out of Ila's door and surrounded the wounded machine. In one swift movement, the light magnetized to the generator and tore it, screaming and screeching, from the ground. Ila stood, frozen, staring at the suspended machine hovering perilously in midair, flailing like a caged animal.

"Out! Everyone, now!" Eve shouted across the blinding light. "Quickly!" The ground of the mines waved and rolled beneath their feet as each of them peeled their hands off the wall and shot toward the door. Eve flew around the open corner and slammed hard into Jay. The door from the mines had opened directly into the courtyard—linking between the mines and the surface. He caught her and steadied her on her feet. In a blink, the rest followed, leaving the mines too hastily to even think about it. With a strangled scream, a rogue beam escaped the machine and shot toward Ila, barely missing her. The heat singed into her leg as if she had been branded. Her leg collapsed beneath her and she fell across the opening. Varsa caught her and pulled her effortlessly to the wall. Single file, the large group slinked away from the opening as the light from below, now integrated and stable, spun itself around the machine again and again.

Across the courtyard, Shree and Anusha continued to draw the dangerous stream to them, wrestling against the pull of the new light on the machine. Behind Anusha, the doorway opened into a long dark tunnel. Ellen peered into the opening and watched as pale green light seeped into the walls and floor. A long shiver ran down her spine as the tunnel morphed and grew before her eyes. A pale green line formed on the ground and spread down the center of the floor, glowing and pulling its way forward, expanding the tunnel further and further away from the entrance. The newly formed tunnel lengthened and lightened as far as her eyes could see. Ellen stepped into the doorway and hovered her hand over the rectangular keypad beside the door. Instantly, she felt a pull. She placed her hand firmly onto the pad. "Welcome, Ellen." Ellen drew in a sharp breath as Shree's voice echoed into the quiet room. She kept her hand firmly on the pad and waited.

Shree's large body, caught in the blended light pulling the machine from below, lifted inches off the ground and began to slide toward Ila's door. Anusha strained, bracing her feet on the ground, and pulled hard on Shree's heart, holding his cells together in her mind as she tried to unhook him, beam by beam, from the pull of the machine. The entire courtyard radiated as if it were daylight. The light from the mines seeped deeply into the generator and began to dismantle it, piece by piece, dragging it against its will underground. Shree's feet touched the ground, and he dug his bare heels into the hard dirt, straining to find a deep anchor. He felt nothing below him, only Anusha across the courtyard. Shree grimaced, desperately trying to untangle his own energy from the treacherous beam, but it had infused itself thoroughly into him. His feet skidded slowly across the ground as the machine inched toward the opening into the mines.

Anusha leaned her entire body backward in a hard angle, struggling against the harsh pull. She slid her hand off the keypad and reached her long brown arm into the mine. Instantly, she felt the pale green flow hook into her being and tether her into the mine. Strengthened, a deep groan escaped her taut lips as she pulled again, moving Shree slightly in her direction.

As they crept along the wall, the entire group felt the building quake and shudder, then vibrate grievously. They tried to pull themselves from the metal but were unable to detach from the magnetism that now filled the metal walls. *Keep moving!* Ila commanded, ducking her head as pieces of the roof began to crash down around them. *Hurry!*

Ellen waved Isaac and the men into the light green tunnel. They darted in and flattened themselves against the wall beside her. Ellen, with her hand still on the pad, reached out to Anusha, and tried to grasp her. They were too far apart.

The building shook and rumbled hard from deep inside. The machine groaned, scraping and piercing their ears as it buckled in on itself. It crumpled grotesquely into a disfigured ball until its form was no longer recognizable. The collapsed generator shrieked one last mushrooming whine, whirring faster and faster, shrieking louder and louder, until all at once, it exploded in a fiery burst that blew halfway up the building. Far up the wall, a dark silhouette slumped momentarily against the small window. Then it slid downward, disappearing completely from sight.

All at once, the severe blast was crushed into one fist-sized ball of light, then inhaled with a deafening, sucking roar through the wide doorway and into the mines below. Anusha flew backward into the opening beside her as the magnetic pull released her. She hit the crystal ground hard and spun around immediately looking for Shree. Unleashed from her connection, he was skidding feet-first toward the roaring opening at the opposite end of the courtyard. He clawed and wrestled, looking for a hold into the dusty ground as the invisible pull of the generator held tight to him.

"No!" Anusha flung herself toward the doorway, but the ground held her feet fast to the crystalline tunnel. She was unable to move forward.

Once the generator disappeared, the building released its grip, and Ila flew towards Shree, launching herself after his swiftly moving body. Varsa and the Others dashed after her. Ila caught Shree's outstretched hands and furiously swung her body around, twisting and torquing herself as she tried to anchor into the ground. Varsa grabbed Ila's flailing legs. Then, one by one, the Others connected, pulling strongly on the magnetic force, desperately straining against the wicked grip.

The world slowed around them as Shree looked at Ila for one long moment, then glanced over her shoulder at the entire line of his kind trailing toward the opening. His dirty face softened as sweat dripped from his brow, streaking down the side of his face. His eyes glistened, bright and clear. *Ila, it's okay.* Ila's heart hammered in her chest as she pulled with all her might into Shree's entangled body. *Ila, I'm going now. Look at me.* Ila gritted her teeth and shook her head. They were slowing, but still moving toward the opening.

No! Shree. Come on! Ila's voice cracked.

It is the only way, Ila. Let me go. It will pull us all in. I know....

NO! Varsa, pull! Anusha! Help us!

Anusha lay helpless, unable to move against the tether holding her invisibly into the ground of the newly formed tunnel.

Shree! Anusha's eyes burned under heavy wet pools. *There has to be another way!* Her voice choked, disbelieving, as a single tear crested and fell from her eye, streaking down her own pale green face.

All at once, Shree ripped his arms from Ila and was swiftly sucked across the threshold, pulling all the light from the machine with him in a blinding flash. He and the light vanished altogether, leaving a darkened void in the arched open doorway. A deafening hiss from the darkness momentarily sucked the air from around them, causing them all to gasp frantically for breath, then it evaporated as mysteriously as it had come. The building shook and lurched hard as a tremendous explosion sounded from far below. Ila watched in horror as the building began to collapse, folding into itself, metal on metal, just as the machine had, crumpling and shrieking wildly into the moonlit night.

The ground below them roared and rocked violently. Ila, Varsa, and the Others stumbled to their feet and sprinted across the quaking ground toward the new tunnel. Behind them, the thunderous growl howled louder and louder until a towering wave roared out into the night, erupting with a deafening crash from the dark opening of the dying building.

"ILA—HURRY!" Eve was already in the doorway, doubled over. She threw her arms out of the tunnel opening, reaching furiously for her racing friend. Her wide eyes focused only on Ila and the Others, ignoring the massive wave careening toward them. Varsa swept her arm into Ila's and flashed with the Others through the small tunnel opening. Ellen ripped her hand from the wall, and the large wooden door flew shut, leaving them in the deadened silence of the pale green light.

STARS II

T he cool tunnel grew warm and humid as its moist, damp air mingled with the dry atmosphere from the surface. Ila's skin coated with moisture. She stood, her heart throbbing, as the realization crept into her shocked mind. She stared at the closed door. *He's gone.* A small wail gurgled from Anusha as she lay curled into a tight ball on the floor. A small glow began to encircle her, radiating a light green womblike field around her. Ila scanned the somber group. The diluted light of each of the Others cocooned them individually into their own bubbles.

Ila backed away and gave them space to adjust to their new circumstances. She rested on the uneven walls a good distance away from the group, feeling comforted by the shadows caressing one side of her body. She was getting used to the hot waves of emotion she sensed around her, but it didn't make it any easier. Especially now— she was having a hard enough time grappling with her own. *He can't be gone. Not like that. He must have planned for something like this.* Ila shook her head back and forth. The slow methodic rocking and her logical thoughts were no consolation.

Beneath their feet, the floor was irregularly smooth, as if time and exposure had polished the newly formed floor to a rugged gleam. Ila stared at it blindly, not noticing the green light spreading out from around Anusha's grieving body. The light widened the upper layer of the entire floor, then descended downward, illuminating the shimmering and transparent depths. More and more of the amorphous floor unveiled itself, revealing within it a complicated configuration of rooms, stairs, and hallways all concealed within the brightening stone. Singular strands of light pulled and stretched the floor into recognizable shapes, as if it were clay being modeled before their eyes. The walls behind them widened as well, enlarging the entire tunnel.

Ila peeled herself off the wall, only then realizing the heat that had accumulated beneath her damp tunic, and fixed her eyes on the scene unfolding below the stone. To her, it looked like one of the snow globes her mother had loved so much—a world within a world.

One by one, the Others locked eyes on the incredible scene growing all around them. Once their attention focused on the mysterious construction, their own unique color stamp added itself into the arrangement, dropping down from the bottom of their feet in thin strands then spreading and filling the strange new world with their own essence. The entire room was bathed in solemn silence. Even Anusha had calmed for the moment.

Beside Ellen, the darkened keypad began to pulse—faintly at first, then brightening progressively to a golden, flashing beacon. Ellen glanced down the hallway to Ila, bent and studying the floor, her face twisted into an equal mix of confusion and awe. Ellen smiled to herself, her heart fluttering in her chest as she was hit with a wave of nostalgia. It was the same look Ila had as a young child, back when the world was fresh and new. She hadn't considered it before, but the scene relieved her tremendously. Even with all that had transpired, her little bug still had that same curiosity, although she was not so unburdened now. Still, she could see it right there in front of her eyes. *My bug.* Her heart swelled with pride as she watched her grown daughter. Ila turned her head and looked back down the long hallway. She caught her mother's eye. A sad smile pulled at her lips. *Hey,* was all she could manage to reply as she straightened herself up to her full height.

Ila's eyes were drawn beyond her mother to the flashing light, now pulsing urgently. With each flash of light, Ila became more and more certain that it was calling her. She stepped cautiously across the still evolving floor, feeling like she was walking on a glass ceiling, unsure that it would hold her weight. She stopped beside Ellen, nodded to the throbbing light, and cleared her throat. "Whaddya think?" she whispered to Ellen, all of a sudden unsure of herself.

"I think you don't really need my opinion." The ground under Ellen's feet shimmered like sunrise. "But I love that you asked."

Moving like thick honey, the shimmering underground light threaded its way up into the wall behind her. It pulled the wall backwards and created a wide and spacious hall, complete with a long table intricately decorated with curves and spirals similar to the ones Ila had seen appear on the doors. Ellen pulled Ila into a deep embrace and hugged her tight. Ila let herself be held again, savoring the deep comfort she had longed to feel for so many years. *Home.* Shree's voice snuck into her head then disappeared like a ghost.

The flashing light quickened, and a high, barely audible chime sounded across her skin, ruffling the short hairs on her arms. "I think I need to get that," Ila whispered into her mother's shoulder.

Ila scanned the room and found all eyes, even Anusha, watching her. In the short span of her mother's embrace, the room had tripled in size. Even the ceiling was high and wide. It was filled with a kaleidoscope of iridescent colored lights raining down into the room, mixing and merging into pockets, as if sunlight were beaming directly underground. Ila felt as if she were gazing at a roomful of jewels: deep green jades, crimson rubies, golden yellow amber. It was all so radiant, beautiful, and consoling, like it called to some deep and unrecognizable place within her. It truly did feel like home, this room between worlds—here but just out of touch inside the stones that somehow created it. She sighed audibly and turned to the keypad.

Ila reached out her hand and hovered it over the blinking pad. Then she looked to Anusha. Her once azure eyes had darkened and were now glistening indigo pools rimmed with red. Anusha gave Ila a tiny approving nod. Ila's mouth pulled up into a wry sideways smile. She had just done the same thing as Shree, asking permission. She had only meant to honor Anusha—but how different was that from the way Shree had asked permission at their first meeting? A dull ache filled her. She peeled her eyes away from Anusha, hesitated only a second, then pressed her hand firmly on the pad.

This time, the door slid open slowly. Shadows danced in the pale light of the waning moon peeking through gently swaying branches. Trees stood in two-lined rows on either side of the doorway, their immature silhouettes swaying awkwardly like shy adolescents. Through the opening, a warm breeze carried on it the scent of sweet familiar flowers. *Tibetan Birch.* The name popped into Eve's mind. Ila, Eve, and Jay stepped toward the fragrance as a large shadow inched across the doorway, spreading its large distorted form onto the room.

Jantu. Anusha's words were low in their heads. *It has been a while, my friend.*

Beast's large head emerged around the corner of the tunnel. Gasps filled the room as one by one the Others recognized the missing animal. Ila inched forward and caught a glimpse of tiny white flowers waving delicately in the air, as if greeting her.

Tibetan birch or birch bark cherry. Jay walked past Ila and surveyed the dark mahogany bark glistening in the silver light. They were just like the trees lining Mave's drive, but much smaller, much younger. Eve held her breath as she stared at the softly swaying flowers.

Jay ... are we ...? Eve edged her way toward the door. Jay's face burst into an irrepressible smile. He reached for her hand and interlaced his fingers tightly with hers. *Shall we find out?*

Anusha, Ellen began slowly, *I don't think—*

I know, Anusha interrupted softly, *I know where we are. We are not in Ariom.* Anusha gave her a weak smile, remembering the stories she and Shree had heard from Ellen and Isaac. Anusha appraised her companions, scanning their fields to see what they already knew. The group shuffled, clearly uncomfortable with the attention, even from one of their own kind.

Finally, Anusha spoke. "My friends, this is the world we have shared with you—the far-off world of Moira, which is no longer so far away. Friends, I know you feel it. I see it inside each of you even as you hold your unique matrix so well. I see you. I know you know, we are no longer bound to the mines"—Anusha inhaled a deep stuttering breath—"because our home—the only one we've ever known—it no longer exists." She exhaled heavily and stared into the unreachable architecture, as if trying to decipher some type of secret code. She felt Shree's essence all around.

Three long shadows bobbed into the opening.

"Oh my God!" Mave arrived first, breathless. She waited for her eyes to adjust to dazzling, translucent light. A shaking hand rose to her mouth as tears of relief gathered, stinging behind her eyes. "Oh, my God," she whispered, rubbing the back of her hand roughly under her nose. She caught sight of Isaac and exhaled sharply, a small cry slipping from the back of her throat. Zoe and Edge trotted up beside her.

"Oh, my Lord," Zoe paused only a second then slipped sideways into the room. Choking back tears of her own, she rushed to Jay and threw her arms around him. *Jersey!*

Edge slipped sideways through the doorway and turned back, reaching an arm through the unseen boundary for Mave. "Turn sideways, remember?" Edge smiled warmly at Mave, frozen and staring disbelieving at Isaac. "Mavel," Edge coaxed gently, "turn sideways and get your beautiful tail in here, you hear?" Edge's grin pulled all the way across his weathered face, deepening the lines around his eyes.

Mave turned sideways, still covering her mouth, and slipped into the enchanting room. Isaac crossed the space between them in the blink of an eye and hugged her off her feet. Mave threw her arms around his neck and buried her head against him.

Zoe searched the girls, as only a mother can, and pulled them into the fold with Jay. Over their heads, she spotted her childhood friend.

"Oh, my!" Zoe dropped her arms and stared, as if she'd seen a ghost. "It has been far, far too long." Ellen grinned from ear to ear, her dark eyes twinkling in the shimmering room as she sauntered up and wrapped her arms around the four of them. She grabbed onto Zoe's hand and squeezed it tight.

Edge's heart felt wide and full as he watched the reunion. He searched the room for Shree and Anusha, but only found Anusha sitting against a wall as deep blue as her eyes. Edge squinted across the room at her, never before noticing her eyes so dark. He distinctly remembered them being light as a robin's egg. Anusha felt Edge's confusion. She was bone weary, her heart as heavy as the stones she sat on. Anusha felt Edge scanning the room. She could not bring herself to explain.

Suddenly, the sound of rushing water filled Anusha's head, drowning out everything else. Her body felt featherlight, as if she could just float away. The thin tendrils connecting her into the ground became a distant memory as the low roar cocooned her. She let herself untether and fall into the luscious feeling of being swept away. She didn't care where she went; she just knew she didn't want to stay here. She heard them calling her name, but she didn't care about that either.

"*Hello, love,*" his voice whispered, as if his lips were resting ever so softly on her ear. "*You didn't think I'd let you go that easily, did you?*"

"*Shree.*" Anusha tried to turn her head, but she was unable to move. "*Where are you?*"

"*I'm right here.*" She felt his breath in her ear. "*But it's not time, not yet. You still have some work to do.*" Anusha could feel a smile tugging playfully at his lips.

"*No, Shree, I want to be with you. Please.…*" Anusha could feel him fading already. "*No. Shree, please don't go.…*"

Anusha's world spun dizzily, the colors of the room pulling around like trails in the wind. She toppled like an abandoned marionette, hitting the floor with a soft thump.

Beast stepped across the threshold facing straight on and glided across the floor, leaving a trail of white light lingering in his footsteps. The room cleared as everyone backed into the solid walls, making a wide aisle for him. He walked straight to Anusha, leaned in close, and nudged her with his large, wet nose.

"Jantu," Anusha murmured through closed eyes, curling herself tighter on the floor. He huffed audibly and nudged her again. With a shaking breath, she peeked just in time to see the entire room darken. The mysterious rooms disappeared, leaving only the steady eyes of the Others, along with the folks from Moira, searching for her across the dark. Anusha had no idea what to do.

One clear and distinctive bell chimed from somewhere deep in the tunnel. It got louder the closer it came, reverberating in their ears and fanning the hairs on their skin. Beast gave one quick nod then turned and walked back out the opening of the tunnel. As he exited, just above the tree line, one fast moving shooting star flew across the sky. Then another and another. Ila leaned into the opening and watched as star after star blazed across the night sky.

In the darkened tunnel, one faint flame of light flew across the ceiling. Then another and another. Each one lodged itself far into the walls and lingered, as if patiently waiting. Again and again, the tempered bursts of light appeared from their unknown source and brightened the darkened tunnel.

"Thirty-three!" Ila turned back into the tunnel. "I counted thirty-three shooting stars...." Her voice trailed off as she noticed the steady beams lodged in the dark walls.

Anusha's brow lowered over her eyes, narrowing them as she looked around her for Beast. He was gone. "Are you certain?"

"I'm positive." Ila nodded. "I'd bet my life on it."

"Okay, then." Anusha frowned, her forehead still creased. She studied the unwavering lights. "That means they're all here." Nobody dared say the words Anusha was thinking.

All at once, the entire tunnel blazed to life—brighter than it had before. The room that had formed before their eyes was still there, now even more lifelike and solid. Colors seeped down the walls and filled spaces that had only been faintly sketched in. Then slowly, as if an unknown combination had been magically found, the separating walls and floors began to dissolve, turning into passages and railings where needed, supporting each person through long-linked hallways on either side of the tunnel. The entire construction became completely and utterly real before their eyes.

EPILOGUE

"**W**hy doesn't Anusha come out and take a rest?"
Ila reached for a slice of cucumber, letting the marinade drip off before she popped it swiftly into her mouth. She tucked her legs back under her and gazed out into the back field. Fireflies were blinking to life across the twilight sky.

"Because," Varsa answered through bites of her own, "she's still trying to find her way back."

Ila leaned her full weight onto the porch swing and rested her head on the aging wood. She sighed heavily.

"You know," Mave chimed in, waving a stick of vegetable toward both Ila and Varsa, "I think she might just be able to do it. She is convinced Shree is in there, somewhere." She shook her head knowingly. "And I know she'll never stop until she knows for sure."

Meena and Jeevan sat quietly, listening, their light skin colorless in the fading light. Eve brought them into the conversation.

"Have you guys been able to grow the tunnels?" Eve didn't mean to embarrass them, but the question made their cheeks glow crimson.

"I'm sorry," Eve chastised herself. She kept forgetting how new all of this was. Only two months ago, they had seen the outside world for the first time. "I didn't mean to pry."

"Pry?" Meena's voice was so soft Eve almost didn't hear her. She brushed her dark, straight hair nervously behind her ear.

Eve was glad she hadn't offended her. She inhaled fully, letting the warm night air fill her lungs as much as she could hold. Anusha had given her that exercise to help her pause and think before she responded to the Others.

"To be nosey. To inquire about someone else's business...." Eve let the last of her breath go with a relieved sigh.

Jeevan smiled, his voice carrying easily across the screened-in porch. "I don't know if we'll ever get used to the idea that you don't read us. I guess that's why we don't have the word 'pry' in our vocabulary. We already know the answers before we ask the question."

Varsa nodded. "But that's only with people. This new mine, it's very different. Anusha is certain that Ariom stands even though the mines, as far as we can tell, are completely destroyed. Shree…." Varsa still had a hard time saying his name without stumbling. They had never had the thought one of them could be gone. It was never a possibility. But now … but now things were different. Varsa cleared her throat, threw her eyes quickly to the sky, and then continued, "Shree found a way to create, just like *He* had."

Ila saw a flash of the smooth metallic building that haunted her dreams. High up on the wall was a small window. Ila quickly looked away, holding her breath to keep herself from impulsively tumbling out the question she had so many times wanted to ask.

Tonight, Varsa answered her unasked question. "*He* was called the Scientist. That's all we know. He was the one who learned how to create humans…. " Varsa paused, pulling her mouth into the wry smile she had learned from Ila. "Well, at least that's what he thought he was creating."

"Oh, honey." Mave leaned forward, her rocker creaking on the loose plank under it, and patted Varsa gently on her knee. "Sweetie, you are human. I'd bet good money on that. You just happen to have traits we haven't quite picked up on. Like that skin changing thing. I'd be interested in learning that one."

Varsa's smile reached up to her eyes. "That still works only in the tunnels." She reached her arm into the warm porch light, turning it over and inspecting the light brown she landed on this time when she exited the mine.

"Maybe one day." Mave chuckled. She gazed out across the low tree line standing like dark sentinels in the back pasture and decided to change the subject. "Ila, has your mom gone to see your dad yet?" It was nice having company on the farm. She was getting used to it. But somewhere deep down, she had a feeling it wasn't going to last.

"Nope. Not yet. I sure hope she does soon. I'm not going to be able to keep it a secret much longer. I feel like if I look him in the eye, he'll just know. I definitely don't want him to find out that way. That's why I've been staying at Eve's most of the summer. Quite frankly, I think he's enjoying the break as much as I am."

Eve's face warmed, turning the same crimson hue that Meena's and Jeevan's had. She brought a hand up to her face, unsure what had happened.

Across the field, a dark figure emerged from nowhere. The last strands of daylight shone on the horizon behind him, offering the group on Mave's back porch a silhouette of his sturdy frame. He ran his hand almost nervously across his hair then scratched the back of his head.

Eve felt the warmth from her face slide down and surround her heart. *Jay, we're over here.* Eve's voice rang through all of their heads.

"Maybe...." Varsa suppressed a giggle, still not used to displaying all of her emotions. "Maybe you're more like the Others than you realize."

www.ingramcontent.com/pod-product-compliance
Lightning Source LLC
Chambersburg PA
CBHW060855250626
47159CB00008B/2741

9 781627 470858